A MURDER AT SEA

A MURDER AT SEA

by

William P. Mack

The Nautical & Aviation Publishing Company of America

Charleston, South Carolina

Library of Congress Catalog Card Number: 2001012345

ISBN: 1-877853-64-X

Printed in the United States of America

Edited by Pamela Ryan
Jacket design by Teddy H. Pound

Acknowledgements

To my son, William P. Mack, Jr., the best author in the family, who suggested a far better ending.

To my editor, Pam Ryan, who did so well.

To my publisher, Jan Snouck-Hurgronje, who took a chance on a new product, a mystery at sea.

To my wife, Elsie Mack, for her love and support.

TABLE OF CONTENTS

A MURDER AT SEA

CHAPTER I

In my dream I am stretched out on the beach at Menton, a seaside resort on the French Riviera. My ship, the destroyer *Lassiter* is here for a two day visit following a week's stay at Naples. We have just completed our five-month tour with the Sixth Fleet and are about to return to our home port in Norfolk, Virginia.

I remembered the small beach I am lying on from a previous visit to Menton. The so-called sand that the beach owner advertises is pushing up under my rented towel almost as badly as the lumps in my mattress back aboard ship. The word sand as applied to this beach is an approximate term. It is either very large-grained sand or small rocks. Either way, the discomfort keeps me awake ensuring that I won't miss any of the lovely sights parading up and down the edges of the narrow beach.

On my first visit to Menton, I asked a cab driver to take me to the nearest topless beach, and with the exception of the rock-like sand, I had not been disappointed. Almost all of the feminine sun bathers were indeed topless. The men wore skinny, colored jock-straps, and I felt a little out of place in my modest trunks. The local ladies were uninhibited and unclothed from the waist up, and wore next to nothing from the waist down. A few of them might have benefited from additional clothing or some form of transparent uplift, but on average, and particularly as a deprived young bachelor, I had no complaints. It was easy to spot the tourists. Their breasts were either milky-white or bright red.

But there is something wrong with my dream. My eyes are tightly closed, while on my previous trips I had kept them so wide open that I developed a slight case of eye fatigue. In my dream I open them slowly. The Riviera sun shines brightly, directly in my eyes, and I squint, trying to make out the scene in front of me.

Suddenly realizing what is before me, I open my eyes as wide as they will go. Standing above me is a beautiful girl. The first feature I search for, and notice, are a pair of large, pointed breasts. Fabulous affairs, two of the best I have ever seen.

She leans over me, and they keep pointing straight at me. I reluctantly raise my eyes to the area north of them and am met by a red mouth under a beautiful face. Her eyes are wide, black, and a little naughty and inviting. Her face is evenly and darkly tanned, just like the rest of her skin. It is obvious from her overall tan that she is a local. Her hair, when I finally get to it, is as dark as her eyes. I lower my eyes discreetly to investigate more interesting territory, but she is now leaning over me so far that her breasts obscure what I only can guess to be is a small bikini bottom.

Behind her head the bright sun slowly begins to turn red and to wave back and forth. She leans over farther, puts both hands on my shoulders, and shakes me, not too gently. I groan with pleasure and anticipation. Heaven is at hand, and I am tingling from head to toe. The Carlsons are a passionate bunch, doing our best to prove that all Swedes aren't cold.

Her voice is low-pitched and seems to have a slight New York accent. "Mister Carlson, Mister Carlson," she says. I wonder how she knows my name.

Then she shakes me violently, and the red light behind her brightens and steadies. Something isn't working out the way I had hoped. "Jesus!" she says. "You could sleep through an earthquake!"

Then I begin to come to. There isn't any sun shining in my eyes. Just a red flashlight almost blinding me.

There isn't any bare-breasted babe leaning over me invitingly and suggestively either. There is only a small, pinched face staring at me. Hands with blue-clad arms attached to narrow shoulders are shaking me. It is Benito, one of the young enlisted men, on watch as a messenger on the bridge.

"Mister Carlson," he whines. "Wake up."

I sit up in my bunk and rub the disappointment out of my eyes. "What the hell do you want? I'm not due to go on watch. Lieutenant Farrington in the bunk below me has the next watch."

"I know," Benito says, "but he didn't come up to the bridge to relieve the officer of the deck when he was supposed to."

"What time is it?"

"Zero zero three zero, and the Exec is mad as hell and about ready to blow his safety valve. You'd better get your butt in a hustle and get up there."

By now, after my few months on active duty in the Navy, I know that zero zero three zero means thirty minutes after midnight. I also know what mad as hell means, but I thought Benito was getting a little too informal. I decide to ignore it.

"What does he want me to do about it? I don't know where Lieutenant Farrington is or why he didn't relieve the watch."

"He says to get out of your bunk and find Mister Farrington."

I think about that for a moment and decide I'd rather go back to sleep and hope to dream about another Menton beach beauty. I start to lie back on my lumpy mattress but Benito pokes his

angry head back in the room and says, "I'm not
kidding, Mister Carlson, the Exec will want to
know what you're doing about it. He's taking the
watch until he can wake someone else up to relieve
him or until you can find Mister Farrington. You
know him. I don't think he's very happy up there
on the bridge in the middle of the night."

I scratched my head a little, but the stimula-
tion didn't help my tired brain. I couldn't think of
any excuse not to carry out his order, so I said,
"Tell him I'll get right on it."

I didn't want to get across the bow of the Exec.
This is a naval expression I had learned recently
meaning don't get in front of a truck unless you
want to get run over. Lieutenant Commander
Joseph Molesworth would have made a good
truck, and personally, he was a real pistol. The
captain called him Joe. The rest of us called him
Commander Molesworth. He called the captain
Captain. So did the rest of us.

The Exec had graduated from the Naval
Academy about fifteen years ago. He was never
without a set of freshly pressed khakis and a
recent and very close shave. When he wanted
something, he wanted it right now and no errors,
please. When you screwed up, and I had done so
on several occasions, he took you aside and gave
you a short fatherly lecture, but he also made it
plain that you'd better not make the same error
again. So far I hadn't made the same mistake

twice, but I had run through the gamut of one-of-a-kind offenses. Somehow nothing I did seemed to please him.

To make matters worse for us average joes, he was a well-built, reasonably good looking guy who treated everyone well. It was hard not to admire him, and I guessed that if I ever managed to improve enough to please him, we might even like each other. At least I was confident I would like him.

Benito left reluctantly, shining his big flashlight in my eyes one last time. I don't think he trusted me. I sat up on the edge of my upper bunk and looked around the room. As an ensign commissioned only six months ago, I was stuck in the upper bunk, while Farrington, six years out of the Naval Academy, drew the lower. It wasn't any softer, but it was a lot easier to get in and out of.

Five months ago, I received my diploma from the University of California at Berkeley and a commission from the Naval Reserve Officer's Training program. I was enjoying my thirty day leave before carrying out my orders to join an aircraft carrier for my first duty. I figured a large carrier would be a good place for a young officer to get lost among all those other junior officers and to be able to make it ashore frequently.

I had enough money to rent a car for the duration of my leave, and a reasonably full black book. I didn't have a care in the world, except for trying to get a date.

Then the yellow telegram had arrived, order-
ing me to join the destroyer *Lassiter* in Norfolk,
Virginia, in forty-eight hours. The rest of my leave
was cancelled, and my carefree days were over. I
turned in my car, tore up my date book, and
began frantically packing what remained of my
uniforms and equipment, remembering that most
of my gear was already on the way to the carrier
by slow freight. I hurriedly bought a couple of sets
of wash khakis and packed a large bag and a small
carry-on. Fortunately, I had forgotten to ship my
sword, so I lashed it to the larger of my two bags.

I took the next flight out of Oakland and a connecting flight from Washington to Norfolk. I had
a little trouble with my sword, but the airline solved
the problem by checking it separately. They seemed
to think it was a dangerous weapon. After taking a
taxi from the airport in Norfolk to the Destroyer-
Submarine piers near the Norfolk Naval Base, I
dragged my suitcases and sword down the length of
one of the Destroyer Piers to the berth where my
new ship was moored. I remember looking up at
the *Lassiter's* staggered twin stacks, one on either
side of the center line of the ship, and wondering
what was wrong with her and why she was lop-
sided. Other than that, she was a beautiful ship. I
hauled my gear up the slim wooden brow, dropped
it on the spotless quarterdeck, and saluted the colors aft and then the petty officer of the watch, who
was standing near the top of the brow.

"Request permission to come aboard," I asked. He looked at me curiously and asked what I wanted. I thought he should have been able to fig- ure that out, since I was standing there with my baggage at my feet and my orders in my hand, but I was too new to question him. There was a slight twinkle in his eyes, and I thought maybe he was trying to give me a little initiation.

I said, "Ensign Carlson, reporting aboard for duty," and handed him a copy of my orders.

The petty officer of the watch read them and looked over his shoulder at a lieutenant junior grade standing forward of us on the quarterdeck.

"Hey, Lieutenant Riley, here's some fresh meat for you."

Lieutenant Riley came over to shake hands with me and then turned on a welcoming grin. I began to feel more at home. He told me I was tak- ing the place of another ensign who had been hospitalized. He directed a messenger to show me down to my room and said someone would square me away in my job after the ship got under way. I was wondering how I was going to get my bulky luggage down below, but he solved the prob- lem for me by telling the messenger to send a mess attendant up to take care of it.

As we went forward, I noticed an unusual amount of activity about the topside area, with men dragging fenders and equipment around and bringing aboard mooring lines. I quickly found out why. Within the hour the ship was underway for the Mediterranean to join the Sixth Fleet. I went topside to watch us leave our berth and head out the channel. I stayed there, watching the large ships at the Norfolk Naval Base as they faded in the distance. Then I went below to unpack. That was a mistake. For the past few days I hadn't eaten anything other than three plastic-looking airline meals and some junk food, and I was tired. The ship began to roll, at first gently and then long and slowly. An hour later, I was stretched out in misery on what I could only assume was my bunk.

Some time later, Lieutenant Charlie Farrington leaned over me and said, "I'm Charlie Farrington, your roommate. If you barf in my bunk I'll throw you over the side. Get in the upper bunk, or better yet, go up on deck and walk it off."

I looked up at him and decided I'd better move. He was about two hundred pounds of well-distributed muscle. His jaw looked bigger than my whole head. My muscles were well-distributed, too, but there was only about one hundred and forty pounds of me.

"Hello," I said. "My name is Carlson. I think I'll go back up on deck."

Later on, after we both agreed that he was the boss, not only because he was a lot bigger but also because he had two stripes to my one, we got along fine.

In the meantime, I went up on deck and found out he was right about sea-sickness. After walking around the weather decks in the fresh air, I immediately felt better. Even the long Atlantic rollers that came at us as we reached deep water at the end of the long channel, no longer made my stomach go up and down with the ship. I was a sea-going sailor now, and I was never seasick again.

* * *

But lying here now in my upper bunk, I had a different problem. Why hadn't Charlie Farrington taken his watch? I forced my sleepy brain back into the present and reached up and grabbed the large beam running over my bunk. I liked to stretch my shoulder muscles with it, and as I twisted around in my stretch, I could see most of our stateroom. It wasn't very big, but it was all ours. Two bunks, two chairs, two small hanging closets (known to the Navy as clothes lockers) and two built-in chests of drawers with pull down desktops in the middle. It wasn't exactly decorated. No pictures. No picture windows. Not even a port. All the furniture was Navy gray, and the walls were a standard beige. But it was home, Navy style, and I soon came to like it.

Charlie always insisted on keeping a small night-light burning. At first I thought he might not like the dark, but I soon learned that it was out of necessity. One of us was always going off or on watch, and at night there was always a steady stream of messengers wanting to show Charlie, who was the Gunnery Officer, some important message or other, or to tell him that some gadget wasn't working. A little bit of inconvenience from a constant small light was better than having a messenger stumbling around in the dark, trying to turn on the overhead lights. Besides, the light was only about three feet from my head.

I had been made the damage control assistant to the engineering officer. This job is usually given to a more senior officer, but for some reason the Exec had other plans for the senior officers. I think he kept a close eye on me because he didn't really think I was experienced enough to do the job. I was in charge of all the equipment and procedures for controlling damage to the ship in both war and peace. The equipment included such things as hoses, portable pumps, wooden shores, and electrical cutting and welding apparatus. Damage could be sudden and severe in wartime. Quickly controlling the flooding or fires that would follow a torpedo or shell hit might mean the difference between sinking and staying afloat.

In peacetime, that kind of damage was less likely, but officers and enlisted men had to be trained and motivated to be ready anyway. Collisions, explosions, and fires were still possible in peacetime, but fortunately not frequent. My job was important, but I wasn't popular with those I had to stay after to keep their damage control equipment and fittings in good shape. Most of the equipment was scattered about the ship in the custody of various division officers. None of these men worked for me directly and only one first class petty officer worked for me full time. One hell of a small personal command. Still, nobody bothered me too much as long as I kept all the damage control equipment markings in order, filled in my inspection forms properly, and showed up for my watches. There were other petty officers who worked on damage control equipment, but they were assigned to other divisions and only reported to me when we were at general quarters. It was a weird chain of command rig, but the Exec liked it.

As I twisted to my right, I could see my sword hanging on a couple of hooks at the foot of my bunk. It was the one piece of military equipment I felt comfortable with. After I had accepted the fact that no college team wanted a hundred and forty pound quarterback, I had tried fencing. By my junior year I had made the team, and in my senior year I was number one on the fencing squad in the saber class. When they needed me, I was pretty good with the foil, too. My dress sword wasn't a saber, which is flat and sharp on the cutting edge and also sharp at its point, but it was made the same way. The edge was dull, but the point was sharp, and it would do in a pinch if I ever had to defend myself, which wasn't likely. But my sword had already cost me money, and not just to buy it. The first week aboard, just after inspection, all the officers had gathered in the wardroom for coffee. As I took off my sword and sword belt before sitting down, Doctor Hasler asked me if I actually knew how to use the sword. I had grown to like and trust Doctor Howard Hasler more than any other officer on the ship. He was somewhat of a kindred spirit, a little non-regulation. His cap always flopped down in the back just a little more than it should have. His hair was always just a little too long, and his mustache never met the Exec's definition of neat. He was well read, intelligent, and witty. As I said, a lot like me.

When he asked me about using my sword, I just assumed he really wanted to know something more about the weapon.

"I'll show you," I said, and I drew it out to demonstrate a few moves. The officers sitting at the wardroom table exploded in laughter. I couldn't see what was so funny. I stood there, sword in hand, looking around the room. Even the stewards in the pantry were looking in the serving door and smirking. Finally, Charlie Farrington stopped laughing long enough to tell me that anyone drawing a sword from its scabbard in the wardroom had to buy drinks for all its

members. Later, ashore in Naples, that little lesson cost me the better part of two twenty-dollar
bills. Everyone ordered the fanciest drink they
could think of. Only the Exec took pity on me
and ordered a beer.

* * *

A quick knock on my door brought me back
to the present again, and Benito's face peered
around the opening.

"Damn, Mister Carlson, I told you you'd better hustle your butt. The Exec wants to know if
you found Mister Farrington yet."

"Well," I said, "he certainly isn't up here in
my bunk, and its the only place I've searched
so far."

Benito sneered, but with a certain amount of
respect. Actually, I thought he had a sense of
humor hidden somewhere beneath his barnyard
vocabulary. I'd dragged him back to the boat landing one night in Piraeus, and he figured he owed
me one. He did. He'd been stinking drunk and
without most of his uniform, and if he'd been
found by the shore patrol instead of by me, his
shore-going days would have been over for a
long time.

"Mister Carlson, I can't hold him off any
longer. Get going."

I started to tell him not to slam the door, but
I was too late. Benito was mad, and the closing
door sounded like a gunshot. I grabbed the beam

above me and swung down to the deck. Now I faced one of those great naval decisions. Should I put socks on, or just shove my bare feet into my shoes? I decided to skip the socks. I put on my cold shoes and added a khaki shirt and khaki trousers to the underwear I had learned to sleep in. I poked my head out the door to make sure Benito wasn't waiting to check up on me again, and headed forward to the wardroom.

As an avid reader of detective stories, I figured this was the place to start my search. After all, Charlie spent a lot of time there. Maybe he had dropped off to sleep in a chair. I looked at my watch. It was one o'clock in the morning, or 0100 in Navy time. Charlie had been due to relieve the watch at 2345. Normally, he would have stopped by the wardroom for a cup of coffee and a sandwich before going up to the navigation bridge, another naval oddity I was learning about. Maybe in the old days the navigation bridge was where the navigating was done, but now it was the area from where the ship was controlled and maneuvered. The officer of the deck was the man in charge of all this activity. The navigator had his own chart house where he did all that navigating stuff like working out navigation sights.

The wardroom was still brightly lit, even though it was empty. This was a little unusual. Most of the time, as soon as the officers going on and coming off watch had eaten their sandwiches and drank their coffee, the messman with the watch would secure from watch, turn out the lights in the wardroom, and turn in.

The serving door, a two-foot square opening between the pantry where the meals were prepared, and the wardroom, where they were served, was wide open, and through it I could see three figures in the pantry. The serving door was used to pass food from the pantry to a buffet in the wardroom. It was so low at the top that I couldn't see the faces of the three men, only their torsos.

"In the pantry!" I yelled, a fine seagoing expression for "Get your butt in a hustle and stick your head out the serving door." Nobody in the Navy ever seemed to do anything in an orderly manner. They were always "hustling their butts."

I saw one of the headless torsos move closer to the door, bend over, and soon the black face of Johnston, one of the non-rated messmen, peered out. "Yes, Sir?"

"Have you seen Mister Farrington?" I asked.

"Yes, Sir. He was in the wardroom about 2330 eatin' a sandwich and drinkin' coffee."

"Do you know where he went from here?"

"Not exactly. A man came in and said somethin' to him. Lieutenant Farrington got up in a hurry and followed the man out."

"Could you hear what was said?"

"No, but Mister Farrington said in a kinda funny voice, 'machine shop?'"

"Who was the man?"

"Don't know, Sir, his back was to me. He was wearin' dungarees and carryin' a baseball cap. But I think he was one of the engineers."

Suddenly Johnston's face disappeared, and there was an angry murmur in the pantry. I bent over, trying to see what was going on. I could make out that the second man was the Chief Steward, Antonio, but I couldn't see the third one. Then Antonio poked his moon-shaped face out of the serving door. He was one of the biggest Filipinos I'd ever seen, about two hundred pounds, some fat, but mostly muscle. I tried again to see past him, but I couldn't see the third man.

Antonio said, "Johnston had to leave. Can I help you?" His eyes were a little shifty, and he didn't look directly at me. Somehow I got the feeling he really didn't want to help me and that he didn't want Johnson to say anything else to me either.

"Do you know where Mister Farrington went when he left here?"

"Musta gone up to the bridge. Don't pay too much attention to anything Johnston said. I don't think he hears too good."

There was something fishy about the whole exchange that had just taken place, but I couldn't put my finger on it. When I left the wardroom, I could see Antonio watching me around the corner of the door leading from the pantry to the corridor outside. I headed up the passageway toward the ladders leading up to the bridge, but doubled back on the weather deck and around to the ladder and passageway leading down to the machine shop. This seemed like a lot of unnecessary maneuvering, but I was uneasy, and I didn't want Antonio near me, especially at my back.

All the way down the passageway and then down the ladder to the lower level where the machine shop was located, something ate at me. Why would Charlie not relieve the watch on time? He was always early, if anything. Why would he go to the machine shop, if in fact he did? Normally he had nothing to do with the engineering department which ran the machine shop. He didn't need to. The gunnery department had a storeroom and a small machine shop of its own.

I turned down the short passageway toward the machine shop still thinking over what had happened. What the hell was Antonio up to? Who came to talk to Charlie and why? Who was the third person in the pantry?

My thoughts were interrupted just before I got to the machine shop door. There was a small, reddish smudge on the linoleum deck. Paint? I leaned over and ran my finger through it. I raised my finger to my nose. It didn't smell like paint. It was still wet, and I knew it was blood. As the smallest kid on the block back in my home town of San Francisco, I'd smelled a lot of blood from split lips in my day. I looked closely at the linoleum-covered deck. There were two parallel scuff marks leading from the area near the blood spot to the machine shop door.

The water-tight door to the machine shop was dogged shut and locked, but that was normal. It was always kept locked at night. The dogs were small handles that could be rotated over shallow fixed wedges on the door. This forced a rubber gasket on the door against a steel edge on the door frame to make the closure water-tight. They were all tightly closed.

With my new-found professional knowledge and keen interest in damage control, I noticed that the dogs were rust-free and well kept. We experts tend to notice such things, even when we are otherwise confused, and confused I was. My tired aching bones told me to forget the machine shop and go back above and look elsewhere. Some machinist's mate had probably cut his finger, and Charlie had taken him to Doc Hasler. Or maybe he had gone off to take care of some emergency in his department. Either way, it made me uneasy. I guess I'd been reading too many whodunits.

Despite all this, I wanted to see the inside of the machine shop. That meant finding the man with the key. A helluva job in the middle of the night. But there was another solution. As damage control assistant, I knew that the chief master-at-arms had a master key for all locks on the ship.

Someone had to have access to them at all times in case of emergencies such as fire or collision. I headed for his office, or shack, as the sea-going veterans called it. It was just a small enclosure where the few men detailed to the master-at-arms force kept their papers, night sticks, and other equipment. It had two chairs and a very small desk with a telephone on it. I didn't really expect to find anyone there except maybe the man with the day's duty, but when I went in the door, the first person I saw was Chief Machinist Novella, the chief master-at-arms. He was talking to a second class petty officer named Whittaker, who obviously had the day's duty. When I came in, Novella abruptly stopped talking and looked at me with surprise. Novella's black eyes and dark complexion were shaded by his chief's cap, which he always wore instead of a baseball-type cap and kept pulled down in front. But I could see his eyebrows shoot up.

"Mister Carlson, what are you doing up at this time of night?" he asked.

"Not my choice, Chief, I'm looking for Mister Farrington. He's supposed to have the next watch on the bridge, but he didn't show up."

"Haven't seen him for hours," Novella said. He seemed sure of his answer, but I noticed that his usually firm jaw was downright rigid.

"I haven't either," Whittaker added. Whittaker was a second class petty officer who tended to be a first class smart-ass. He was a well qualified ship-fitter, but not as good as he thought he was. As I stared at him, he reluctantly stood up.

I decided to use the old Carlson diplomatic technique and come right out with it. "Chief, I need to borrow your master key."

The chief's mouth opened slightly while he thought this one over. "Sir, I can't do that for anybody. What do you want it for?"

"I want to look around in the machine shop."

Whittaker smirked, "Want to practice a little night damage control?"

I'd remember that. Some of the petty officers liked to put down the junior ensigns when they could. They forgot that we also stood watches on the quarterdeck in port, and some day when they were going over the side on liberty, we could retaliate by making a slow and detailed inspection of their persons and uniforms. They might even miss a boat that way.

I silenced Whittaker with one of my famous Carlson put-down looks. "No," I said, "and I'll bring it right back to you."

Novella knew when he was beaten, but there still was something strange about his manner and his eyes. He looked uneasy. But then who was I to judge? I was uneasy, too.

Novella said, "All right, we'll come with you." He opened the right-hand top drawer of his desk and pulled out a bunch of keys. I noticed that the master key had a red tag on it.

When we reached the area outside of the machine shop, I carefully stepped over the small red patch on the deck and asked Novella for the keys. He passed them to me and I turned the dogs off the door. Then I unlocked the padlock with the master key and pushed open the door. The lights were all on.

I stepped inside. Then I sucked in my breath as my foot caught on something soft. I looked down, barely breathing. There lay a prostrate body clad in dungarees. My foot was pushing against it. The man was lying on his stomach, and seemed to be unconscious. I bent down and felt for his carotid artery. His pulse was beating strongly. On the back of his head was a nasty gash, apparently from a blow with a blunt instrument of some sort. It wasn't bleeding much and the blood in the hair on his scalp was drying. I figured he had at least a concussion. I could only see the side of his face, and I didn't want to move him. I pulled back the top of his collar and read the stenciled name. His name was Garrity, a third class petty officer who stood watches in the engineering department.

I figured I had found the man who had come to the wardroom to see Charlie. But where was Charlie?

I stood up and looked around the crowded room. The big lathes and drills appeared to be in order. The machine shop contained an impressive array of machine tools with which the ship's machinists could turn out spare parts if needed or repair damaged pieces of equipment. All of the machines were arranged in aisles so that each one could be used without interfering with an adjacent one. In spite of the fact that the *Lassiter* was far more spacious than the average destroyer, the machine shop was crowded with the bulky, glistening machines. The smell of the machine oil was overpowering, and the strong smell coupled with the tension of the moment made my stomach churn. I pushed back the feeling, took a deep breath, and concentrated on the problem at hand.

When I had finished scanning the large machines, I looked at the aisles at floor level. Something unusual caught my eye. It was more than unusual; it was frightening. Two feet clad in brown shoes were sticking out of one of the aisles. I knew the shoes. One had a large piece out of the heel. I had seen it many times parked on the edge of Charlie's desk. I stepped forward and looked down at Charlie's body. Seeing Garrity was bad enough, but this was far worse. If he wasn't already dead, he was at least very badly injured. And unlike Garrity's, his muscles were slack.

When my heart started up again, I turned to Novella, who was still standing outside the door. "Get the doctor down here right away!" I shouted.

Whittaker stood behind Novella, looking confused. "Whittaker, wake up the Exec and tell him to get his ass down here on the double!"

Whittaker's mouth fell open in disbelief. "Yes, sir," he said.

Both men left on the double, and I apprehensively walked further into the compartment. Charlie was lying face down. I bent over him and felt his neck for a pulse. It was rapid and weak, but he was still alive. I gave a little prayer of thanks. I didn't think I should move him. I gently tore his shirt open, starting from the edges of a small hole in the back of it. There was a hole about an inch long just below his lower left rib. The opening was not sharply defined, as it might have been if it had been made by a sharp knife, but dull and ragged. As far as I could tell, he had been stabbed in the back with something blunt, like a screw driver.

His shirt was bloody where it had covered the wound, but there was no blood gushing from the small hole. It was seeping out slowly and running down his side in small rivulets. I got a clean rag from the rag bin and pressed it over the wound. I don't think it did any good, but I wanted to do something for Charlie. I was still pressing on the wound when Doc Hasler ran in the door, looked down at Garrity, and then over at Charlie.

"Jesus," he said. "What happened?"

"Garrity looks like he was hit on the head, but his pulse is strong. Charlie has a bad stab wound in his back. Don't know who did all this."

Hasler looked at Garrity first and bent over to feel his pulse. "He'll be all right." He straightened, pushed me aside, and walked over to Charlie. He looked at him for a second or two, shook his head, and got down on his knees to examine him.

I had to move back to let Hasler by, and as I did so, I leaned back against the low work bench behind me and put my hands out to steady myself. As I did, my left hand came in contact with a metal object lying on the bench. It was hot, but not enough to burn me. I turned around to look at it. It was an electric soldering iron with the cord wrapped around the handle. Next to it was a coil of metal solder. The end of the solder roll was bright, and I knew it had been used recently. I gingerly picked up the soldering iron and the roll of solder and put them in my pocket.

Meanwhile, Novella had followed Hasler into the machine shop and was standing next to me. As I picked up the soldering iron, his eyes narrowed, and he said, "What are you taking that for?"

"Might be evidence," I said.

"I don't think you should do that," he said.

"If it isn't important, I'll bring it back. Tomorrow you can tell the man in charge of the machine shop I've got it."

About the time Doc Hasler had Charlie's shirt cut off, the Exec burst in the door. He was so angry he didn't even see Garrity's body at his feet.

"Carlson, what the hell are you up to now, and what do you mean by sending me a message like that?"

Once again, I was back in his dog house. I wondered in passing if ensigns ever got passed over for promotion, but the thought went away quickly. There was work to do. Before I got to it, I looked at Whittaker.

"Did you relay my message to the Executive Officer exactly as I gave it to you?"

Whittaker's mouth hung open in embarrassment. "Yes, sir," he said quietly.

The Exec frowned at me. "If he did, I want an explanation."

I pointed at Garrity and then at Charlie's body, still lying face down. Doc Hasler was listening to his back with a stethoscope. "Quiet back there!" he yelled.

I held my breath in the silence. The Exec's face was clouded with emotion, and his jaw was working rapidly as he tried to take in the situation. I knew he wanted to ask a lot of questions, but he contained himself and kept quiet.

After the longest three minutes of my life, Doc Hasler straightened up, the stethoscope dangling from his neck. He looked at the Exec and shook his head slowly, "He's gone."

A MURDER AT SEA

CHAPTER II

The Exec stared down at Farrington's lifeless body for several seconds. No one spoke. The Exec's hands opened and closed convulsively, and he shook his head. Then he took a deep breath.

"Doctor, can Garrity be moved?"

Hasler moved over to Garrity, kneeled next to him, and ran his hands over Garrity's body while listening to his back with his stethoscope. As he was doing this, I noticed that the heels on Garrity's shoes were new, with sharp edges. In all likelihood they had caused the scuff marks on the linoleum-covered deck outside. I guessed that Garrity had been left outside by Farrington while he investigated something going on inside the machine shop. Whoever had killed Charlie must have gone outside and hit Garrity from behind before dragging him inside.

After examining Garrity, Hasler stood up and took a deep breath. Doctor Hasler was one of my closest friends on the *Lassiter*, and I never admired him more than I did right now. He was obviously shaken, but he was in control of his emotions and knew what to do professionally. His tall, slim body seemed to vibrate with energy, and his mustache shook slightly as he said, "He's probably got a bad concussion, but he can be moved. We'll take him up to sick bay on a stretcher."

"Good," the Exec said. He turned to Whittaker. "Get two stretcher parties down here on the double. Take Garrity up to sick bay and tell the pharmacist's mate to get him ready for Doctor Hasler. He'll be up there in a few minutes."

"Doctor, use the other stretcher to take Lieutenant Farrington's body to the refrigerator. Tell the supply officer I said to move crates around in there if you need room. There will be an autopsy after we arrive in Norfolk. I know you can't disturb the body now, but can you give me some idea of what might have happened to him?"

Hasler took off his stethoscope and rubbed the back of his slim neck. I knew he had seen death before. It was part of his profession. But he was badly shaken in spite of his outward appearance of calmness. The energy he had shown when he first arrived seemed to have drained away. I thought this was natural, but I sensed some other disconnect. Hasler took off his glasses and wiped the lenses. I tried to see the pupils of his eyes, but he turned away from me and put his glasses back on.

Charlie was a close friend of all three of us,

and seeing his lifeless body lying there was like looking at a member of one of our own families. Perhaps Hasler felt the loss of Farrington as deeply as I did. I gave him the benefit of the doubt.

Then Hasler took a deep breath and ran his hand through his thinning hair. His hand steadied. "Looks like he was stabbed from behind with some kind of weapon, but not a knife. The entry wound is not sharply defined. Maybe a screw driver. The weapon must have hit one of the major vessels. He never had a chance. The internal bleeding was steady and severe. The autopsy will answer some of these questions."

From what I had seen, I agreed with his diagnosis and his estimate of what had happened. I did not think this was the time or place to give my opinion about what I thought had happened to Garrity. There was something more important that should be started right away. The short course in Naval justice I had been given during NROTC at the University of California was very clear about requiring that an investigation be made as soon as possible whenever there has been a death, serious injury, or damage to equipment. I thought I'd better speak up in case it slipped the Exec's mind.

I said, "Sir, we're still three days out of Norfolk. As required by the Universal Code of Military Justice, somebody on the ship ought to be appointed to begin the investigation of this death and injury right away."

The Exec looked at me patiently. "I'll take care of all that, Carlson." Molesworth was a very cool customer. He was obviously deeply pained by the loss of Farrington, just as Hasler and I were, but he kept his head and did what he had to do. I decided right then and there that I'd like to have him on my side anytime, even if the feeling wasn't mutual.

The Exec turned to Novella, who was standing in the doorway. "Lock this door when we leave and post a guard in the passageway. No one is to enter this space except the Captain or myself."

Novella said, "Aye, aye, Sir."

I did not like the look in Novella's eye, nor his manner. He was too cool about everything. He seemed relieved when he heard the Exec's order to lock the door. He had not seemed surprised enough when I had turned to him after I had discovered the body, and he had not even asked me what was wrong when I sent him off to get the doctor. Although he couldn't see inside the room, he acted as if he knew what was there. Experienced chief petty officers do not usually take the word of inexperienced young officers that easily. I know. I had found out the hard way on several occasions.

The Exec said, "There isn't much more we can do now. All of you turn in as soon as you have carried out my orders. Carlson, you come with me."

I followed him out the door and up the passageway. As we walked along, feelings of guilt flooded my mind. I thought of all the time I had spent stalling in my bunk before I had started my search. Maybe If I had started sooner, Hasler could have saved Charlie. I knew I'd have to ask Hasler about this. But the problems of the moment pushed these thoughts aside. Now I had to help the Exec carry out his responsibilities, which were to inform the Captain of what had happened and then to start an investigation. The fact that there had been a murder also gnawed at me. If someone had killed Charlie, were the rest of us safe?

I watched the Exec striding along in front of me, the squared heels of his well-polished shoes playing a tattoo on the linoleum deck. When we were out of hearing range of the others, I said, "Sir, I don't think it's a good idea to have Novella put one of his men on guard outside the machine shop. He has the master key and I think he may know something about what happened."

The Exec kept right on walking down the corridor, but he turned his head and looked at me. "Carlson, that's the most sensible thing I've heard you say tonight."

I knew he was still stinging over the brash way I'd summoned him down to the machine shop.

But I did not have any time to explain, and I thought my approach would get him down there in the shortest time possible. It had, but I'd have to pay for it as soon as he recalled my insolence and decided to extract his revenge.

The Exec said, "Carlson, I expect you'll tell me, and the Captain when we see him, why I should not use Novella's men. We'll be there in a few seconds."

I was in over my head now, but we Carlsons are not quitters, and I made up my mind not to hold back when I reported to the Captain. The Captain, Commander Evan Faraday, was actually a commander. In the Navy, anyone in command of a ship, no matter what size, is called captain. Sometimes I thought the Navy was a little off the beam. They seemed to want to promote everybody, even though they did not wear the stripes or draw the pay. Not only was Commander Faraday called captain, but the executive officer, Lieutenant Commander Molesworth, was called Commander. To make it even more confusing, the Division Commander, who was in command of the four ships of our division, was a four stripe captain, but was called Commodore. Very confusing, but they all seemed to like it. I was an ensign, and like all other ensigns, I was just called Mister Carlson. That bothered me for a while, but then I remembered that the President of the United States was also called Mister President, and that made me feel a little better.

Even without a title, Captain Faraday would have intimidated me. He was a real bear of a man, about six feet four, size seventeen collar, and even that sometimes bulged. He was not fat, just big. His voice was strong when he needed it to be, but most of the time he spoke slowly and plainly, almost as if he were addressing a class in naval tactics. I found out later that he had come to the *Lassiter* from the Naval War College where he had been doing just that. I figured I had better have my homework ready and listen carefully to what he had to say.

We were on our way up to the Captain's sea cabin near the navigation bridge. The sea cabin was a small but comfortable room with bunk, head, and shower. It was here that the Captain spent much of his time at sea when he was not out on the bridge. It was where he ate and slept and he never went to his larger cabin down below except when we were in port.

As we walked along, I recalled that I had made a few good points with the Exec recently, particularly tonight, but the Captain was a different story. I had seen him up close on many occasions when I had been on watch. He usually sat in his bridge chair and did not say much to anyone. After three months of standing watch as junior officer of the watch on the bridge and as combat information center watch officer, the senior watch officer had, probably with apprehension, proposed to the Exec that I be put on a few daytime officer of the deck watches. This meant I would be in complete charge of a multi-million dollar ship wheeling about the ocean and of about 280 officers and men.

When we were maneuvering with the other surface ships of our battle group, this ship and its men were usually hurtling about in a tight formation at high speeds. Sometimes we spread out in a circular screen around the carrier we escorted. But this wasn't any easier. Long signals came threading through the static on the voice radio requiring that I take the ship from one station to another in the screen or even leave it altogether to go off on some other mission. I thought I was getting pretty good at it until I noticed that the Captain never left the bridge when I had the watch. Sometimes I tried what I thought were dashing maneuvers, using a little more speed than was called for by the tactical publications. After all, the *Spruance* class destroyers are gas-turbine propelled and can accelerate like a souped-up motorcycle. Once or twice the Captain groaned faintly, and once he said in a somewhat exasperated but patient voice, "Carlson, what the hell are you doing?"

"Just displaying speed, dash, and initiative," I had said.

This time the Captain groaned loud enough

for all of the men on the bridge to hear him. There were several snickers from the younger enlisted men watch standers, but a glare from the older boatswain's mate of the watch silenced them quickly. I guess he'd seen a lot of young officers come and go.

I had developed the feeling that the Captain was less than impressed with me, but I was going to go down fighting, doing what I thought was right. As we clattered up the last passageways and ladders, I used the few extra minutes I had trying to think of what I could say to change the Captain's opinion of me, but I gave up. The Captain was not the kind of man to be impressed by mere words.

The Exec stopped outside the Captain's sea cabin and knocked loudly. I stopped behind him. There was a muffled sound inside the cabin, something like the growl of a disturbed bear. I couldn't decipher the noise but the Exec seemed to be able to interpret it, and he opened the cabin door.

"It's bad, sir," the Exec said, "Lieutenant Farrington has been found. He's dead. Been stabbed, I think. I need to talk to you about it."

"Come in," said the Captain.

We stepped inside the cabin, and the Exec turned on the overhead light. The Captain swung his feet over the side of his bunk. This was the fastest I had ever seen him move and the first time

I had ever seen him less than calm.

He had about three quarters of a head of dark brown hair which now swirled in all directions around his strong face. His eyes were spaniel-sized and the same color as his hair. Before tonight either I had not found the courage to look at him directly, or else his eyes had been half-closed or behind dark glasses. At first they were sleepy looking, but as the impact of the Exec's report sunk in, they got bigger and brighter.

He shifted his solid body down to the floor. This was also the first time I had seen him when he was not completely dressed, and I noted that he was a little hairier in the body than we Swedes and that his legs were in good shape for a man who was not able to exercise much.

"Sit down," he said.

Thirty seconds ago he had probably been sound asleep. Now he was wide awake and in complete command of the situation. I had a lot to learn about waking up and about being a naval officer.

"Tell me about it," he said.

The Exec told him what he knew and what he had done. He was a little easier on me than I had expected. When he finished talking he turned to me and said, "Tell the Captain what you know."

I started my report with just the facts, beginning with my wake-up call from Benito, but omitting the delay I now regretted in starting the search for Farrington. I ended my report with the message I had sent to the Exec via Whittaker. I did not state the exact words I had used and the Exec let me off the hook by allowing this omission to slide by. He looked at me out of the corner of his eye and I was certain I'd hear from him later. Still, I owed him one. I did not include any of my feelings or speculations in my report. I just stuck to the facts.

The Exec looked at the Captain and said, "On the way up here Carlson advised me not to let Novella set a watch on the machine shop using his men. I did not have time to ask him why. Carlson, what do you know about this, and why did you make your recommendation about Novella?"

The Captain swung his liquid brown eyes toward me, and I felt like I was under a brown sun lamp.

"Sir, I think Lieutenant Farrington was killed because he stumbled on to something in the machine shop that he was not supposed to know about. As I told you, I found a small smear of blood on the deck outside the machine shop and two scuff marks leading to the door. That's why I decided to go inside. When I went up to the master-at-arms shack, Chief Novella was there. Normally only the man with the day's duty would have been there. Novella should have been asleep. I've never heard of a chief petty officer being up at that hour."

There was a slight lessening of the tension around the Captain's eyes, and he looked at Molesworth. But he did not smile.

"Go on," the Captain said.

I tried to think of some facts other than those I had already reported that would support what I was about to say, but there weren't any. I knew I just had to give him my impressions. I cleared my throat and plunged ahead. "When I tried to get Chief Novella to give me the master key, he was very reluctant to do so and insisted on accompanying me down to the machine shop. When I opened the door, I went in and looked around. Chief Novella was behind me and could not see inside. When I saw Garrity's body and turned to Chief Novella to tell him to get the doctor, he did not seem surprised. It was almost as if he knew what I would find."

The Captain looked at me without any change of expression, but when he spoke, there was a new tone in his voice. "Hmmm, I can follow your logic."

He turned to the Exec. "Do it, Joe. Make the necessary arrangements so that nobody can get into the machine shop except you or me. Then go down to the ship's office and bring back all the manuals which deal with this sort of thing. There are several. Wake up Chief Snodgrass and bring him up here. We'll be making reports to every body and his brother."

"Aye, aye, sir," said the Exec. "We won't be able to get in to Norfolk for about three days if we stay at sixteen knots. After they get our report, the Office of Naval Intelligence will be going ape, and they'll want to bring the FBI into the case to help them. I think we should hold up on conducting an investigation until we hear from higher authority."

"Right," said the Captain. "First, I'll make a report by visual message to the Division Commander and request permission to speed up. We might be able to get in a day early at twenty-four knots."

We were steaming across the Atlantic toward the entrance of the Chesapeake Bay in company with three other ships of our division, and the Division Commander was the senior officer of our formation. Our Captain was expected to report all unusual events to him and would need his permission to speed up and leave the formation. Fuel is very costly, and in most instances all Navy ships crossing the oceans are required to steam at what is considered an economical speed of about sixteen knots. This did not make much sense to me after all the hours we had spent racing around the Mediterranean on exercises and maneuvers, but I guess the big shots knew what they were doing.

The Captain stretched and yawned. I won-

dered how he could shift emotional gears so fast.
I couldn't. I also knew I probably wouldn't sleep
the rest of the night. But then he'd had half a lifetime of practice. When we left his cabin, I noticed
that the slightly amused looks the Captain and
the Exec usually exchanged when dealing with me
had been replaced by another kind of look. Not
exactly one of respect, but at least neutral, as if I
were now part of the team. I hoped so. It was a
good team and I wanted to be on it.

A MURDER AT SEA

CHAPTER III

The night was almost over by the time I climbed into my upper bunk, and my body felt like a deflated tire. I was exhausted, but even then I could not get to sleep. I kept turning over the incidents of the night in my mind, trying to make some sense out of them. The loss of Charlie Farrington was a blow to me. I had liked him, and he had helped me whenever he could, which, in my state of professional innocence, was quite often.

I did not wait for my alarm clock to go off the next morning at 0630, and got up earlier. I had the watch from 0800 to 1200 as officer of the deck and I needed about forty-five minutes to take a shower, shave, eat breakfast, and get up to the bridge by 0745 so that I would have at least fifteen minutes to absorb all the information possible before relieving the watch. I was not fully qualified to stand watch in a formation at night, but the Captain allowed me to take the deck in daytime.

When I got to the wardroom for breakfast, the atmosphere was silent and somber. By now the other officers must have heard about Charlie. But I could tell by the way they were acting and by the quiet conversations, that they were full of questions. They probably knew that Charlie had been killed and where it happened, but that was about it. If easy-going Charlie could buy the farm, they might be thinking that any one of them could be next. As for me, the more I thought about it, the more concerned I became for my own safety. I was involved in something I did not know much about, and I had visions of myself ending up next to Charlie in the refrigerator. The thought made me lose all interest in breakfast.

Doc Hasler came in and sat down next to me. He was the mess treasurer, and as such occupied the seat at one end of the table. As mess treasurer, he collected money from all the members, paid the bills for the food, and supervised all the stewards. The head steward, who worked directly for him, made up all the menus. He sat at the end of the table. This morning I was sitting in the last chair on the left next to him because I was junior man in the mess and also due to go on watch. For other meals, I ate with the second sitting because the table was not big enough to seat all of the officers at once. In port, the Captain sat at the head of the table, but at sea he ate almost all of his meals in his sea cabin or out on the bridge. When he was not at the table, Lieutenant Commander Molesworth, the Executive Officer, sat at the head of the table and presided as acting president of the mess. This morning, as usual, he was shaved down to the quick, and his spotless khakis had been starched and pressed by the mess attendant assigned to him. The rest of us wore ship's laundry-ironed khakis which were always slightly rumpled.

I lowered my eyes discreetly and looked down at my uniform. It was passable, but it wasn't even close to the Exec's. I had dressed in my best uniform, cap, and shoes for my watch, but had already managed to get a spot of egg on my shirt pocket. Doc Hasler was more like me. There were lots of spots on his shirt, and his hair was not very well brushed. His small mustache was poorly trimmed, although the rest of his mid-western farmer's face was cleanly shaven. Hasler was about six feet tall and of medium build. He knew the benefits of physical fitness and prescribed it for everyone, but didn't follow his own advice. This morning he seemed to be a little preoccupied and if he had been ashore, I would have said he had a slight hangover. But after all, his night had been every bit as confusing and emotionally draining as mine, and my head ached.

Hasler stopped shoveling in the eggs and asked me a question. "Carlson, what made you insist on entering the machine shop last night?"

I watched as the officers at our end of the table strained to hear my answer. I spoke a little louder than normal to accommodate them but not loud enough for the Executive Officer to hear.

"Just instinct," I answered. "And, there was blood on the floor outside the machine shop."

"How did you know it was blood?"

"I put my finger in it and smelled it. It did not smell like paint."

"Yes, but it could have been ketchup from someone's midnight snack."

"Very funny. It was blood alright. I've smelled a lot of it in my time. I used to do a little Golden Gloves boxing, and I didn't usually win."

At that, a couple of the ensigns at our end of the table had heard enough. They got up and left, leaving the remains of their breakfast cooling on their plates.

Hasler put down his fork and turned to me. "When I was in medical school, one of our professors used to make us taste our urine. I'm sure glad you didn't taste the blood."

"I'm not stupid," I replied.

I looked up at the Executive Officer. I think he had been following our conversation, even though I had tried to keep my voice down. "Excuse me please, Sir, I have to go on watch."

"Excused," he said, "and when you have an opportunity, remind those two bumpkins who just left to ask to be excused next time before they leave the table."

"Sir, I don't think they were feeling well."

"A lot of us aren't," he said.

The watch was easy, even for me. By the time I took over, we had been detached to proceed independently to Norfolk and the other ships of our division were already just gray dots on the horizon astern. Twenty-four knots still was not my kind of speed, but it would get us in a day early. About 0900 the Captain lumbered out of his sea cabin and wedged himself in his chair. Like the rest of us, he looked like he had missed some sleep. But he missed sleep all the time. It was a way of life for a destroyer captain.

I nodded familiarly, smiled in his direction, and said confidently, "Good morning, sir."

Maybe I was too familiar, for his reply seemed just a little distant after his almost friendly attitude during the meeting in his sea cabin the night before. But in spite of his lack of sleep, he appeared to be in a good mood.

The sea was reasonably calm, and the sky a brilliant blue, somewhat unusual for the mid-Atlantic. With all that good weather, and the Captain in a good mood, the morning could be interesting. I set about doing all I could to show the Captain what a good watch I could stand. I scanned the empty horizon frequently with my binoculars, tapped the glass face of the gyro-repeater knowingly, and inspected the uniforms of the members of the watch. Their uniforms were spotless, and all the equipment was in good order.

After about an hour he left the bridge, apparently impressed by my efficiency. This was the first time he had ever left me alone in charge of the watch, and it felt good. I was almost glowing with confidence before I remembered that it was full daylight and there were no other ships in sight. I could not even change speed, and I was dying to. This beautiful ship with its gas turbines and variable pitch propellers would respond almost instantly if I asked it to. But all I could do was watch it cruise along at a steady twenty-four knots.

My upbeat mood dissolved when I remembered poor Charlie Farrington lying all alone in the refrigerated spaces between the other slabs of meat. I sighed deeply, but the sheer beauty of the day and the gently throbbing deck under my feet brought back my good feelings, and I turned my thoughts to the wonderful piece of machinery I was now in charge of. The propulsion system was fantastic. The ship could cruise with one gas turbine connected to each shaft. When full speed of over thirty knots was needed, a second turbine could be added to each shaft in ninety seconds. This relatively simple power plant drove two large, seven bladed propellers capable of having their pitch changed quickly. Both pitch and turbine speed could be changed from several positions on the navigation bridge, and there were an infinite number of combinations of speed and power. You could shift the propeller blades completely and the ship would slow rapidly and then go astern so fast that you had to have a good grip on something or you'd hit the deck. But this morning the best I could do was caress the controls.

I remembered arguing the relative merits of nuclear power and gas turbine power in a bar in Naples with a couple of engineering officers from a nuclear cruiser. I finally told them that nuclear power was a thing of the past, that gas turbines were the answer to surface power, and that they could tell that to Admiral Rickover. Evidently they did. In about a month I got a letter with a return address on the envelope which read simply Rickover, Nuclear Reactors, Navy Department. I opened it, wondering what the great one could possibly want with me. I had forgotten my rash remarks of a few weeks ago.

He was blunt. He said, "Dear Carlson: I understand you do not know what nuclear power is all about. I hope this is the extent of your lack of knowledge. The next time you are in Washington I want to see you in my office."

The signature was equally short and simple, just Rickover. I resolved to avoid Washington at all costs for a good many years. Maybe he would forget.

After being relieved, I went down to the wardroom for lunch. There were only a few of us in the second sitting, but the atmosphere had lightened a bit and there were a couple of feeble attempts at jokes. Most of the conversation was speculation about exactly what would happen when we reached Norfolk. All the fresh air I had taken in up above had sharpened my appetite, and I put away a good-sized lunch.

I decided to visit the one man who would know how the enlisted men on the lower deck were taking all this. After only five months in the Navy, I had learned that enlisted men should be consulted and listened to. Most of them had a fundamental wisdom brought with them from their particular part of the country and their individual culture. Add to that the years of practical experience in their specialties and you had a powerful force. My readings in naval history told me that the Japanese Navy in World War II had not trained or encouraged their enlisted men to show initiative. When their officers were killed, the men were paralyzed. Our American enlisted men, on the other hand, have always contributed greatly to our success.

I had expected that enlisted men would ignore a young, inexperienced officer. The reverse was true. Ask a good question and you get a good answer, and I asked a lot. Treat them with respect, and they'll treat you the same way.

My main contact with the enlisted men was Damage Controlman First Class E.I. Howlett. No one in the rest of the crew knew what E.I. stood for. Another petty officer had asked if his first name was Elmer. That was a one-blow-black-eye mistake. Since Howlett worked for me, I looked it up in his service record. Sure enough, the initials E. I. stood for Elmer Ignatius. I sympathized with him. Trying to explain why I was named Carl Carlson, as is the usual Scandinavian custom, was bad enough.

Howlett had driven heavy equipment, bull dozers, back-hoes, and cranes, for about five years before joining the Navy. One day, when we were sitting in the damage control locker shooting the breeze, he told me that a holding company had taken over the little operation he had worked for. Their aim was to sell the company assets and fire all the employees. The day the sale was final and the firing notice had been posted, Howlett had started up a bull dozer and leveled the company office. Then he had flattened the automobile of the head of the holding company that just happened to be parked in front of the office.

A few days later, in another state, he joined the Navy. He was almost thirty, making him a little older than his contemporaries, and in six years service in destroyers, he had risen to first class petty officer. He was catching up fast. I knew he'd make chief petty officer in a few years, and I tried to help him in every way possible.

Howlett was a hell of a sailor. Five ten, one hundred eighty pounds of muscle. Solid muscle. I had seen him pick up a one hundred-pound pump as easily as I could lift a six-pack of beer. He was always dressed in a clean, neat uniform and when he went ashore in his dress blues, he looked like he just stepped out of a recruiting poster. A well-fitting uniform, clean white undershirt with a tuft of black chest hair peeping up over the top of it, and a perfectly tied neckerchief. His white hat was almost square on his head, but not quite. Just enough off to look great, but not so much as to excite the shore patrol.

Howlett's well-trimmed black hair framed a square, tanned face. His regular white teeth were part of a strong mouth and a square chin. Howlett had only one weakness; his speech was not very refined. But that was to be expected of a man who had never finished high school and had lived in a poor section of a west Texas town. Stripped of the usual below-deck slang and obscenities, it still was not good. Howlett knew it, and he was unusually quiet around officers. After I had gained his confidence, I gave him a few good books to read on speech and English composition and tutored him as best I could.

We held our tutoring sessions in the damage control locker. Actually, it was officially titled the "Forward Repair Station." When we were at general quarters, manned for battle, it was my station. In addition to Howlett, I was assigned two other men who were technically qualified to weld and repair machinery, wiring, and piping. Our job was

to go to the scene of any battle damage or peacetime casualty and try to repair it.

Over the years, Howlett had expanded the
original damage control locker by cadging some
space from an adjoining storeroom. During a yard
overhaul and while the keeper of the space was
away on leave, Hewlett took over part of the passageway. The result was a nice little room which
easily held all the tools, pumps, and welding
equipment we were assigned. By building efficient
shelving and using a few arcane storage methods,
such as hanging large tools and pumps from the
overhead, Howlett had freed enough floor space to
hold two canvas folding chairs and a large box
which he placed between the chairs as a side table
of sorts. A drop light with a home-made shade
completed Howlett's living room.

Of course all of this had to be unrigged and
quickly hidden for Captain's inspection. In the
Navy, and particularly in destroyers, enlisted men
are not entitled to either comfort or privacy. There
are seats at the tables in the mess hall for the crew
to use when writing letters and reading, but only
when they are not in use for meals. Even then,
most masters-at-arms chase the men out so the
floors can be scrubbed over and over again. There
are also seats in the head, but not many, and they
are at a premium for more important uses.

Most senior petty officers have learned over
the years how to make folding chairs. If made

cleverly enough, they can be taken apart quickly and the parts hidden or disguised for inspection. Howlett's version came apart in seconds and the parts looked like pieces of wooden shoring and canvas for patching holes, their original intended use.

Captain Faraday was understanding about such things. He knew what Howlett did, and though he couldn't officially condone it, he was proud of Howlett's ingenuity. Still, the compartment had to pass weekly inspection, and it always did. It was my duty to stand by the compartment when the Captain came by to inspect, and I always shifted nervously from foot to foot when he was there.

Even the Executive Officer became one of Howlett's fans. One day he spied a battered aluminum coffee pot on a shelf. "Aha!" he said. "Howlett, you know you are not supposed to have a coffee pot that I have not approved."

Howlett's eyebrows shot up. "But, sir," This was all he got out before Lieutenant Commander Molesworth lifted the lid of the coffee pot. Over his shoulder I could see a collection of nuts and bolts filling it to the top.

Howlett found his voice again. "Sir, I'm just trying to save the ship money. That old pot made a good storage container. I could have requisitioned an aluminum box, but they cost fifty dollars."

"No," The Exec said. "This is just fine. Well done."

An hour later the nuts and bolts were back in an old canvas bag, and coffee was boiling in the pot, which was heated by two soldering irons.

Howlett always borrowed thick white coffee mugs from the enlisted men's mess hall and took them back the day of inspection so the Captain would not find them. After inspection he would just "borrow" them again.

When I got down to Howlett's digs, I found him at home, feet on the box, studying one of my books.

"Howlett," I said, "can I have a few minutes of your time?"

"Sure, Mister Carlson, pull up a chair."

Actually I couldn't have moved the chair more than an inch. I think Howlett was just practicing his conventional manners on me.

"Howlett," I began, "what do the men think happened to Lieutenant Farrington?"

"Well, down below all we know is that he must have been murdered. The guys have taken it hard, too. He was a nice guy, and he treated us all real well."

"Does anyone have any idea who might have wanted him dead?"

"No, but you can bet we'll all keep an eye out for anything unusual."

"Thanks. I'll be down to see you from time to

time. Let me know if you hear anything. I'd particularly like to know if you hear anything about someone bringing anything illegal aboard ship."

Howlett shook his head firmly. "I don't think anyone would do that, Mister Carlson. That's bad joss. Booze, yes, but drugs, no. Too much chance of getting caught and too high a penalty if you do get caught."

I did not know exactly what "bad joss" was, but I got the general idea. I decided I did not want to tell Howlett what I knew or suspected just yet.

After talking to Howlett, I went back to my room and stretched out on my upper bunk for a little deep contemplation. That usually meant dropping off to sleep in about two minutes, but today I was wide awake. I thought about moving into the lower bunk, but couldn't do it when I thought of Charlie. Maybe in another day or two after his body was off the ship.

I went over the events of last night looking for some sort of pattern, but there didn't seem to be one. No one in his right mind would have stabbed someone like Charlie Farrington. Could there be some nut aboard who had done it without reason or provocation? It didn't seem likely, so I put that theory back on the shelf. Why else would a man or men kill? For money? Not the kind Charlie had in his pockets, but a lot of money. And that's something Charlie didn't have. I knew he had been sending checks back to his aging parents and sometimes he had to borrow small amounts from me to cover his daily expenses.

So if not for Charlie's money, then what? Modest amounts of money might be made from smuggling alcohol aboard ship and selling it to thirsty sailors. But that didn't make sense either. There wasn't enough money in alcohol to justify murder. And where would large sums of money come from? The first thing that came to mind was drugs. Maybe Howlett was wrong and someone had taken a high risk for an equally high return. What kind of drug? Heroin, or maybe cocaine? Between the two it was more likely heroin, which came from Asia and was usually refined in European countries like France. Cocaine came from South America and was not used much in Europe. Besides, pure, uncut heroin with a street value of over one million dollars could fit inside a basketball.

The drug abuse program aboard ship had taught us all about this sort of thing. It had also identified Naples as one of the places in the Mediterranean where heroin was readily available, in large amounts or over the counter. We had spent six days there just before leaving the Mediterranean, and we had stopped there once before about two months ago. Plenty of time to pick up some heroin.

I got out of my bunk and walked around the room. My feet still hurt from over four hours of standing during the morning watch, so I sat down at my desk, a pull down affair under a chest of metal drawers. I thought more about Naples. I had had a good time there. I spoke a little Italian, picked up in my youth in San Francisco. There are still many Italians in certain districts of San Francisco. My elementary school population was about half Italian. I had liked most of them a lot, and I liked to think I understood them and the Italian culture.

The kids playing on my playground used Italian terms and all the swearing was done in Italian, too. This was easy to learn, and it held me in good stead in Naples. The taxi drivers always tried to take advantage of anyone they thought was a gullible American tourist. I could argue a little with them in Italian, and knew what they were saying when they began to swear. One very bad driver, whose mother I called a hairy goat, threw my change in my face, much to the delight of the ever-present Naples street urchins.

Still, I liked the Italian people, and even if I was right, I wasn't about to become a bigot over-all this. If heroin was aboard, it didn't necessarily mean that a crew member of Italian descent had collaborated with Neapolitans. With that much money at stake, anyone could have been foolish enough to take the risk. But a quantity of expensive heroin had to be paid for by someone, and nobody I knew aboard would have that kind of dough. That meant someone needed to finance the buy, which in turn meant that someone in Naples probably had connections in Norfolk. The scenario I was envisioning kept getting more and more complex, and I still didn't have the least bit of evidence to support all this conjecture.

I left my room and made my way along the steel passageways to the ship's office. It was a compact affair to say the least. It had three small desks along one side of the narrow room, and a platoon of file drawers standing at attention on the other bulkhead, leaving a small corridor in the middle of the room. The desk nearest the door was held down by a third class yeoman, busy with a pile of the Captain's correspondence.

At the desk in the middle sat Chief Yeoman Snodgrass. I always thought his name suited him and his specialty. Snodgrass wore steel-rimmed glasses that sat on the end of a prissy nose over a slim mouth. He was of medium height and build, which was fortunate, because there wasn't much room between his chair and the edge of his desk. But whenever he got up, he still had to pull in his stomach, which was the closest thing to fat about him. He was a Chief Yeoman, an expert in typing, filing, and telling each man who came to the office why he couldn't have what he wanted. Leave, a change of beneficiary, a school assignment, it didn't matter. Any of these meant additional paper work for Chief Snodgrass, which he could avoid if he convinced the applicant that there was little chance for approval of his request.

I broke the ice. "Good afternoon, Chief. I'd like to have a copy of the ship's roster, and then I want to look at some service records."

Snodgrass did not give in easily, and I knew he didn't want to have a green ensign nosing around in his files. He opened his mouth to give me some reason why I shouldn't bother him, but I beat him to the punch.

"The Executive Officer is going to make me the head of the board to administer rating exams next week, and I want to be prepared."

This was not exactly true, but I would volunteer to the Executive Officer as soon as possible in order to cover myself.

Snodgrass closed his mouth, not clearly beaten, but at least more agreeable, and said, "Yes, sir, I'll get the list for you. And you can take that desk in the back. It used to belong to Ensign Fillmore, the man you replaced numerically. He was the ship's secretary."

That was naval personnel talk. He meant that I had replaced Fillmore in the total number of officers aboard, but was not to take his job as ship's secretary. At present Chief Snodgrass fulfilled this role by working several extra hours a day. Under the circumstances, I could see why he was negative about processing extra requests.

I looked at the desk I would be using. Not

bad, double the size of my room desk.
Comfortable leather chair and more room than
Chief Snodgrass had. It would be a great place to
spend some afternoons when the Captain didn't
need me. I could imagine leaning my head against
the bulkhead behind the chair, alternately snooz-
ing and catching up on *Playboy* magazine. I filed
the information away for future action. The plan
was a definite winner.

When Chief Snodgrass had laid the long list
of the ship's crew in front of me, I started down
the columns, making tick marks in front of every
name I judged to be Italian. Not that I was all that
convinced the crime had been committed by
someone of Italian descent but I had to start
somewhere. I felt a little guilty about singling
them out for investigation but it was hard to know
how else to begin.

I noted in passing that Chief Antonio's name,
which was of Spanish origin, could also be
Italian, Spanish, or even Filipino. Filipino names
were often of Spanish origin.

When I got through, I had four names in
addition to Chief Novella's, and Antonio's. Three
were young firemen and seamen. It was the fourth
name that really gave me something to think
about. Daviglia was the chief commissary steward,
and as such, in charge of feeding the crew. This
included responsibility for the refrigerator spaces
and the storerooms where all the dry provisions

were kept.

I waited until Chief Snodgrass was occupied trying to explain some arcane point about insurance to a second class petty officer, and then I went to the file cabinets and took out the files for Daviglia, Novella, Antonio, and the others.

I knew Daviglia. He wasn't very well educated, but he was good at his job and worked hard. He had a medium but husky build, his most prominent feature being a Roman nose of almost staggering proportions. Maybe not to him, but to the casual observer, it was a biggy. Then something I read in his file made me sit up and take notice. His father was listed as next of kin and guess where he lived? Naples.

Novella's record took a little more searching. He had been in this country for at least forty years and was a citizen by birth. In the back of his file I found a copy of a telegram asking that he be allowed to visit Naples for the funeral of his grandfather. I left his name on my "suspect list" and moved on.

Just on the off-chance that I might find something, I decided to go through Antonio's file. As it turned out, he was Filipino, but only on his mother's side. His father was Italian and from Naples. He stayed on my list, too.

I felt that maybe my hunch had been right. I knew enough about Italian history, culture, and politics to know that Neapolitans were second only to Sicilians in their feelings of family loyalty and closeness. I also knew that any violation of this loyalty meant instant and heavy punishment, perhaps even death. Naples was also a center of Italian crime and a gathering place for hundreds of young Italians looking for trouble. The streets were full of pimps, pushers, and punks looking for a mark of any kind. It could get even worse just a few blocks off the main streets, or into some of the residential districts inland from the main city. Actually, it wasn't much worse than many American cities. Just better organized.

I put the files back, taking care to see that Snodgrass didn't see which ones I had been looking through. I didn't suspect Snodgrass of anything, but the chiefs were notorious gossips. Anything they knew was soon common knowledge in the chief's quarters. Also, they tended to forget that the young seamen mess cooks who served them had ample opportunity to listen to their conversations and spread the resulting dirt throughout the ship.

Then I realized that I was being a little unfair. I had only searched the enlisted files. Maybe an officer was involved. I sat back in the comfortable swivel chair reserved for the ship's secretary, put my hands behind my head, and mentally went over the roster of officers. Yes, there was one of Italian descent, Lieutenant Carlos Abrizzi. He had been the ship's supply officer for the last two

years, and had just been relieved by Lieutenant
Barnaby before we arrived in Naples. For some
reason he was not flying back to the States but
was returning with us as a passenger. I thought
this was strange, and I added him to my list of
possible suspects.

All I knew about Abrizzi was that he was dark-
haired, dark-eyed, and had a Roman nose second
in size only to Daviglia's proud prong. He was a
loner and seldom joined in the conversation during wardroom meals. Afterwards he would disap-
pear quickly, probably to his room. Many times he
didn't come to meals at all.

This was not much to go on. I decided to ask
Doc Hasler what he knew about Abrizzi.

Then I turned my attention to the other officers and non-Italian members of the crew. In reality, any of them could be involved, because the
Neapolitans would sell drugs or other contraband
to anyone who had the cash. But that was too big
a field to cover, and I decided to stick with my
more narrow search. It seemed like the only way I
could get anything accomplished before the professional detectives took over after our arrival in
Norfolk.

I stuffed the listing of the ship's crew and my
notes in my windbreaker and went back to my
room. After dinner, I skipped the movie and
climbed up in my bunk at about eight o'clock. My
physical limitations were beginning to affect my

mental abilities and my emotions. I was tired as hell, but I couldn't sleep and I tossed in my bunk for hours. Mostly I thought about "the case," although now and then I remembered parts of my past, at least the best of them.

I remembered my days in grammar school in San Francisco and all of my Italian friends. I hoped I was not insulting them by my initial conclusions regarding the case, and I resolved to try to be fair.

I remembered my time at the University of California and particularly Candace Terry. I had been completely hung up on her. I met her my sophomore year at a sorority dance, and she liked me, too. But only up to a certain point. I could never manage to get past that point, and many nights I went back to the fraternity house both physically and mentally frustrated. The mental stuff I could take, but the gears of my sexual system were growing rusty from disuse.

Candace was only about one hundred pounds, but they were very well-distributed. She liked to jog and was a physical fitness buff. She also had a white belt qualification in karate, as I found out on our first date. I asked her out to dinner, and she countered by suggesting a picnic. I put together a blanket, wine, and some other odds and ends, and she brought the chow. We went up into the hills behind the city of Berkeley and found a secluded spot in among some pine trees. We could faintly hear the automobile sounds from a nearby freeway infiltrating our bower, but nobody could see us. The picnic was great, and the wine strong. It cranked me up, but it did not seem to affect her. When I put on my best campaign, all I could do was get her shirt open a little bit. She was like an octopus. Whenever I opened something, she closed something else. Everything seemed to be inter-connected. We were headed back to the car when she told me about her white belt in karate.

She offered to have me enrolled in her class, and I accepted. She turned me on so much I was willing to try almost anything. I took a lot of throws and got a lot of bruises over the next few weeks, and I finally decided it was time to try out my new-found skills. Again the picnic was great, and I had fortified the wine with some alcohol, but the results were about the same. We had a fine time for an hour or so, including a few passionate kisses. Unfortunately, it seemed that those kisses would be the high point of my day. Then, in a fit of supreme over-confidence, I dropped my trousers. If I had anticipated a quick surrender, it was not to be. With a quick leg trap she threw me completely off the blanket, landing me in a patch of poison ivy. On the way back to the car, she explained that while I was earning a white belt, she had advanced to a black belt. For two weeks I scratched my poison ivy welts surreptitiously, and when I could stand it no longer, openly.

Our romance was down hill from there, and ended when I abandoned karate and began to concentrate on fencing. I was definitely an indoor guy, and she was just as surely an outdoor girl.

Up in my bunk and once more back in the present, I turned over on my back and groaned, scratching the memories of my poison ivy. I looked at my wristwatch under the glow of the night light. It was 0200.

Then I was aware that the light in the room had increased. I opened my eyes wider and looked toward the door. It was opening slowly, and the light from the corridor was coming in around its edge. When it was about half way open, two figures slipped quickly past it, and the second one eased it closed behind them. The two figures looked like something out of Disneyland, only bigger. They were above-average size and they were wearing bags over their heads and faces. The bags were stretched so that their features were distorted, giving them the appearance of cartoon characters.

One had a large wrench in his hand and the other carried a good-sized butcher knife. Jesus, I thought, this is a hell of a way to go, trapped in an upper bunk. I wondered idly if the knife or the wrench would get me first.

A MURDER AT SEA

CHAPTER IV

The two giant characters sneaking around my room would have amused me if I had not seen the ten-pound wrench and the ten-inch knife they were carrying. They meant business, and I knew I would be on the receiving end. I hoped they just wanted to rob me, but then nobody in his right mind would expect a new ensign to have any money, especially at the end of a Mediterranean tour when everyone had spent all available money on good times, women, and booze. Then it occurred to me. Maybe they were looking for something. I thought about the soldering iron and solder I had picked up in the machine shop. If that was it, they'd never find it here. I had hidden it in the repair locker when I was talking to Howlett.

The taller of the two men was carrying the knife and he came over and stood near my bunk, obviously standing guard. I stayed still, watching the proceedings from under my partially closed eyelids.

The other man nosed around the desks,

quietly opening all the drawers and trying not to disturb anything. That made me feel a little better, because it meant that they probably weren't going to kill me. If they were, they wouldn't care what they did to my personal effects. When the searcher came up empty handed, I figured I had to make a move. By keeping my eyes almost shut, I hoped they would think I was still asleep. I had been throwing in a slight snore for good measure.

I did not want the bastards to get away with this, but I wasn't about to face two men, one heavy wrench, and one long knife barehanded. All I had for a weapon was my trusty dress sword. It was hanging from two hooks across and above the foot of my bunk. I could see its gold hilt sticking out of the scabbard, but it might as well have been a million miles away. My amateur karate ability would do me no good in the confines of my bunk, and I couldn't get up without arousing the intruders who were now either going to take their frustration on me, or hopefully, just leave quietly.

I had no reason to believe they would just leave quietly, so I had to do something. I had no intention of dying in my bunk.

That was it, then. The sword or nothing. I decided to use something I had learned in karate class. I stored up a full breath at the end of one of my better snores and held it. Then, ready or not, I let out a gigantic roar that would have fazed even Candace Terry. At the same time, I rose up in my bunk and reached for my sword. Then everything dissolved into darkness.

* * * *

I came around slowly. At first there was just total blackness. Then waves of darkness began to alternate with glimmers of light, and a wavering sea of faces. They weren't covered by bags, so I assumed they were friendly. I couldn't focus on either one, but my opening eyes must have triggered them to speak.

The one with the mustache asked, "How do you feel?" I opened my mouth to reply, but my whole head was pounding. My forehead hurt worst of all. All I could say was, "Fine."

The mouth under the mustache said, "Horse shit. You've got ten stitches in your forehead and a helluva lump to go with it. You must hurt."

If he knew so much, why did he bother to ask me? Then I recognized the voice. It belonged to Doc Hasler.

The other voice sounded vaguely familiar. It said, "Do you know where you are?"

Another stupid question. I had no idea where I was, except that I was in a lower bunk. I also knew that I was not on the beach at Menton. I wasn't in my room either. Then I recognized the voice. It was Molesworth, our Executive officer.

I stifled my desire to make a smart reply and said calmly, "No, sir."

Doc Hasler reached over and felt my wrist for my pulse. "Strong," he said. "He'll be all right in a few minutes."

For a moment I thought he was talking about my physical development, but as my foggy brain began to clear, and I realized he was talking about my pulse. My last conscious thought had been about Candace Terry and so was my first one now. That explained my galloping pulse. He listened to my chest and examined a few other parts of my body I could not see.

"He's one tough Swede," he said. "I think you can ask him some questions now."

The Exec cleared his throat and started with a brilliant one. "What happened?"

My awakening memory remembered the intruders. I could see their threatening forms skulking about my room. "There were two of them. They were wearing plastic masks," I said.

The Exec looked at Hasler inquiringly. "You said he was all right?"

Hasler shrugged. "About par for him. Let me try to question him." He leaned forward and put his hand on my chest in his best physician's bedside manner. I sighed. Even this small movement hurt.

Hasler said, "You have a large gash in your forehead. When we found you, you were lying half out of your upper bunk and almost ready to hit the floor. From the shape and location of the cut and the blood on the beam above your bunk, I would guess that you had a nightmare, sat up too fast, and banged your Swedish gonk on the beam. Does that make sense to you?"

"It does, but that's not the way it happened. I was trying to get to my sword to defend myself against two guys who were ransacking my room, and I must have straightened up too fast. I'll buy the bit about hitting the beam. I must have forgotten that it was up there."

When I got to the part about the intruders, Molesworth's eyes had rolled up in his head, but Hasler put a hand on his arm and stopped him from saying anything.

Hasler said, "What's this bit you keep bringing up about intruders?"

"Just like I said. There were two of them. About two hundred pounds apiece, I would guess. They were wearing plastic bags over their heads."

The Exec looked unconvinced, shook his head, and said nothing.

Hasler smirked. "Carrying weapons, I presume."

"Yes, they were carrying weapons. A butcher knife and a monkey wrench to be exact. Big ones."

Molesworth stood up. "Let me know when he's back in this world," he said, and left.

In retrospect, I can understand his lack of faith. I think Doc Hasler stayed just because he remembered his Hippocratic oath.

Since Hasler seemed to trust me, I decided to try again. Besides, my memory was coming back.

I took a deep and careful breath and started off. "I was lying in my bunk about 0200 trying to get to sleep. My door slowly opened, and two men came in. They were masked and armed just like I said. One went through my desk and Charlie's desk, and the other stood guard over me. I do not think they planned to stop at searching desks. I think what they really wanted was to examine my liver with that knife. They must think I know something about Charlie's death, or at least something connected with it. Maybe they were looking in our desks for some type of evidence linking them to Charlie's murder. I don't really know. But now that I think about it, maybe they were looking for the soldering iron I found in the machine shop the night Charlie was killed."

"What's this about a soldering iron?"

"Down in the machine shop, while you were examining Charlie, I found a warm soldering iron and some recently used solder on a work bench. I thought it might be evidence and put it in my pocket."

"Where is it now?"

"Don't worry, they didn't get it. I hid it."

"Does anyone know you have it?"

A small light went on in my foggy head. I grinned tentatively which made my stitches hurt.

"Novella knew." I began to think a little harder about what all this meant and tried to sit up. Hasler pushed me flat and said, "Slow down a minute." He took my pulse. "In addition to your bruises and cut, you've probably got a slight concussion. I don't think you're ready for all this thinking."

"I'm as ready as I'll ever be." I replied.

Doc grinned and his mustache twitched with the grin. It was funny that way. When he grinned socially the mustache stayed fixed. When he really meant what he was saying, the mustache moved. When I hit him with a good one, it danced.

From the way the mustache moved, I could see that he believed me. Hasler said, "From my room, which is just down the corridor, I heard one hell of a howl. Was that you?"

"Must have been," I said, "but it was a karate cry, not a howl."

Doc looked at me out of the corner of his eye. "I won't argue about it. All I will say is that it woke me up. It took me a minute to get oriented and then I heard the sound of running feet. Maybe two or three men. When I opened my door, no one was in sight and none of the other guys living on this passageway came out of their rooms."

"Mostly Annapolis grads living near us, I think. Those bastards really know how to sleep.

Nothing wakes them up. Even a karate yell as good as the one I got off probably didn't even make them turn over. But then, most of us line officers are either on watch, going on watch, or coming off watch. We can all sleep pretty well. It's only you non-watchstanders that have trouble."

Hasler said, "Anyway, I could see that your door was half open. I came down here and walked in. You looked like one of the chickens my mother used to kill back on the farm. Your head was hanging down, and you were bleeding all over the deck. I pulled you the rest of the way down, checked your bleeding and your pulse, put you in the lower bunk, and called the Exec."

I grinned, even if it did make my head hurt. "If you really want him in a hurry, have the messenger you send tell him to get his butt down here on the double."

Hasler frowned. "Now I'm sure you have a concussion. I can't give you any pills to make you sleep, but I'll see you early in the morning. In the meantime, either my pharmacist's mate or I will be taking your pulse every hour. We'll try not to wake you up. Leave that night light on."

"I'm going to see the Exec now, and when he hears your story, I'm sure he will put an armed guard on your door."

"Tell him not to let Novella, Daviglia, or Antonio get anywhere near me."

"Why?"

"We'll talk about it later. Doc, before you go, I've got to get something off my mind. It's tearing me apart. I could have found Charlie at least fifteen minutes earlier if I'd gotten out of my bunk sooner last night. Could you have saved him if you'd gotten to him that much earlier?"

Hasler didn't hesitate. "No. Forget it. I would have had to cut his chest open to get at the source of bleeding. I don't have that kind of equipment aboard. And there was no other ship or shore base near that we could have helo'd him to. Now go to sleep."

That eased my mind a hell of a lot, but I still could not sleep. I could really have used a sleeping pill. Without one, I could only doze on and off and try to ignore my throbbing head. As Hasler had promised, someone came in every hour to take my pulse. After a few of these visits, I began to feel better. When the door opened on one of the visits, I thought I recognized Doc Hasler's after shave lotion. I figured I'd get him good. I stayed quiet, and when my wrist was picked up, I grabbed the hand that held it and heaved two amorous sighs, or what I thought might be amorous sighs.

There was a loud laugh, but it wasn't Hasler's. I opened my eyes. It was the pharmacist's mate. I guess he bought his after shave lotion at the ship's store just like Hasler did.

"Er, ah, Oh!" I said, "I thought you were Doctor Hasler."

The pharmacist's mate laughed again. "I'll tell him you want him."

"No, no, you don't understand. I was just kidding around."

"Well, I guess I'll buy that. I saw you two ashore in Naples making like Laurel and Hardy scattering the local women. If you two were any straighter, they'd make yard sticks out of you."

"Thanks," I said, "I owe you one."

When Hasler came in an hour later, I played it straight and opened my eyes. After he had taken my pulse and flashed his light in my eyes, I said, "What do you know about Carlos Abrizzi?"

"Why do you ask?"

"Just thinking. Abrizzi is Italian, and we shouldn't leave him off of our suspect list."

"What suspect list? You're getting way too involved in this. You ought to stay out of it. It's not really your business."

"Anything involving the death of my room mate is my business."

"Maybe so, but be careful." Hasler thought a minute. Then he said, "I know a lot about Abrizzi. I've been trying to help him get adequate medical treatment for his family. He has a sick wife, a sick child, and two other slightly handicapped children. He does not trust the Navy medical system for some reason he won't tell me. I think his wife's religious beliefs have something to do with his attitude. As a result, he's run up about fifty thousand dollars in medical bills. He has no outside income, and I don't know how he expects to pay them."

"Maybe I do," I said quietly.

"What was that?"

"Nothing, just a suspicion. Go on."

Hasler looked at me closely, but he went on. "Abrizzi was relieved as supply officer by Ross Barnaby just before we got to Naples, but he asked to stay on and come to Norfolk with the ship. Doesn't like to fly."

I said, "Did you ever see him ashore?"

"No. I don't think he ever went ashore."

"Not in any other port, but he was ashore every day in Naples."

"Now that you bring it up, you're right. But I never saw him ashore."

"Neither did I, and we went ashore in Naples every day, too, except when I had the duty. When I had it, you went ashore without me. We covered a lot of territory, but we never saw him around."

Hasler stroked his mustache. "You're trying to tell me something."

"Yes. From what you're telling me about his family medical history, he's got a motive to try to come up with money to pay his bills."

Doc rose, stretched his arms over his head, and said, "I don't think we need to bother taking your pulse anymore. You're about as okay as you're ever going to be. Which isn't saying much. Good night, Carlson."

* * * *

In the morning there was a knock on my door, and Hasler poked his head in. "Are you decent?"

"Very funny. Get your butt in here."

Hasler opened the door. The Exec was standing just behind him. "Good morning, sir," I said, hoping he hadn't heard my impertinent remark.

He had. He clouded up a little and said, "Well, Carlson, I see you're back to normal. What is this obsession you have with fast-moving butts?"

I colored a little. "Just an expression I learned in the Navy, sir."

"Well, try another one, like 'bear a hand'."

I had no idea what he meant, but I filed it away in my nautical phrase memory anyway.

Behind the Exec was a messman with a tray of what smelled like breakfast. "Thanks," I said. "You can put it on the desk."

Hasler said, "I'm going to take a quick look at you and if you're all right, I want you to tell Commander Molesworth what you told me last night."

After poking and prodding me, Hasler said I was fit for limited duty, but that I couldn't stand any watches for a few days.

"Why not?" Molesworth asked.

"He might still have some occasional dizziness."

Molesworth raised his eyebrows. I knew he had a zinger for me in there somewhere, but he held it in. Once or twice I had seen him laugh, and I was grateful now that he kept his reaction in check. He couldn't keep it all in, and he finally said, "So what's new about that? It happens frequently."

"Sir," I said. "That's unfair. I'm improving rapidly as a watch stander. After all, the biggest piece of machinery I ever drove before I got to the *Lassiter* was my uncle's pick-up truck."

The Exec took pity on me. "Take it easy Carlson. Why, just yesterday the captain told me that he had left the bridge when you had the watch."

That wasn't exactly the compliment I had hoped for, because we both knew that there was no way I could have gotten in trouble unless a submarine had surfaced directly under us. The weather had been unusually mild for the North Atlantic in the winter, and the ship had hardly rolled. I decided to take his remark in stride.

"Thank you, sir." I said, hoping the eggs on the desk weren't getting too cold.

Hasler and the Exec sat down next to me and Hasler brought the breakfast tray over and said. "Eat this."

"Good idea," the Exec said. "He looks like he needs a little fuel."

Hasler said, "He's much better. He can get up

and around and do limited duty for the next two days."

"But no watches?" the Exec said hopefully.

"No," said Hasler, trying not to smile. His mustache decided to twitch anyway. "Go ahead, Carl. Start from the beginning."

I was a little pissed at Hasler, and I ate a few bites of egg while I cooled off. "Should I include the night at Naples?" I asked innocently.

Hasler's mustache drooped. We had had several good nights in Naples, but on one in particular Hasler had been in his element trying to show some Italian babes how to do the Tarantella. Afterwards the girls had taken us out to Ottiavana for supper. When Hasler disappeared with one of the girls, I hadn't minded. If he didn't want me to interpret for him, then that was his loss.

Hasler came back around and said, "Start with the two men in your room."

I told the Exec all that I could remember exactly as I had seen it, trying to avoid any smart remarks. Evidently I was successful. When I got through, I had the impression that he believed me.

I was sure of it when he said, "Carlson, evidently you know more than you told us before."

"Yes, sir, but a lot of it is just speculation."

"Go ahead."

"Well, last night I was pretty sure that the two in my room were Antonio and Daviglia. One bag covered a moon-shaped face, and the other failed to disguise a helluva nose. That one might have been Daviglia. Even the weapons were characteristic. Antonio had the kind of knife a messman would pick out, and Daviglia had a wrench. But I don't have any concrete evidence, other than suspicions. There is also possibility that the man with the large nose was Lieutenant Abrizzi, or even someone else."

The Exec bristled. "Why Lieutenant Abrizzi?"

"It's possible. He is deeply in debt for medical bills and needs a large amount of money to cover them. Plus, he was ashore every day in Naples."

The Exec was not quite convinced, and Hasler changed the subject. "Isn't Daviglia a commissary steward?"

"Yes, but he transferred to that rate from the engineers."

Now the Exec was really listening, and I think he had put his personal feelings about Abrizzi aside. He was bent forward from his usually straight posture. Surer of my audience now, I went on.

"Yesterday I went down to the ship's office and searched through the personnel records."

"Snodgrass told me about that. Some story about getting ready to give the rating examinations."

I swallowed hard. "Yes, sir, I've been meaning to volunteer for that job. I'm interested in personnel and ship's administration."

"Ah, we'll see," Molesworth said.

"Go ahead," said Hasler, obviously not interested in my future.

"I found that Novella, Antonio, and Daviglia
all have connections in Naples. We were there a
few days ago. In our drug abuse orientation we
were told that Naples is a big source of heroin."

The Exec cut in, "You mean you listened to all
that stuff?"

"Yes sir. I paid attention to all of your lectures,
particularly the ones on drugs."

The Exec's eyes narrowed. I am sure he was
trying to recall all the times during his lectures
that he had seen me doze off. Before he could
count too high, I broke his concentration.

I said, "I think the only thing that would
make a man, or men, want to kill someone like
Charlie Farrington is money. Maybe one million
dollars worth of heroin, or the profit to be gotten
from smuggling it into the United States."

"Given to him on consignment in Naples,"
Molesworth said. Now he was with me, and I
raised the level of my voice, a Carlson technique
for regaining the initiative. "There wouldn't be any
problem in getting it aboard. No one searches the
effects of the officers or the chief petty officers
when they come back to the ship. It could have
been accumulated in small packets over a period
of several days."

"And collected where? In the machine shop?" Hasler asked.

"That's what I'm thinking," I said.

"You could put a million dollars worth of heroin in almost anything. Even a basketball."

"Well, it doesn't make sense. Those dogs the customs agents will bring aboard in Norfolk will sniff it out in a minute no matter what it's in."

I paused a moment, intent on getting in another 'sir.'

"Sir," I said, "When we were in the machine shop the other night, I found a warm soldering iron and some solder on a work bench."

Hasler followed my line of reasoning "They could have been soldering some type of metal container when Charlie walked in on them," he said.

The Exec looked at him and rose out of his seat. "Then we'll need to search the ship!"

"Sir," I said, "I think we should wait a few days. Whatever it is is probably hidden in a metal container. Let's look for it quietly for a day or so. The agents and the dogs that will board us will do a better ship search than we can do. Besides, all we have is a theory. Maybe in another day or so we'll turn some real evidence."

Hasler came to my rescue again. "He's right. I'd like to do a little research on whether dogs can really smell drugs through tightly sealed metal. And we can do a little covert searching first so as not to warn the suspects."

Doc was talking like a real whodunnit fan now and his mustache was twitching rapidly.

The Exec was still dubious, but he gave in. "All right. Nobody talks to anyone. I'll alert the captain. Carlson, you stay in your bunk today. You can get up tonight but your armed guard goes where you go. And don't get in any trouble."

As he headed out the door, closely followed by Doc Hasler, I wondered how much more trouble I could get into. After all, I had discovered a dead body, a possible drug smuggling plot, and I had narrowly escaped my own funeral, all within twenty-four hours.

I sat up, resting my aching head, and went over to the desk. Although the eggs were cold, the toast was still warm and crisp. My jaws hurt, but I managed to eat it all. I'd need all the strength I could get. I knew I had to stay close to my bunk for a while and couldn't even think of leaving my room except to visit the head. But I had time to plan, and when my strength returned, I'd have a lot to do.

A MURDER AT SEA

CHAPTER V

It was a long night. I tried not to turn over too often in order to ease the strain on my aching head. By early morning I felt a lot better, and I got up and did a few light exercises. Everything worked all right, and I got back in my bunk.

I decided that if I had to stay in my bunk for part of the day, I'd spend the time doing a little thinking drill. I had read a lot of detective novels and books on the subject of deduction. Sometimes I imagined myself a combination of Sherlock Holmes, Charlie Chan, Mike Hammer, and Spenser. Forget Spenser. He got shot at too many times. Sherlock Holmes was more my type. Sit back, think about the clues, make deductions, come up with lists of suspects, and then manipulate the peons. Great stuff!

My mind kept going back to that night in the machine shop just after I had found Charlie. The warm soldering iron and the roll of solder had to mean something. If heroin was involved, someone could have been soldering the top back on a metal container which had been filled with drugs.

Maybe Charlie Farrington had surprised him, or them. Doc Hasler could help. He'd volunteered to do a little research on the ability of dogs to sniff drugs through metal, including through soldered joints and container closures. He'd be first on my call list.

If the heroin was sealed in a container, what kind of container would it be? Metal, of course, but a lot of small ones? A single big one? My intuition told me it was a large five-gallon or so, tin container.

Where would one of these come from, and more importantly, where could one be hidden? Most likely, among others just like it. Or maybe alone in some out-of-the-way place. But there were not many out-of-the-way places on a destroyer that did not get looked at often, and if the culprits wanted to pass the customs inspection we would be subjected to when we arrived in Norfolk, they would hide it among others that appeared to be identical. Again Doc Hasler could help. He'd come back from Mediterranean tours before, and he would know what customs inspections were like. From the talk I'd heard in the wardroom, I guessed that they were very thorough and that several dogs would be used to sniff for hidden drugs. Drug abuse in the Navy had been getting steadily worse, and the Navy's drug abuse program was going full speed ahead.

I thought about what parts of the ship con-

tained five-gallon tins. The commissary storeroom
would probably have the most, with lots of five-gallon tins of salad oils, cooking oils, and other liq-
uids. Maybe even some filled with solids.

The paint locker had cans of paint and paint
thinner. Maybe a good place. As damage control
assistant, I had a key to the paint locker. Getting
in would be no problem.

There were places about the ship that used
special lubricants, such as gunnery supply storerooms, but they were not high on my list. I could
get Howlett to search those.

Getting in any compartment without the
knowledge of the person having the key, with the
exception of the paint locker, would be difficult.
At this stage, the fewer who knew about what I
was doing, the better. Maybe my theory was all
wrong and someone else was watching my moves.
I stored all these possibilities in my slightly aching
head and looked for more candidates. I couldn't
think of any.

After seeing Doc Hasler I thought I'd go see
my friend, the new supply officer, Ross Barnaby.
Then on second thought, I figured I should try to
look in these storerooms myself before letting any
other officers and enlisted men know what I was
doing. Particularly Lieutenant Abrizzi.

So how does one get into all these locked
rooms? Simple. One makes a copy of the master
key. And where is this key? Again, simple. In

Novella's top drawer. How to get one's hands on said key? Not so simple. There is always somebody in the master-at-arms shack when it is unlocked. I thought in circles for almost an hour, thinking up scenarios only to discard them.

At noon there was a knock on my door, and a messman brought a tray of lunch in to me. It was good old *Lassiter* chow. According to the more senior officers who had served in other destroyers, the quality of food on a destroyer could range anywhere from foul to good. On this ship it was very good. It never ceased to amaze me how the cooks for the general mess could turn out so much good food when the ship was rolling and pitching like a rodeo bronco. My food came from the wardroom mess, cooked by a separate but equally talented expert.

I felt stronger after finishing off a full ration of pork chops, mashed potatoes, gravy, and peas. It was not until after I'd finished the last bite that I remembered that Antonio was one of my leading suspects, and possibly the one who had been after me with a knife. He could just as easily have slipped some roach poison in my gravy after the wardroom cook had prepared it. I poked my belly tentatively, trying to push that worry aside. I had enough others to keep me busy for the rest of the cruise.

I settled down for an afternoon nap. I was getting the hang of going to sleep in a hurry even for short periods. The guys from Annapolis were great teachers and accomplished sack-artists.

Later in the afternoon, I decided to overlook the Exec's order to stay in my room and just hoped he'd be too busy to check up on me.

I put on my uniform, carefully added my base-ball-type cap while trying not to disturb the bandage over my stitches, zipped up my blue windbreaker, and opened the door.

The first thing I saw was Benito's mournful face. He was standing across from my door, trying his best to conceal the fact that he was leaning against the bulkhead instead of standing erect as men on watch were required to do. When he saw me, he eased to attention.

"Good morning, sir," he said in the middle of a sloppy salute.

I started to correct him, but I didn't have the heart. Besides, it was taking all the control I could muster not to laugh. Benito was barely over five feet tall. He was wearing clean but faded dungarees with a web belt around his waist. On one hip was a holstered .45-caliber automatic pistol. Balancing the other side was a long night stick, reaching almost to the deck. I was impressed. The armament was great, but the wearer was a little less than qualified. I remembered Benito's record from the ship's office. He had not qualified with a rifle and had never fired a pistol, although he had been instructed in how to fire one before he was assigned watches where he might have to use one. He was one of the young Italians on the list I had compiled, but I had dismissed him as probably not involved. He had been restricted in Naples and never got ashore. I still felt that he was not any threat on his own, but that he could be part of a group. I decided not to turn my back on him when we were in any isolated location.

"Benito," I said, "I'm sorry you got stuck with this job." Benito smirked.

"Don't worry, sir. It beats scrubbing paint or standing watch on the bridge. It's also warm down here."

"What are your orders?" I asked.

"To follow you around and make sure nobody bothers you," he said.

"Well, let's go. Keep your gun in its holster and your trigger finger loose, and if you need to, just use the night stick. It won't go off."

"Very funny," said Benito as he moved off close behind me.

"Just be careful."

"Where are we going?" Benito asked.

"To the paint locker. I have to check the condition of all the damage control fittings and the water sprinkler system."

The Navy quite rightly is afraid of fires aboard ship and does everything it can to minimize or prevent them. Long ago it decided to concentrate all paint, which used to be highly flammable when it was all petroleum-based, in one storeroom called a paint locker. Now most but not all paint is water-based, which makes the whole locker safer. In the Navy the word locker can be used for anything from a small clothes locker to a large storeroom. This room, or locker, is usually located in a non-vital part of the ship and is protected by an automatic sprinkling system. There was still enough petroleum-based varnish and other paints in the locker to necessitate special precautions. A fire is dangerous no matter what its origin, so the Navy still maintains paint lockers with sprinkler systems.

Benito was clearly puzzled. As we walked along, he said, "Jeez, you officers never quit, even when you're banged on the head. If I had all those stitches holding my gonk together, I'd be lying in sick bay checking out some skin mags."

"C'est la guerre, Benito."

"What ever you say, sir, but I think your Italian is lousy."

I couldn't think of any reply to that gem. We walked in a loose column down to the paint locker, and I unlocked the door.

"Benito, you can come in if you want to, but this place really smells. I suggest you stay outside, close by the door."

Benito poked his nose inside, sniffed the effluvia of a hundred paint pots and mouldering paint brushes, and said, "I didn't know there was this much paint in the whole Navy."

"There is a hell of a lot more on other types of ships. This one is specially designed to need a minimum of paint. You're lucky to be on it."

"You couldn't prove it by me," Benito said. "If we don't paint it, we have to scrub it. I'll guard the door from the outside."

"Suit yourself," I said, and I went inside. There were many cans of paint, stacked on high shelves. All were one gallon size. And although a single can would be easier to handle, I thought I'd find what I was looking for in a five-gallon can.

The only five-gallon cans were labelled paint thinner, and there were about ten of them. I took them down and hefted each one, shook it, and put my ear to it. All of them gurgled quietly.

I figured I had struck out, so I walked outside, locked up, and motioned to Benito.

"All okay," I said.

"You smell like a thousand paint stores," Benito said, wrinkling his nose.

"The Navy calls, I do my duty," I said.

I started back to Hasler's room. We went up a ladder and down a long passageway, heading aft, Benito trailing behind me. Just as I was turning a corner, I heard a whizzing sound. Something brushed the back of my windbreaker and thudded against the bulkhead beyond me. Then it clattered to the deck. When it stopped bouncing, I could see that it was a long knife of some sort. I turned quickly and looked back up the passageway. No one was in sight. but there was a cross passageway about twenty feet back.

Benito unlimbered his night stick and started back up the passageway with me in hot pursuit. We made the turn but saw no one was in sight. The knife thrower had gotten a good head start while we were still looking at the knife. Now we had a choice to make. There was a ladder leading up to the next deck about half-way down the cross passageway, which continued across the ship and connected with another fore and aft passageway on the other side of the ship. We decided to go across the ship, or rather Benito did. I debated for a moment whether we should split up, with me going up the ladder, but I decided in favor of staying close to Benito's gun. Not only didn't I want him to shoot an innocent person, I also wanted its protection, and didn't want to go off by myself and run into the knife thrower alone. He might have another one. Benito had not prevented the first attack, but by the law of averages, he might be able to ward off another.

We were both mistaken. After dashing madly up and down in both directions in the long fore and aft passageway, we found nothing but a badly startled seaman cleaning a storeroom.

We trudged slowly back to the scene of the attempted crime, both of us breathing heavily. The knife still lay on the deck among some of the paint chips it had removed from the bulkhead. I pulled my handkerchief out and picked up the knife with the handkerchief around the handle. I ignored the paint chips, but with Benito the important things came first. "Some poor bastard will have to paint this," he said.

My blood pressure shot up, which pained my head. "Good God, Benito, I've almost been killed and all you can think of is painting."

"Well, the knife just missed me, too."

"Maybe, but I don't think it was meant for you."

I looked at the knife. I need not have bothered with precautions to preserve finger prints. Both the handle and the blade were too rough to retain any.

The knife was about fifteen inches long and made out of a steel paint scraper or a rough piece of steel of some sort. The blade was ground so that it had a needle-like point, with and the edges that were just as sharp. The shape of the blade reminded me of a stiletto. The handle was formed of two small pieces of metal placed on either side and bound with a winding of black electrical tape. The whole knife was one hell of a weapon. Cheap, but effective. It was balanced well enough to throw, and it could have made a big hole in my back.

Benito bent over the knife and looked at it more closely. "Cristo!" he said. "That thing could have plugged me!"

Then he let out a long string of Italian oaths that once again took me back to my San Francisco playground days. Some I had never heard before, even in Naples.

"My sentiments exactly" I said. Then I tried my best to match his artistry by doing some swearing in Italian myself. I must have done pretty well. His eyes widened, and he looked at me with new found respect.

"Hey!" he said, "You cuss good in Italian, even if you don't speak it so good."

"What kind of cabra do you think did this?"

"Goat? No goat did that."

"I don't mean literally, Benito, I know no goat threw that knife. But who could throw it so hard and straight?"

"Almost anyone. It has a heavy handle to give it power when it hits. Also, most throwers grip it by the point and throw it so it turns over once and then when the point comes around it gigs you like a fish.

"You don't have to be so specific. I heard it hit the bulkhead."

I ran my finger over the edge of the blade. It cut me slightly, and I pulled back.

Benito raised his eyebrows disapprovingly and said, "Mister Carlson, you're lucky to be alive. Just holding that thing is dangerous."

"Thanks, Benito, now you tell me. This thing looks like it could have been made in the machine shop out of a paint scraper."

Benito pursed his lips. "Maybe, but you can buy one just like it on the streets of Naples. They make them out of old automobile springs."

I looked back up the passageway. The thrower must have stepped out of the cross passageway after we had passed and waited for me to turn up the next passageway. He'd had to wait for me to turn just enough so that I would be clear of Benito. Then he had a second or two to spare before I disappeared around the edge of the bulk-head. It had been a difficult deflection shot, as Charlie Farrington would have described it. I thought about Charlie, and for a moment I felt like just locking myself in my room until we got in port. But I knew I couldn't let Charlie's killer get away, and I hitched up my Carlson courage and decided to get on with it. I wrapped the knife in my handkerchief to protect myself from the sharp blade, stuck it in my belt, and headed back to the ladder in the cross passageway. I wanted to see if there was anything we might have missed by going the other direction a few minutes ago.

Now that it was too late, Benito put on an Indian scout act, poking his nose carefully around each corner and glancing back over his shoulder at frequent intervals. We managed to get up the ladder safely and started aft. There were mostly locked storerooms along the way, but after going about fifty feet aft, we came to the chief petty officer's messroom which doubled as a lounge between meals. I pushed aside the curtain covering the door and looked in. A solitary figure was sitting at one of the tables. His back was to me, but I could see and his shoulders moving a little more than was required to move the cards he was playing with. Maybe he was breathing hard, but then again, maybe he was just breathing normally for him.

I walked around to see who it was. It was Chief Novella, playing solitaire. The way the cards were arranged indicated the game wasn't very far along.

"Hi, Chief, just starting a game?"

Novella looked a little surprised. "No, this is my third and last. I've got to get back to work. Want a cup of coffee?"

"No, thanks, I was just walking by." I noticed that Novella did not have a cup in front of him. Somewhat unusual, I thought. No chief petty officer ever missed a chance to drink coffee.

I walked out of the CPO lounge, picked up Benito, and started off for Doc Hasler's room. I had done all I could. Now I needed help. This was getting too serious to go it alone.

I stopped abruptly at Doc Hasler's door, and Benito ran up my heels. The long night stick kept going and rammed into the back of my knee.

"Not so close," I said. "I'll be in here for a few minutes."

"Sorry. Next time say something before you

stop. You ain't got no brake light."

I knocked on Hasler's door and entered when he answered. He was working at his desk with a pile of books at his elbow, and papers piled in between. Doc was not the neatest person I knew, and when he was really concentrating on something, he just pushed anything he had finished with aside without putting it away.

He took off his glasses, rubbed his eyes, and looked at me with what I guessed was his best physician's manner. "You look as well as could be expected. How do you feel today?"

"A typical quack's diagnosis. My head is fine, and you can put away those glasses. How come you never wear them ashore?"

"When I'm ashore I can smell the booze and feel the broads. Don't need the glasses."

"In that case I suggest you bring the glasses next time. You weren't doing very well without them. Some of the babes you picked out weren't exactly first class. And just a few minutes ago you might have needed them to sew me up."

Hasler looked puzzled. "What the hell are you talking about? Did I let you up too soon? And I thought you were to stay in your room until later today."

I dodged the last question, and told him what had happened. When I had finished I showed him the knife.

He whistled softly, picked up the weapon, hefted it, and gave it back. "Jesus, somebody's really after you. By the way, you'd better lock that thing up. It's evidence. And if you want more advice, you ought to retrieve that soldering iron and give it to the Exec for safekeeping, too."

I decided I'd keep them hidden for a while longer to see what developed.

I changed the subject. "I know someone's after me. Who do you think it is?"

"Sounds to me like Novella is a good suspect. Maybe Abrizzi." Hasler seemed to keep pushing Abrizzi as a suspect even though we did not have much evidence against him. Maybe he knew something I didn't.

"Maybe, but it could be someone else I don't even know about."

"True. You could make the Italians on this ship very unhappy if they realize what you are doing. The Navy does not like racial discrimination. You'd better find a few non-Italian suspects. Also, you'd better not try this Lone Ranger stuff anymore. Get help."

I said, "All right. I'm here for help and to get some questions answered."

"If the first one is about the olfactory ability of search dogs, the answer is that no one knows exactly why they are so good. They just are. There are some experts who claim that enough drug molecules pass through metal for dogs to recognize the distinctive odors of the major drugs even when they are sealed in cans or cans hidden in gasoline tanks."

"Do all experts think that?"

"No. There are as many others who claim that the test results are questionable or that odors are passing through poorly soldered joints or closures."

"What does that mean?"

"It means there is a lot of doubt. Maybe some of the drug remained on the outside of the metal container or there are not enough normal masking odors present. Those conducting the tests may have cleaned the container too well. No one will ever know what the answer is until dogs are taught to talk."

"That brings me to another question," I continued. "Suppose a metal container was placed in a room where a lot of odors, more then just what you called masking odors, were present. Wouldn't that complicate the process or even make it impossible for the dogs to come up with something?"

"Sure. It might make it impossible for a dog to pick it out, but there are some real experts in the field who will even dispute that. I think they are dog lovers and are therefore unduly influenced."

I began to think that Doc Hasler really believed these little excursions into fantasy. Maybe he liked dogs, too, as I did.

I said, "Thanks. I might know where the container is hidden. I'll see you later."

Hasler's icy blue eyes and twitching eyebrows stopped me even before his voice roared, "Like hell you will. You're my patient, and where you go, I go."

I knew he meant business. I said, "You'd better step outside and see part of the problem." I opened the door, and Benito was standing there, twiddling his night stick in small circles, and waiting expectantly for us.

Hasler closed the door and said, "What the hell is this?" "Don't you remember? The Exec put an armed guard on me. And I told you Benito was there when the knife was thrown at me. Are you losing your memory?"

We went back over to Hasler's chairs and sat down.

Hasler's mustache twitched violently. "All right, I guess I wasn't listening closely enough. But if Benito takes that thing out of its holster, I'm leaving."

"I told Benito to use the night stick instead of the pistol. We'll be safe. Besides he can't swing that long a stick very hard."

"I hope not."

I said, "Okay, I told you I won't try to do it alone. We need to find a way to make a copy of Novella's master key. Can you rig an emergency situation near the master-at-arms shack so that you can quickly order the duty master-at-arms to come help you for a minute or so?"

"I guess so. What will that do to help?"

"I'm going to use the Candace Terry plan."

"You're always talking about that broad. What the hell is that?"

I laughed. "You would have liked Candace. She was a great tactician in the field of love. Never lost a battle. She knew how to divert attention by attacking. When I unbuttoned something, she buttoned something else."

"What has that got to do with Benito?"

"Benito is following me around like a lap dog, but I'll figure out a way to shake him for the same period of time you draw off the master-at-arms. Then I'll slip in and make an impression of the key."

"How?"

"Simple. In a soft bar of soap."

"Where the hell did you get that idea?"

"Mike Hammer, I think. Maybe someone else. I read a lot of that stuff."

Hasler groaned. "You read too much."

We talked over the scam for a few minutes, and then I left, trailed by the ever-present Benito. I stopped by my room and picked up the bar of soap, which I had been warming in water in my wash basin. It was soft enough to do the job, but a little slimy. I wrapped it in the celophane covering it had come in and slipped it into my pocket, hoping the slime wouldn't soak through.

As we walked down the passageway toward the master-at-arms shack, I tried to set Benito up for the coming scam. I said, "Benito, do you feel all right?"

"Sure."

"I smell something unusual."

Benito sniffed obediently. "Don't smell nothing except for the wax on the linoleum deck. We use too damned much of it."

I deliberately staggered a little.

Benito said, "The ship ain't rolling that much. Maybe you ought to go back to your room."

"No, I need the exercise."

We went on up the passageway and past the master-at-arms shack. As I had expected, the duty master-at-arms was sitting behind the small desk reading a copy of *Playboy* magazine. He was so absorbed in memorizing the charms of some babe that he didn't even look up when we passed. I turned the corner beyond the shack, stopped suddenly, and bent down to tie my shoe lace. Benito stopped beside me.

In a few seconds, as planned, Doc Hasler burst around the corner forward of the shack and said to the startled master-at-arms, "Quick, follow me! I have an emergency, and I need your help!"

The duty master-at-arms made a move to lock the shack, but Hasler grabbed his arm and hurried him off. I straightened up from tying my shoe, blinked my eyes, and leaned on Benito.

"Damn, I feel awful! Go get Doc Hasler, quick." I slumped down to the floor. I was a histrionic success, for without hesitation, Benito took off like a small spaniel after a wounded duck. I got up, moved quickly into the master-at-arms shack, and pulled open the upper drawer. Sure enough, the keys were lying there, and I grabbed the ring and found the one with the red tag. In less than a minute I had uncovered the sticky soap, pressed the key into it, re-covered the soap with the cellophane, stuffed it back into my pocket, wiped off the key, put the key ring back in the desk drawer, and returned to the passageway.

I sat on the deck for a minute or so until I heard the sound of running feet. Doc Hasler wheeled around the corner, closely followed by Benito, night stick flapping, and the duty master-at-arms. Hasler bent over me. "What's the matter?"

"I almost passed out," I replied. "Fortunately Benito's prompt action saved me from another bump on the head and maybe serious injury."

"Yeah," said Hasler, "You've had your quota of those. I think you're wacky enough already."

I thought this was a bit of an exaggeration. Doc Hasler helped me up and said to Benito, "Let's get him up to sick bay so I can examine him."

The duty master-at-arms looked a little mystified. "But, sir, what about your emergency?"

"Oh, that. I think my pharmacist's mate can take care of it. Thanks for your help."

When we got to sick bay, Benito stayed behind as I went inside. I asked Hasler if I could see Garrity.

"Sure, he's conscious. He started opening his eyes about an hour ago."

Garrity lay in a lower bunk, his head wrapped in a turban-like bandage. He was pale, but his eyes were open, and they followed me as I bent over him.

"Can you hear me?" I asked.

"Sure," he said. "The pharmacist's mate said you found me. Thanks."

"Can you tell me what happened?"

"More or less. Some of it is still foggy. I was going on watch in the engine room, and I passed by the corridor to the machine shop. Two men were going in the door. There may have been a third man in front of them. The two I could see were fairly large and were wearing dungarees. They were carrying some paper bags and a large can. I started down the corridor to see what was going on, but before I could get there, the door clanged shut.

"Then I thought better of it. I was only a petty officer third class, and I figured I needed some help. I went up to the wardroom and found Lieutenant Farrington sitting there. I told him what I had seen and then followed him back down to the machine shop. He told me to stand guard outside the door while he went inside. He opened the door, went in, and closed the door behind him. I kept my eyes up the corridor, waiting to see if anyone would show up. Nothing else happened, but in a few minutes I heard the door open behind me, and I started to turn around. The next thing I remember, is waking up here."

Hasler had been listening to all this, and said to me, "That's about what you guessed."

"Please," I said, "I didn't guess, I deduced. There's a difference."

Hasler snorted. "Baloney. It sounded like guesswork to me."

"How would you like it if I called your diagnoses guesswork?"

"Sometimes they are. Call what you did whatever you want. You were right, but that still doesn't help us very much."

"Yes, and now we know that there were at least two men, maybe three, involved, and we have a better idea of what they were doing in the machine shop."

Hasler looked down at Garrity. "He shouldn't talk any more now. Maybe later."

"All right," I said. "I've got some other things to do."

While Hasler looked on with silent disapproval, I borrowed some bone files, bone cutters and saws, and a few other assorted instruments from the pharmacist's mate, stuffed them in my shirt, and went back to my room. On the way, Benito looked at me anxiously. "Are you all right, sir? You look a bit swollen."

"Good as new," I said. "Doc Hasler fixed me up with some new medicine and a dose of sympathy."

"Jeez," Benito said. "I could use some of that." "I'll be working in my room for a while." I said. "Please see that I'm safe."

As gunnery officer, Charlie Farrington had had custody of a lot of keys to various storerooms, magazines, and other assorted rooms. I found a key that had the same longitudinal grooves in it as the impression in my bar of soap, and that was big enough to allow me to cut it down. I set about transforming it into a copy of the master key. Charlie always kept a few small tools in his desk, and those and the tools I had picked up in sick bay would have to do.

Four hours later I had the finished product. I had ruined most of Hasler's instruments and had screwed up the front part of my desk. My hands were cut, scraped, and bleeding in three places because I didn't have a vise to hold the key in, but the finished product was worth it. It may not work, but at least it looked like a professional job.

I went back to Hasler's room, followed closely by Benito. Hasler was less than pleased when he saw what I had done to his instruments, but he didn't say much. His twitching mustache was in its mad mode, but he controlled himself well, took the instruments from me, and promptly threw them into his waste basket.

I said, "Let's start with the commissary storeroom. It's the most likely place after the paint locker, which I've already looked at."

"You what?"

"I searched the whole paint locker. There wasn't anything there in five-gallon tins but several cans of paint thinner."

Hasler's mustache quivered. "Thanks for telling me. I thought we were in this thing together."

"We are. I just didn't want to bother you until we were ready to take on a more important job. Let's get on with it. I'll give you the key I made, and after we get there, I'll draw Benito off around the corner. You can unlock the storeroom and take a look around to see if you can find anything unusual."

"Unusual? What the hell does that mean?"

"Anything that doesn't seem to belong there. Specifically a five-gallon tin recently soldered, top or bottom. Or an amateur soldering job. Or anything else that doesn't seem to belong there. That's the way Holmes searched a room."

"Holmes?"

"As in Sherlock Holmes."

Hasler groaned. "Enough of that detective stuff. Let's go."

We went down to the storeroom in column with me in the lead and Hasler bringing up the rear. When we reached the door, I kept on going and when Hasler stopped, Benito didn't even notice he was missing. Around the corner, I put on another act, and stopped and leaned against the bulkhead.

"I feel a little faint, Benito, hold me up." Benito grabbed my arm and looked around for Doc Hasler, but saw nothing but empty passageway behind him.

"Don't worry, Benito. I'll be all right if I just sit down a minute."

I was still sitting with Benito hovering over me when Hasler came around the corner. There was a pained expression spread between his mustache and his eyes.

"Let's go," he said. "Enough of this amateur sleuthing. We're off to see the supply officer."

"What happened?"

Hasler pulled out the key I had made. It was twisted and bent. "Couldn't even get it all the way in the lock," he said disgustedly.

In a few minutes we reached the supply office. Lieutenant Ross Barnaby was sitting just inside, immersed in a pile of papers. I think he had to catch up on all the stuff that Abrizzi had left undone. Barnaby had been a wide receiver on the football team at the Naval Academy. All-East, I think. We University of Californians don't really keep up with eastern football. Barnaby was African-American and shorter than I would have expected of an All-East receiver, but he made up for his lack of height by mobility and speed. As a quarterback in a touch football game in Naples, I never could pass the football far enough to get it past him. He was a smart supply officer and a very nice guy. He had only been aboard a short time, but he was already well liked.

He looked up when we entered. "Hi. What can the supply department do for you? We buy, sell, or trade anything, as long as you own it."

"We'd like to talk to you about something very important, but we need some privacy."

He pushed back his chair, grabbed his cap, and said, "Let's go up on deck."

We found a quiet place on the main deck. Except for a group of sailors working nearby and Benito, we were alone.

"Benito," I said, "Go over there and guard that missile launcher."

Benito looked uncertain, but he moved away out of ear shot.

"All right, what's the mystery?" asked Barney.

"You know about Charlie Farrington's death and about my trouble?"

"I know that Charlie is now in my refrigerator, and you lost an argument with a large beam. Did you have any more trouble than that?"

"Yes," Hasler said. "Someone tried to stick a

homemade shiv in Carlson's back."

"And there's even more than that," I said. "We think that the person or persons who killed Charlie are involved in smuggling heroin for eventual delivery to some group in Norfolk. I don't have time now to tell you all we know, but we think that Daviglia may be involved."

"We do?" Hasler said.

"Yes, I haven't told you everything about my investigation into the ship's roster. Daviglia has connections in Naples. If he's involved, it's probable that his role is to hide the tin can filled with dope in the provision storeroom. There are a lot of similar containers stored in it, and I would guess there are enough different smells in the storeroom to mask the characteristic odor of heroin or any other drug from search dogs."

"Dogs?" said Barnaby, "Are you sure you guys haven't been in to something? If not drugs, maybe some of Doc's medicinal brandy?"

"Doc says the ship will be searched in Norfolk by customs agents using dogs capable of sniffing out drugs," I said.

Barnaby said, "Well, there are a hell of a lot of strong smells down there. I feel sorry for those poor dogs. I take it you'd like to go down there?"

"Yes, we'd like to look around."

"At your service," Barnaby said.

We made our way down to the store room, Benito guarding our rear. Barnaby hauled out his master key and opened the door. When the lights had been turned on, we stepped inside. The room was a cramped version of an old country store. There were shelves of cans and cartons and burlap bags from overhead to the deck, with narrow aisles between the shelves. The smell was overpowering. I didn't think a dog could smell his own dinner or even another dog in there. The smells of spices, coffee, mold, and cotton and burlap bags mingled with smells I couldn't even guess at.

I started to walk up and down between the rows. There were cans of all kinds of foods. One kind, which stopped me was tomatoes. The cans were big, but not big enough for only one to be sufficient. I ran my fingers along the tops of all the cans and then along the bottoms. They were as smooth as Candace Terry's bottom, or at least what I had been able to feel of it.

Farther down was a row of five-gallon tins without labels. All they had to identify them was a string of numbers and symbols on their sides.

"What are these?" I asked Barnaby.

Barnaby bent down and looked closely at the numbers. "Salad oil."

I gave the tops of the cans in the front row the Candace Terry bottom test. They passed. I asked Doc Hasler to help me lift them down off of the shelves. His enthusiasm was flagging, but he came around when I threatened to take them all down myself. I don't think he wanted to have to help carry me up all those ladders if I passed out.

"Okay, I don't have time to fix the hernia you'll get," he said.

"Very funny. I lift weights all the time. You should, too. You're getting a little thick in the middle."

Hasler snorted. "That concussion must have affected your vision."

"Then let's get to work."

We began lifting the cans down together. One of the cans that had been in the back was suspicious. The soldered joint around the edge of the bottom was smooth enough, but the solder was newer than the others. I picked the can up and shook it. It was not as heavy as the others, and it did not give off the same gurgling sound. I put my ear to it and could hear a peculiar swish when I moved it. Not a liquid swish. More like cellophane rubbing together. It was a likely candidate.

"Doc, does this sound like something rubbing together to you?"

Hasler picked up the can and gave it the same shake I had.

"Maybe," he said. "We can tell more if we open it."

"No, we need it for bait. And it's the only evidence we have except for the soldering iron. Let's put it back and leave it."

"Good idea," Hasler said without any argument.

We had found what we were looking for and it was time to go. Besides, our sense of smell might never get back to normal if we stayed down there any longer. We put everything back the way it was when we came in, stepped outside, and Barnaby turned the lights off and locked up.

Benito was outside and hadn't seen anything that had happened inside the storeroom. Only the three of us knew about the can.

On the way back topside, I cautioned Barnaby about keeping quiet. After we had dropped him at his office, we headed for the Exec's stateroom. I had talked to the exec more in the last forty-eight hours than I had in the past six months, and I hoped he'd take the latest news well. My stock ought to be rising, and I hoped to do even better in the future.

A MURDER AT SEA

CHAPTER VI

Hasler and I continued up forward to the Exec's stateroom. I could hardly wait to tell him the news. I made sure that Hasler stood back so that I could enter first. I knocked boldly. I was getting the hang of this highlevel stuff now.

The Exec said, "Come in," and when he saw my face he almost smiled. I think I was getting him trained Carlson style. But then again, maybe he was just remembering some of the time he'd had to gig me.

We sat down without being invited. The Exec never turned a hair. A good sign. First, Hasler told him what Garrity had told us. Then, I gave the Exec a complete run down on my earlier search of the paint locker and the subsequent lack of results, and then a complete description of our visit to the commissary storeroom.
Hasler interrupted and said, "Tell him about the knife." The Exec said, "What knife?"

I had hoped to keep this quiet so that I could persuade the Exec to cancel the guard he had placed on me, but now I was forced to tell him the details. As I talked, his eyes grew wider and wider.

When I finished, he said, "Jesus, what is this Navy coming to? You'd think this was 1880. We've got to stop this diddling around before we all get killed."

Hasler said, "I don't think it's that bad."

"Don't worry, sir," I said. "The guard you put on me is working fine and we'll be in port soon."

The Exec wasn't happy with the situation, and he got up and paced back and forth. I knew now he would continue the guard detail. Maybe his conscience was bothering him. His choice of Benito as my guard showed he hadn't taken the risk to me very seriously. He gritted his teeth and sat down.

"Go on, Carlson."

I told him that although the search of the paint locker was a bust, the payoff had come in the search of the commissary storeroom. I included all the details, giving Doc Hasler as much credit as I could. The Exec asked a lot of questions, all penetrating and to the point. He got more and more enthusiastic, and soon was on the edge of his chair, his eyes sparkling.

"Let's go down to the storeroom so I can see the can," he said, rising eagerly out of his chair.

"Better not, sir," I said. "We've stirred up the water enough. I think we should let the evidence stay where it is until the authorities come aboard in Norfolk. I assume somebody will be coming aboard by helicopter early tomorrow morning."

The Exec was nodding and taking in what I was saying. "That makes sense," he said, but he didn't sound completely convinced.

I decided to give him another salvo. I said, "I don't think anyone knows we've found it except Hasler, Barney, and myself. Benito was outside all the time we were searching, but he never saw what we were doing inside."

"Yes you're right. We'll be getting investigative help from the Fifth Naval District staff, the Office of Naval Intelligence, and probably the FBI. They'll be arriving via helo about 0800 and will start their inquiry while we're on the way in and traveling up the channel. We're now scheduled to arrive at the destroyer piers about noon."

I liked his attitude. We were now talking about the whole affair man to man and not lord to vassal. Haser kept looking at me out of the corner of his eye as our conversation went on. I think he expected the Exec to bring me to heel any time. Hasler's attitude slowly turned to what I thought was newfound respect, or maybe it was just a slight case of indigestion.

The Exec sat down reluctantly. "All right," he said, "We'll leave it there. Hopefully the professional investigators will know what to do."

I was a little put off by his use of the word professional. Maybe we weren't professional, but I thought we were doing pretty well.

"I'm sure you're doing the right thing, sir," I said hopefully.

As we got up to leave, the Exec said, "Oh, Carlson, what is your first name?"

"Carl, sir," I said.

"No, your first name." I think he thought the "sir" was "son".

"Carl is my first name, sir."

"Oh. Isn't that a bit unusual?"

"No, sir, not for Scandinavians. Carlson means Carl, son of Carl. They do that a lot, like Swen Swenson, son of Swen."

"I see. Well, Carl, keep up the good work."

Hasler didn't say a thing until we were well down the passageway. Then he sneered, "Carl! You sold out to the enemy. What the hell has happened to you? A little success has gone to your head."

"Calm down, Doc. I'm the same guy I always was. Just a little more experienced. Besides, we haven't got this case solved yet. We have a motive and some suspects, but we don't have enough evidence, and what we do have we can't connect to any of the suspects. I'm afraid we need the help of the experts ashore. Apparently only they will be allowed to question the suspects. I asked the Exec about starting an investigation, and he put me off. Until an investigating officer is appointed, no one else can legally ask questions of any of the suspects."

Hasler snorted. "I can see why. We don't have any experts in that line aboard."

"What's wrong with us? You're as bad as the Exec. We haven't done badly so far. If we could just question the suspects, I bet we'd solve this case."

Hasler laughed, "Forget it. You've been reading too many detective stories. Go out on deck and get some fresh air. It will help your headache and clear your overinflated head. That's a medical order."

"Okay," I said. I missed being in the fresh air on my bridge watches. Most of the officers looked on standing watches as a chore, but I always liked them. They were a challenge. The officer of the deck, and even his assistant, known as the junior officer of the watch, had the best seats in the house when maneuvers were going on. Granted, as officer of the deck, you could lose your shirt if you made a mistake and went the wrong way in answer to a signal, but if everything was done properly, the results were spectacular, with all those big ships wheeling around just like an aquatic ballet. I never could get enough of it, even in bad weather.

The wind in the North Atlantic got damned cold if you had to spend much of your watch out on the bridge wing in the open, but the inside of the bridge was warm and pleasant. I figured that if a man didn't like standing as officer of the deck watch, he didn't like being in the Navy. After all, maneuvering small, fast fighting ships was what the Navy was all about. John Paul Jones said so, and I agreed with him.

Benito was still tagging along in my wake, obviously disappointed that someone hadn't done something either to relieve him of the job of guarding me, or to give him a chance to use his pistol. I had hoped that the Executive Officer would have answered his conscience and replaced Benito. Maybe he just hadn't gotten around to it yet.

"Come on, Benito, we're going topside for some fresh air."

As we were going up the passageway, I spotted my petty officer Howlett coming my way, and he saw me at about the same time.

When we met, he looked at Benito. "Is he following you or after you?"

"Don't be funny, he's guarding me. Someone tried to kill me last night and again this morning."

"That's what I wanted to talk to you about. Can you call him off for a minute or so?"

I turned to Benito. "Benito, please go ahead and make sure the passageway is safe. I'll be along in a minute as soon as I talk to Howlett."

Benito looked at me and walked off.

"What's new?" I asked.

"I just heard about what happened last night

with the guys in your room. The whole crew knows, and they don't like it."

"Thanks, I didn't know they cared."

"They know I do, and that's all they need to know."

"Someone also threw a knife at my back a few hours ago."

"Damn! Do you have any idea who was in your room last night, or who threw the knife?"

"Maybe Antonio or Daviglia. Maybe not. Maybe Novella threw the knife. Maybe someone else."

"Okay, we'll watch all three of them."

"It could be anyone, really. Before long you'll have half the crew watching the other half."

"We'll watch as many as we have to. I think a guard is a good idea, but I don't know about Benito. I'll pass the word around. Also, I think it's time to add my own guards to Benito. He's not good enough, even with that gun. I'll get back to you."

"Thanks," I said, as I hurried on to join Benito. Benito was a little put out, but at least the next passageway was safe and clear.

Benito's black eyes sparkled with indignation. "Jeez, Mister Carlson, if we're going to be knifed together, the least you can do is to trust me."

"Sorry," I said. "It was a private matter between Howlett and me, just business."

I went up to the weather deck, Benito following like a small, disgruntled dog. On the *Lassiter* there is a continuous deck, all on one level, known as the main deck, from the bow almost all the way aft to just behind the helicopter deck. Then there is an additional small deck at a lower level aft to the stern. The main deck is narrow in some areas, wide in others. I found that I could go up to the forecastle, out the door in the forward bulkhead, and then turn to cross the ship, keeping close to the bulkhead so that I couldn't be seen from the bridge above being trailed by Benito. I felt a little foolish being escorted by an armed guard, even though I seemed to need one. Then I could move off the forecastle through the door in the forward bulkhead, walk aft past the stacks to the helo pad, cross over the deck, and make my way forward again. On the first lap, I counted my paces and figured I could do a mile in seventeen laps.

After the eighth lap, Benito was puffing, and I stopped on the starboard side, just below the after deck house, for a few minutes rest. The deck was quite narrow there, and I was tempted to lean on the lifelines and watch the swirling wake pass by. Then I remembered the advice of an old chief boatswain's mate who had been an instructor in seamanship at the University of California NROTC. He told us never to lean on the lifelines. He never said why, but I figured he knew what he was talking about. I stood back against the bulkhead with Benito literally leaning on the bulkhead a few steps aft of me. He was really breathing hard. All that running around in Piraeus was telling on him.

"What's the matter?" I asked. "Too much shore time in Piraeus?"

"Nah," he gasped. "Too short legs."

"You got around pretty fast in Piraeus."

Benito snorted. "Them Greek women was easy to catch."

"So's the clap, particularly if you're full of ouzo." Ouzo is a sweet, anise flavored drink which is a favorite of the Greeks and some American sailors. I couldn't stand it.

Benito laughed. "I didn't drink much ouzo, only wine. I used the ouzo to prevent the clap. Only a damned fool would drink ouzo."

That one stopped me. "How's that?"

"I rubbed it on my tool after I left the women."

"Did it do the job?"

"I guess so. It hurt like hell, but I didn't get the clap." Ask a foolish question and you get a foolish answer, at least from Benito.

I decided to give him a little recovery time, so I stepped over near the lifeline, looked down, and watched the ship's wake boiling back along the side. I'd heard the Atlantic was usually rough as hell and very cold in December. Today, in the lee of the ship's side which sheltered me from a wind out of the south, the temperature was comfortable. The wind was whistling over the top of the deck house thirty feet above, but down on our level it was almost calm. The sun was starting down in the west, and felt very pleasant shining on my windbreaker. I took off my cap and gingerly felt the area around my stitches. The swelling was going down.

I liked watching the endless succession of waves generated by our bow's twenty-four knots spreading away from our side. Today they were in good form, running at an angle in serried ranks, and occasionally cresting with little whitecaps. We were close enough to the coast to be crossing the Gulfstream, and I spotted a few pieces of gray-green floating seaweed, known as Sargasso weed, which had been carried thousands of miles north in the slowly flowing Gulf Stream current headed for Ireland. Even a few sea gulls were wheeling about, looking for unwary fish or pieces of garbage. They squawked and squealed at each other as they fought over their catches. I never tired of watching their graceful movements.

After I had watched a turning gull nearly touch its wing tip in the sea, I decided to walk over to Benito to see if he was ready for a few more laps. I had only taken a step aft when there was a hell of a crash behind me. I turned around. A large, galvanized bucket was bouncing along the deck, spewing heavy metal objects behind it.

"Jesus, Mister Carlson! That thing missed you by inches!" Benito yelled.

I looked up. Thirty feet above, I could see just the top of a man's head as it was pulled back. His hair was black, and he was not wearing headgear.

Benito was frozen in place, his mouth wide open, and his eyes staring at the bucket.

"After him, Benito!" I shouted. Right away I regretted my order. Benito's legs began working, but he wasn't making much headway. He turned forward and started hauling his pistol out of its holster. "I'll get the bastard!" he shouted.

"No! No! Don't try to shoot him! Just find out who it is! Go up the ladder!"

Benito reluctantly pushed his pistol back into its holster and took off for the nearest ladder. He sprang at it like a miniature Tarzan and shot up the first four steps. On the fifth step his night stick got tangled in the rungs of the ladder, and he crashed to the deck, a flailing mass of stick, holster, arms, and legs.

I ran over to his struggling form and tried to untangle him from his weaponry. It was a lost cause.

"Never mind, Benito," I said. "It's too late. The man is long gone now. He could have gone below decks through the hangar and then almost anywhere. We'll never catch him. Let's go see Doctor Hasler and find out if you've broken anything. Can you get up?"

"I dunno. My knee hurts. Musta caught the damned night stick in the ladder. Shoulda used the pistol."

"You'll be all right," I said. "I'll help you stand up." We started off slowly, Benito leaning on me. He was limping a little, but I got him to Doc Hasler's room.

When we went in his door, Hasler looked at us with a pained expression. "Some exercise," he said. "It looks like you've worn each other out."

"Don't try to be funny. You're lucky you aren't down in sick bay trying to put me back together again."

"Yeah." said Benito. "Some sunnabitch tried to drop a bucket of iron pipe fittings on Mister Carlson. Musta weighed fifty pounds. If he hadn't moved just in time, he'd a been shorter'n a pile of hamburger. Maybe even shorter'n me."

I shuddered. Benito was right. If my head had been hit, it would have ended up between my ankles. I felt weak, and I sat down on Doc's bunk in a hurry.

"Doc," I said through a slight haze. "We've been through a hell of an experience for the second time today. Benito and I both need a shot of medicinal brandy." Hasler peered at me. "Damned if you don't. You're pale as a Greek woman's belly. I think I'll take one, too."

"Why a Greek woman?" I asked, not particularly caring why. For once I had lost interest in women. "They never wear bikinis."

"Oh yeah. I remember you saying that Greek

women are very modest."

"That's right. They wear one piece suits," Hasler said. "You can't be too bad off if you can still think about women. Maybe you don't need the brandy."

"Oh, no you don't. I need it."

Hasler walked over to a locker with a large pad-lock on it, opened it, and drew out three small bottles of medicinal brandy. He handed us each one and kept one for himself. Benito drained his in one gulp. As an after thought he said, "Downa hatch," and smiled. It was the first time I had seen Benito smile.

Hasler drank his slowly, his mustache twitch-ing contentedly, and he was apparently lost in thought.

I said, "Even at a time like this, you're think-ing about that woman's belly."

I shouldn't have said that. He looked at me like he had been hit with a wet rag, and he didn't even bother to answer my thoughtless comment.

I sipped mine slowly, too. It felt warm all the way down, and the haze slowly dissolved. The drink was the best thing that had happened to me all day. I could still see that heavy bucket rolling around on deck and hear the heavy thud. I shud-dered and savored the last drops of brandy.

When Benito, now miraculously recovered, and I got back to my room, a relief was waiting to take over the watch from Benito. He was a tall black man named Helms. He saluted and said, "Good evening, Mister Carlson, I'm here to relieve Benito."

I was glad the Executive Officer had finally gotten around to relieving Benito. I though he needed a relief and after the last hour he deserved one. I looked at Helms. He was a strong looking, capable man. His intelligent face topped a tall, muscular body. I said, "Any relation to Senator Jesse Helms of North Carolina?"

Helms laughed, "No, not that either one of us would admit to. Besides, I'm from Louisiana."

By now he and Benito were going through the bit of transferring the belt holding the gun and night stick from Benito's short form to Helms's lanky one. The night stick looked better on Helms.

Benito said to Helms, "This guy is unlucky. You might have to use these things."

Helms looked confused and his eyes widened, but he didn't ask any questions.

I pointed to the .45 caliber automatic Helms was adjusting over his hip. "Have you ever fired one of those things?" I asked.

"Not this particular kind of gun. As a watchstander, I've been instructed in how to use it, and I don't think I'll shoot you or me if I have to take it out of its holster. I've shot many a gun, and I used to throw a lot of sticks."

"How much experience have you had with a gun?"

"I used to shoot my daddy's thirty-eight back in the fields on our farm. Mostly at snakes. Sometimes a rabbit. Ammunition cost so much, most of the time I had to throw sticks or rocks. I'm pretty good with sticks. This one here is too long to throw well, but it'll do if I have to defend you, particularly tomorrow when we get into port and some girls come aboard."

A real wit I thought. "What girls?" I asked, ever ready to play the stooge.

"Guy I know in the radio shack said there might be some bitches coming aboard tomorrow."

Just as I was about to go into my room, Howlett came running down the passageway.

"Jesus, Mister Carlson, I just heard about the bucket. Are you all right?"

"Yes, it missed me, and Doctor Hasler has treated me for a near miss."

Howlett looked puzzled for a minute. Then he looked at Helms appraisingly. "I didn't like Benito very much. Helms, here, will do better. I'm putting a backup of my own on you."

"Any dope from the crew?"

"No, I didn't have time to get my guards set or to do much investigating. They definitely think drugs are involved. No one would try to kill you twice for cheap."

I didn't know exactly what he meant by that, but I could guess. I thought I'd include a little more vocabulary in our next English lesson.

"Thanks," I said.

Howlett left, muttering to himself.

Then I had a thought. Could the man who had dropped the bucket have been Lieutenant Abrizzi? Probably not. But what if he were trying to divert suspicion from him to an enlisted man? I decided I needed Doc Hasler's help to find out more about Abrizzi.

I went to Hasler's room, Helms following. When I opened the door, Hasler didn't looked too happy to see me. He closed the safe he had been standing in front of and turned to face me.

"Don't worry," I said. "This time all I want is something simple."

"Go on," he said.

"I need you to give Carlos Abrizzi a physical exam. Tell him you have to give him a predetachment physical, or any other excuse you can think of."

Hasler snorted. "He won't go for that. Besides, what's the point?"

"I want to search his room."

Hasler's face seemed to brighten. I think he thought Abrizzi was involved. He said, "Don't tell me any more. I don't understand any of this. What about his roommate?"

"He's on watch," I said.

"All right. Give me a few minutes head start."

I sat quietly for ten minutes and then went outside to pick up Helms. There didn't seem to be any way to get rid of him, so I decided to bluff it out. I went directly to Abrizzi's room. As I went in, I said, "Wait here. I'm going to visit Lieutenant Abrizzi."

"He ain't here," Helms said.

"I know. I'm going to wait."

I went in and looked quickly in his hanging locker. There was a pair of jeans and a blue shirt hanging in the back. They were just civilian clothes, but they would look like dungarees if he were trying to look like an enlisted man. I walked out Abrizzi's door and picked up Helms. Helms said, "I haven't seen him out here."

"Guess he's delayed," I said.

I went back to Hasler's room and waited until he returned. He raised his eyebrows questioningly.

"He's got clothes he could have worn to pass himself off as an enlisted man," I said. "He's still on our suspect list."

"Maybe you're right. You ought to talk to him. When I left the wardroom, he was in there nursing a cup of coffee."

"I'll go right now," I said.

I picked up Helms outside and told him I was going to the wardroom to see Lieutenant Abrizzi.

"Could of told you he was there when you went to his room."

"Why didn't you?"

"You didn't ask. You officers never do."

"Oh come now, Helms, you know I'm not like the rest of these guys."

Helms smiled, and I think he had a real put down ready, but he didn't use it. Instead he said, "Maybe not. Sorry. He went up there over an hour ago and hasn't come back. If he had, I would have seen him. He has to pass right by here to get to his room."

I thought about that on the way up to the wardroom. I hadn't realized how close to me Abrizzi lived and how easy it would have been for him to keep tabs on my movements. Abrizzi was sitting all alone in the wardroom with a fresh cup of coffee in front of him. I turned to Helms before I entered. "I'll be in here for a few minutes. Why don't you go to the pantry door and ask Antonio to give you cup of coffee."

Helms screwed up his face, "Not me. Benito says he is a bastid. Benito said he tried to be friendly with him, ashore in Naples, but that Antonio told him to get lost in a very unfriendly way."

So Benito and Antonio didn't get along. That meant they probably weren't collaborators. But then maybe this was all for show, staged for Helms's benefit. They knew that Helms would be guarding me.

"Well, suit yourself. I think I'll be safe in here. Go where you want to go."

I entered the wardroom and sat down across

from Abrizzi, stopping on the way to pour myself a cup of stale and lukewarm coffee.

I drank a little. It was awful, but anything in the line of duty. Abrizzi didn't even look up.

I said, "How's it going?" A great opening gambit, worthy of Mike Hammer.

"Ugh," he said slowly, his eyes still fixed on his coffee cup.

I tried again.

"I guess you're glad to be getting back to Norfolk tomorrow?"

He raised his eyes and looked at me. It wasn't an unfriendly look, just a pained one. He looked unhappy. For a moment I felt a tinge of sympathy. Then I remembered that I might be sitting across from a man who had twice tried to kill me. With this thought in mind, it was easier to go on with my questions. A Mike Hammer question might work for a starter, but the next one had to dig a little deeper. I needed a Sherlock Holmes type probe.

"I guess it will be a relief to get back to take care of your family."

Maybe no one had bothered to be sympathetic to him recently. He almost warmed up as he answered, "Yeah, I've got a lot of problems with my family. And sometimes I think there are no solutions."

I dug a little deeper. "Can't the Navy medical system help?"

Abrizzi made a sound like a cat sneezing. The only difference was that a cat, like anyone else, enjoys a good sneeze. Abrizzi was definitely hurting.

He said, "I don't trust those Navy doctors. Neither does my wife. They can't even take your temperature right."

The way he said this convinced me that this was probably his wife's opinion, and that maybe he was just going along with it.

"You seem to get along with Doc Hasler, and he's a Navy doctor."

Abrizzi got up, and for a minute I thought he was going to leave, but he went over to the coffee pot and refilled his cup. Then he sat down and drank a sip of the coffee. He screwed up his face in disgust and pushed the cup away. "He's a little different. I like him personally, but I wouldn't let him treat my family."

I probed some more. This one had to hurt him or I wouldn't get results. "You must have run up a lot of bills going to civilian doctors."

Abrizzi's eyes narrowed. I was getting in dangerous waters. "Don't worry about me," he said. "I'll manage."

"How so?"

Abrizzi clouded up. "That's my business."

With that he pushed back his chair and left the wardroom. I noticed his coffee cup was still full. If Sherlock had deduced that I had asked a pretty good question, he would have been wrong. He left the cup full because the coffee was lousy. Anyway, I was satisfied that I had done all that I could.

I sipped a little more of my cooling coffee. It was just as bad as when I first poured it. Yes, Abrizzi had a motive, but I wasn't sure he was the kind of person who would kill for it. He could certainly use the money from the heroin, but maybe he had another method of paying his bills. A rich uncle, perhaps, or maybe he was leaving the Navy to go into business with his father-in-law. I mulled over the possibilities, but couldn't reach any definite conclusions. The only sure thing was that Abrizzi was still on my suspect list. I abandoned my cold cup of coffee, pushed it over next to Abrizzi's, and left the wardroom. Helms was leaning on the bulkhead as far away from the pantry door as he could get.

"Let's go," I said.

"Fine with me," said Helms. "I don't like the air around here. But first, Howlett wants to see you in the damage control locker."

"Can't it wait?"

"He said you'd ask that, and he said to tell you it's for your own safety."

I gave in, and we headed down to the damage control locker. As we approached it, I could see Howlett and three other men standing outside laughing and talking. Each man had one of Howlett's coffee mugs gripped in his hand.

Howlett saw me coming and waved me into a seat in his locker. I recognized three men and returned their salutes and greetings. Howlett took the seat opposite me and the others crowded around the door.

I looked across at Howlett. "Well, Howlett, what's this all about?"

"Mister Carlson, if we're going to protect you, we've got to set some rules, and you've got to know something about your protectors."

"I know them," I said. "Dubek, here, is an engineer, and he..."

Howlett interrupted. "Sure he is, but he's also an expert with a wrench."

"Aren't all engineers..."

"See, you don't listen very well, and you don't understand. Look at Dubek."

I did. I saw a big, husky sailor wearing a windbreaker and a baseball cap. Below his broad face was a wide mouth punctuated with a gold tooth. "What's so different about Dubek?"

"Look again," Howlett said.

Dubek lifted the front of his windbreaker. A large wrench was stuffed in the front of his trousers. Almost as big as the one the intruder had used in my room the other night.

I said, "He'll have a lot of trouble bending over."

Howlett looked at me patiently. "You still don't get it. Dubek can pull that thing out and hit a fly with it at fifty feet."

I looked at the wrench again and shuddered as I thought about the poor fly. I looked at the three men with new respect and decided to take Howlett and his gang more seriously. I don't think they appreciated the Carlson wit, and I decided to keep it in check.

Howlett pointed at the second man. "You know Wiltsie. He's a deck hand."

"Yes. I think he's the one who's always swiping our watertight dog pipe wrenches." These were eighteen-inch long sections of heavy pipe kept on hangers near each watertight door to use in closing the big dogs that made the doors watertight. It was some of the damage control equipment that I was responsible for.

Wiltsie laughed, which made his heavy jowls and ample belly jiggle. "I lost the others over the side practicing."

"Practicing?" I asked.

Howlett said, "Yeah. Wiltsie can hit a target, too. Although maybe not a fly."

Laresa was different from the other two. He was only about five feet five, slim, and nervous. I knew he was from Mexico, since I had found his name in the list of the crew and had checked his record to make sure his name wasn't Italian. He was serving as a messman. Messmen worked in the mess hall, serving food, helping the cooks, and cleaning up. He wore the white uniform of a messman, so I didn't see any place where he could conceal a weapon. There was a large aluminum coffee pot at his feet which he had obviously brought from the mess hall. Howlett seemed to notice that I was looking at it. He grinned and said, "I see you know about Laresa."

I was puzzled. "What do I know? All I see is a big coffee pot."

Howlett said, "Show him, Laresa."

Laresa picked up the container, took off the top, and pulled out a wicked looking knife. It was the twin of the one that had been thrown at me.

"You get that in Naples?" I asked.

Laresa looked at Dubek. "No. Dubek helped me make it after Howlett told me I might need one."

I looked at Howlett. "And he can hit a fly?"

"Sure can. He's been practicing. He hit the target every time except once."

"What happened then?"

"Dubek came around the corner just as Laresa let go."

"And Laresa hit the monkey wrench?"

"Yeah, how'd you guess? Didn't hurt Dubek at all."

I said, "Maybe I don't want to know, but what were you using for a target?"

"An old life jacket."

"Good God, you must have ruined it. If the Exec finds out, he'll raise hell."

"Don't worry. We recycled it. You're sitting on it."

I realized Howlett's chair was a little softer. I looked down and saw that there was a red canvaslike cushion on it. "You cut up what was left of it up and made cushions out of it?"

"Yep. Wiltsie is good with a sail needle."

"He must be. These things have a lot of stitches in them."

Howlett reached over and patted my knee solicitously. "Don't worry, Mister Carlson, you're worth it. We all want to keep you healthy and comfortable."

Dubek cleared his throat. "Of course. Mister Carlson, we're counting on you to keep chief Snodgrass in line. We don't want him losing our special liberty requests again."

I sat back in my chair and tried to relax on my red cushion, but it was difficult, particularly with the cushion pushing up at me. I knew I'd be safer with these guys, but the cost might be high.

Howlett broke my short reverie. "Dubek will be near you when you're below deck. Wiltsie will cover you when you go topside, and Laresa will be with you in the mess hall. In order for the plan to work, you will have to tell Helms here where you are going."

"What do I do when Helms is relieved?" "He won't be. He's volunteered to guard you as long as the Exec wants him to."

I sighed. "Howlett, how can I ever thank you?"

Howlett looked at the overhead, avoiding my eyes. "Don't worry, Mister Carlson, I'll think of something."

I knew he would, and Helms and I left before he got the chance.

* * * *

I slept a little better that night, even though I knew there were still several persons who might be after me. I hoped I was safe, at least as long as Helms didn't go to sleep and Howlett's guard maintained their throwing accuracy. Somehow I trusted Helms more than I had Benito. Tomorrow would be a big day, and I wanted to be ready for anything that might come along. There was still a lot to be done before we got into port and the real experts took over. If the Exec wasn't going to suggest to the Captain that an investigating officer be appointed, I had a clear field to make a lot of moves. If I succeeded, who knows what my future might be in the Navy. If I failed, I might end up in the refrigerator with Charlie.

My headaches had stopped, the stitches were beginning to itch, and I was ready for anything provided I could get a little rest first. More than anything, I wanted to find out who that bucket-dropping bastard was. I could still hear the sickening crash and the heavy parts of pipe bouncing around the deck. But I was bushed and needed sleep, and finally I dropped off.

In spite of my tiredness, I slept restlessly, waking up now and then to turn over in my subconscious mind the elements of the case and wondering what Mike Hammer would have done that I hadn't. Nothing, I suspected, since there weren't any beautiful women in this case. He didn't usually take cases with just men and endless expanses of water involved. I didn't have any choice in the matter, so I tried to dream about my old schoolmate and karate partner, Candace Terry. But she was a long way off, and now just a faint dream to me.

Then I thought about Benito. He was off watch now and free to come and go as he pleased. I didn't think he was involved in the case, but he might be talking to his Italian friends. They were always a close knit group and would know that he had been following me around. They could easily get from him all they wanted to know. He knew where Barney, Hasler, and I had been this afternoon. Anyone who knew where the heroin was hidden and heard that we had been there would react strongly and quickly. Maybe they would come after me. Maybe they would remove the can and hide it somewhere else. The last thing they would do was throw it over the side. No one would do that to a million dollars.

Then I thought about who "they" was. Was it Novella, Daviglia, and Antonio? Or just two of them? Was Abrizzi part of the group? There had

to be at least two because two men had been in
my room. But what connection would Abrizzi
have with the machine shop? Maybe the man
helping Abrizzi was a machinist with a key to the
machine shop. By now I couldn't be sure of my
tentative identification of the two men in my room
as Antonio and Daviglia. There were a lot of men
and officers on the ship who were big, with broad
faces and big noses. A lot of men had black hair,
too. I tried to recall Abrizzi's hair, head, and face.
His hair and forehead could have been those of
the bucketdropper, but Daviglia, Novella, and
many others had similar hair and foreheads. Only
Antonio could be eliminated. That didn't help
much. The possible combinations of suspects confused my overworked and tired brain.

Then again, maybe there was someone else
masterminding the whole thing. That happened
all the time in most mystery novels. But this was-
n't a novel and I had nearly been the second vic-
tim. I started to get out of my bunk and do something about preserving our best piece of evidence,
the five gallon can. I knew it was important, but
my head began to hurt again, and I settled back
in my bunk instead. To hell with it, I thought. I'd
rather think about Candace Terry. The Navy
didn't do much for your sex life. It was all or nothing with the Navy. Nothing aboard ship, and all
you wanted ashore, provided you could find and
persuade someone to play. Or maybe you had to

pay for it, and I wasn't for that.

I thought about Candace's perfumed hair, her smooth, tanned skin, her well proportioned body, its firm muscles sheathed in just the right amount of padding. I fell asleep dreaming that I had her pinned to a blanket in the Berkeley hills. But I was so tired that, just as I was about to enter Nirvana, I fell deeply asleep.

A MURDER AT SEA

CHAPTER VII

The next morning my headache was gone and the bump under my stitches was almost flat. The stitches were itching like crazy, but I knew they'd be there for another week. I got up with my usual bounce and headed towards the shower. Then I went up to the wardroom and ordered a full breakfast. Lots of fuel. I figured it would be a full day. My thoughts turned to Antonio out in the pantry. If he were one of my pursuers, poisoning my breakfast would be simple if I made it easy for him. I called the mess attendant back and changed my order to grape fruit, corn flakes, and toast. Not as much energy as in my usual breakfast, but harder to poison.

Hasler watched me carefully, and after hearing the size of my first order, he said, "Our growing boy is back in business."

When he heard me change it, he said, "Now that's better."

I couldn't let him get away with that. I looked down at his waist. Hasler noted the direction of my glance and sucked his stomach in slowly.

"Yes," I said, "but I won't be growing sideways." Hasler colored a bit. He was getting sensitive about his expanding waist line, although his overall weight was going down.

About half way through my breakfast, I heard flight quarters sound over the loud speaker. That meant the crew members detailed to help a helo land aboard would be gathering quickly on the helo deck. I finished the last of my spare breakfast quickly, stuffed a second order of toast in my windbreaker pockets, and headed up to the helo platform on the after part of the ship. The platform, or pad, as the sailors called it, is a flat deck cleared of all obstructions aft of number two stack. A big bull's eye is painted in the middle of it for the helo pilots to aim for, and forward of it is a hangar in which our own helo is housed after its blades are folded.

Helms had been secured from watching over me early that morning. I guess the Exec figured I was safe during daylight hours, or else he needed Helms for some other important duty. I felt the same way, as long as Antonio hadn't slipped arsenic into my cereal. I felt fine with a load of calories in my gut, but maybe arsenic took time to act. I tried to remember the details of a similar case solved by Sherlock Holmes, but I finally thought to hell with it. If I keel over, it'll be Doc Hasler's problem.

As I reached the top of the deck house aft,

just forward of the helicopter landing area, a Navy helo came around our stern to make its approach and land aboard. It was so low that its rotor blades were whipping the green coastal waters into foam. I joined a couple of officers who were already standing next to the rail just forward and above the helo pad watching the aircraft approach.

One was the communications officer, Lieutenant Joe Barrows. Joe was a big guy who liked to talk. Raised on a ranch in Montana, I think he spent so much time alone with cattle that all he wanted to do now was make up for lost time. He'd talk nonstop about anything, as long as it wasn't confidential or secret. When he started to talk, his eyes got that faraway across the Montana prairie stare, and he wouldn't stop talking for anything. Only once when some smartass in the wardroom had yelled, "stampede!' did I ever see and Barrows stop talking. And that was as he headed for the door.

As communication officer, he would know all about the dispatches that had come in overnight. I wanted to get him talking so that I could tap his knowledge.

I started with, "Joe, what are they going do to us when we get in?"

Barrows kept on looking at the slowly approaching helo but his mouth started moving just like I had hoped it would. I did my part as an earnest listener ready to absorb his every word.

"That helo is carrying an advance party of five officers. Two FBI agents, two Office of Naval Intelligence agents, and one commander legal specialist from the Fifth Naval District Headquarters."

Joe sounded like he was reading a dispatch. The words just kept coming. "They will use the period of time during which we are approaching Norfolk and passing up the channel to begin the investigation."

I knew from looking at the charts and from having been aboard when the ship had gone out the channel, that the trip alone would take two hours. I hoped they would be easier hours than the seasick period I had experienced almost six months ago. After all, I was an old salt now.

Joe went on. "We'll arrive at the destroyer piers at the Norfolk Naval Base about 1100 and moor at a south side berth all by ourselves port side to the pier. We'll be guarded by a platoon of Marines and be isolated and in effect quarantined. Nobody goes ashore and only those persons authorized by the Office of Naval Intelligence or by the FBI will be allowed to board the ship."

"Including some bitches," I said in a low voice.

Joe looked away from the helo and said, "What was that?"

"Nothing."

I guess my smart remark had turned Joe off.

He clammed up and in a few minutes moved aft and down the ladder to the helo pad to meet the passengers from the helo. I think he told me all he knew anyway, or at least all I wanted to know, so I stayed back with the others. All those not directly connected with helo operations are required to stay well clear in case of an accident.

The helicopter slowed its forward motion as it approached the ship. By now we had changed course and were headed so that the relative wind would be blowing across our deck at an angle of about forty-five degrees and the helo could come at us into that wind. I could sea the pilot staring at the white marks on our deck and manipulating the controls. I knew from my one helo ride that he had both hands full of controls and both feet busy on the rudder pedals. Landing a helo required much more skill and attention than bringing a regular aircraft into an airfield ashore. Landing on a carrier's short, pitching deck was much harder than landing ashore, but landing a helo on a small ship was the most difficult flying job in the Navy. I wanted to try it some day and maybe even become a naval aviator if I made the Navy my career. In the meantime I liked the *Lassiter* and the surface Navy. They were challenge enough for the moment.

Watching the pilot, I saw firsthand the skill needed to make a landing at sea on a pitching postage stamp of a deck. The pilot was good, and the sea was relatively mild. Through the plexiglass side panels of the helicopter, I could see him delicately manipulating all of his controls just prior to the touchdown on deck.

After a few seconds of jockeying, he made a perfect landing, the helo engine slowed down, and the rotor blades slowed and drooped like gigantic insect antennae. As Joe had predicted, an officer wearing a commander's three gold stripes on his sleeve and four men dressed in civilian clothes got out of the helo. They made their way forward clear of the rotor wash, holding on to their hats as they skittered across the deck, fighting the cross wind. Joe greeted them Montana style and escorted the party up to the bridge.

The helo pilot revved up his engine, the blades whirled horizontally, he pulled up on his collective control, and the helicopter took off, rising slowly before veering off and heading for shore. The ship changed course to head for the Virginia Capes guarding the entrance to the channel, and we sped up a little to make up for the time we had lost bringing the helo aboard.

I decided to go back to my room so that the Captain would know where to find me when he needed me. Before I went to my room, I knocked on Doc Hasler's door.

Hasler looked up from his usual pile of books and papers. He seemed pleased to see me. "I'm glad you stopped by. I told the Exec all about your encounter with the bucket. He was whizzed off that you hadn't told him about it yourself, but I calmed him down. He questioned a lot of men who were topside at the time. A signalman on watch saw a man standing by the edge of the deck around the after stack. He couldn't identify him. Too far away. Said he was wearing dungarees, nothing on his head, and his hair was black.

"Could have been anyone, from a chief petty officer in the engineering department to a fireman. Maybe even an officer," I said.

"What was that about an officer? They don't wear or have dungarees."

"Nothing, just a theory. Go on."

"It probably was an engineer. The Exec doesn't like anyone except engineers wearing dungarees, end even then not topside. That's why the signalman noticed him, the dungarees."

"Could have been Novella, or one of many other guys," Hasler went on.

"That's how I figure it. We're no closer to a solution than we ever were. As a matter of fact, it could even have been Abrizzi. He has some civilian clothes in his locker that look like dungarees."

Hasler brightened. "Abrizzi? How do you know what's in his locker?" I told him all about my trip to Abrizzi's room when he had agreed to keep Abrizzi busy and what I had found. As I talked, his mustache began to twitch, and he seemed almost pleased. When I finished, he said,

"My money's on Abrizzi, not Novella." That didn't seem exactly logical to me, but then Hasler wasn't always logical.

I changed the subject slightly. "After all that has happened, I'm just glad to be alive."

Hasler looked at me closely and grinned. "More or less," he said.

"You don't look so well yourself." And he didn't. There were dark shadows under his eyes, and his hands shook a little as he toyed with some of the papers on his desk.

Hasler put the papers down. I think he noticed that I was looking at his hands. "Haven't had much sleep. I've been worrying about what might happen to you."

I sighed. "At least someone cares."

"So does the Exec," said Hasler. "He wants to keep you out of harm's way."

"Only because he'd have to fill out a lot of reports if the guys who are after me succeed."

"Maybe, but I had to talk him out of your armed guard as of this morning."

"Thanks," I said.

"It was nothing. I figured you were safe in daylight as long as you stayed away from places where knives could be thrown at you or another bucket could be dropped on you. Also, most of the crew will be running around topside getting the equipment on deck ready for the ship to enter port, so you won't be alone."

That was enough for me. I thanked Hasler and went back to my room. I settled down in my chair to wait. After I had my feet arranged on my desk, I went over the facts and theories I hoped I would be called upon to present to the group. I finished in about five minutes and to fill in time, I began to recall the delights of past days in Naples and Menton.

A young, bachelor ensign could live a good life in a destroyer operating with the Sixth Fleet. We usually dashed around the relatively calm Mediterranean waters on ten-day to two-week exercise periods. These exercises were real, twenty-four-hours a-day workouts, and most of the officers usually were so pooped that they caught up on their sleep during the first day in port following the exercise period. After that, the pleasures of the Riviera awaited us, from Monaco to Villefranche and Menton. Particularly Menton, although there were many topless beaches elsewhere in France. The Italians were still a little hesitant about going topless, and the Greeks never did. I looked at my watch, wondering why I hadn't been sent for. I shrugged and went back to my reveries.

We also went to Naples and to ports in Greece and Turkey such as Piraeus, Benito's favorite watering hole. We rarely visited ports in North Africa. These were good ports for shopping, but not for much else, particularly for healthy young men with active glands. Most of the women wore veils. Those who didn't should have.

On the way into the Mediterranean, we stopped at Gibraltar. It was a strange mixture of British culture, Spanish influence, and African aromas. But reviewing its history and standing at the base of the menacing rise of the Rock, made it worth the trip.

Monaco was the place I liked best. Someday after I retire and have both the money and time to enjoy all of its attractions, I'm going back for a long visit.

Our first visit was short, just four days. We entered the small, crowded harbor on a beautiful day. I was standing at my entering-port quarters aft on the help platform, commanding my one-man division, Petty Officer Howlett. Doc Hasler, who was free to go any place he wanted to go for entering port, had elected to join me. We had a good view of the fantail, the aftermost deck of the ship. I couldn't figure our why Doc Hasler wanted to watch part of the deck force hustling about, moving big mooring lines around the small space below us. I'd have gone to the forecastle to get a better view of the beautiful yachts we were passing. But maybe he knew something I didn't know. He had been to Monaco before.

From my position aft we could see the rising, terrace-like hills of Monaco, topped by Prince Rainier's palace.

From conversations in the wardroom that

morning, I had learned that we were going to
make a Mediterranean moor. Most
Mediterranean ports are small, crowded, and limited in pier space. To use this pier space most effi-
ciently and to crowd in the largest number of
ships and larger boats, a system has evolved of
mooring ships and boats with their bows riding to
an anchor out in the stream, and their sterns teth-
ered to a narrow segment of pier. Then a brow is
run from their stern to the pier giving easy access
to the shore. For a small vessel, the
Mediterranean moor is easy, but with a ship as
big as the *Lassiter*, the process is more complicat-
ed. The ship has to drop its anchor at just the
right distance from the pier. Too far out, and the
anchor chain, when let out, won't permit the stern
to reach the pier. Too close in, and the anchor
and chain won't have enough holding power.
Whatever it took, I was betting on Captain
Faraday to do it right.

The *Lassiter* was so big that there was only one
berth that would accommodate us. We
approached it heading in. At the proper place, the
anchor up forward was dropped, and we could
hear the rumble of chain as the ship moved forward. At the same time, the rudder was put over
full and one engine backed while the other continued ahead. The ship began a graceful twist,
with the anchor, rudder, and the engines all working together to bring her stern around just short

of the section of the pier we were to use. I scanned that part of the pier, and noted that it jut-ted out a little beyond the adjacent structure, obvi-ously designed for still larger ships. Then I looked beyond the pier. Barely twenty yards away was a large swimming pool and beyond it a small park. My eyes widened. There were at least a dozen bronzed girls lying about the pool enclosure on chaise lounges. All were bare-breasted. I dug an elbow into Hasler's side. "You dirty old man! So that's why you came back here with me. You've been to Monaco before!"

"Sure. There's nothing wrong with my hor-mones. Don't you like the sights?"

I did, and so did the sailors down on the fan-tail preparing the small messenger lines to send the larger hawsers over to the pier. I could hear some low murmurs of appreciation and a few the-atrical groans.

Charlie Farrington, as gunnery officer, was in charge of the fantail. He was watching his men stumbling over the line as they tried to divide their attention between the lines and the swimming pool. Even a couple of barrell-chested boatswain's mates were having a tough time getting them to pay attention to their jobs.

Charlie finally lost his patience. "All right, you farmers, keep your eyes in the boat!"

I turned to Hasler. "What the hell does that mean?" He laughed. "An old Annapolis expression, I think. A command the old boat coxswains used to tell their oarsmen to watch the man's back in front of them and not look ashore."

"They must have missed a lot of scenery."

Hasler sighed. "That's the idea. These Naval Academy guys seem to survive, though."

Charlie's admonition seemed to do the trick, and the lines were soon secured and a large brow brought aboard.

The beautiful view ashore was causing a stirring in my underused loins, and I knew I would have to become better acquainted with Monaco. Up until a few months ago, all I knew about it was that it had a reputation for having large and beautiful gambling casinos, and I had expected to lose a few bucks. Now I had other plans. Where there was smoke there had to be fire, and at least from this distance, I liked the smoke.

Hasler seemed to sense my mood. He said in a stern voice, "The venereal disease rate in Monaco is moderate, but take every precaution."

That brought me down to earth, but as my mother used to say, you can't bake a cake without breaking a few eggs. Just thinking about my mother calmed me down a bit, and I decided to play it cool. Maybe I could win some money if I stuck to the casinos.

The next morning Hasler banged rudely on my door before flinging it wide open. Luckily, Charlie Farrington was up and out of the room, or he might have flung the door back in Hasler's face. I stretched and looked at Hasler. "What the hell is the trouble?"

Hasler sneered. "Nothing, if you took my advice. You look pretty pooped to me."

I let him stew for a few seconds. "The casino was pretty nice," I said. "I made a few bucks."

Regardless of where we went ashore, the trick for me was to stretch out an ensign's pay, not to eat the wrong foods, and to avoid the professional girls who were waiting at every bar. The few dollars I had won would help build up a little nest-egg for the States.

Doc Hasler was also a bachelor. His higher rank and extra doctor's pay helped fill out our combined financial resources. Two drinks, and all the money he had with him was mine, too. He also had a good eye for judging the ladies, and, as long as he was sober, he wouldn't let me get into trouble.

Now and then he drank too much, and his judgment would falter. Then he'd go after anything in skirts, with the exception of Greek soldiers. When he got too far off the beam, I'd have to get an arm-lock on him and drag him away from whatever doll he was chasing. I had the duty aboard ship every fourth day, but Hasler, as a doctor, was free to go ashore every day. On those occasions when I couldn't go with him, he would sometimes come back pretty much the worse for wear. I tried to find out where he had gone and what he had done, but he was never very forthcoming about it. Either he would say nothing, or he would joke about it.

When I asked other officers who had been ashore what had happened to Hasler, I couldn't find anyone who even remembered seeing him.

When we went ashore together we had one hell of a time. I was chuckling over one such incident when there was a knock on my door. The messenger barged in without waiting for my reply. "Sir, the Captain wants to see you in his lower cabin right away."

"Thank you," I said, suddenly jerked back into the present. I got up, checked my uniform in my mirror as far down as I could see from my limited height, brushed my hair, patted down the bandaid over my stitches, and went out my door. The messenger was still standing there, with an expectant look on his face.

"What now?" I asked.

"Benito says not to trust you. Sometimes you go back to sleep"

"I'm awake now. You can go back to the bridge."

As I walked down the corridor, I tried not to hurry in a manner unbecoming to a star witness. The ship was rolling gently in the coastal chop, and I had a little difficulty in walking a straight line. When I arrived at the cabin I knocked with a firmly closed fist.

The Captain said, "Come in."

I entered, hat in hand, and said, "Good morning, Captain. Good morning, Commander Molesworth." I had seen the Exec out of the corner of my eye and wanted to give him equal billing. The Captain harrumphed slightly and put down his empty coffee cup.

"Gentlemen, this is Ensign Carlson. Carlson, this is Commander Knight, the Fifth Naval District Legal Officer."

A pleasant-faced commander wearing glasses nodded in my direction. His blue service sleeve bore the legal corps insignia above the stripes. I noticed something else about his uniform. It was clear of all medals and campaign ribbons. Until now, I was the only officer I knew who had none. Legal officers don't go to sea much, but maybe this one had never been to sea at all.

The Captain turned to the next person, a chunky civilian of about fifty with steely gray eyes and a trap-like mouth. "This is Chief Agent MacIntyre of the FBI."

The penetrating eyes stared at me closely, and the mouth opened momentarily like a frog waiting to catch a fly, but he didn't say anything. His two hundred pounds was mostly muscle, but beginning to turn to fat. Tough as he looked, I liked him, and I wanted to see him in action, as long as he wasn't after me. He wore a dark gray suit

and vest, with a plain blue tie. A white handkerchief peeked out of his pocket. He was cleanly
shaven.

The next man was a little slimmer and
younger than his boss. He had a large black mustache, better than Doc Hasler's scraggly bush. I
looked him over carefully. He was still working
out, I thought, and not beginning to get out of
shape like his boss. But like his senior, he wore a
medium gray suit and vest and a lightly figured tie.

The Captain said, "This is agent Ligosi of the
FBI who will be assisting Mister MacIntyre."

Jesus, I thought, with a Italian name like
Ligosi, he isn't going to like my theory about the
shipboard mafia and their probable involvement.
Ligosi nodded slightly, the mustache so rigid that
it nodded too.

The other two were introduced as agents
White and Theron of ONI, from the Navy's
Office of Naval Intelligence. They wore nonde-
script brown suits without vests and with loud
ties. Both had small, straggly mustaches. Not quite
on the first team, I thought. There also seemed to
be some connection between mustaches and
investigating. I momentarily thought about growing one of my own, but remembered that
MacIntyre didn't have one. That was good enough
for me and I gave up on the idea.

They both nodded ceremonially and without
enthusiasm. I sensed that someone, probably

Commander Knight, or his boss, the Commandant of the Fifth Naval District, had called the FBI in on the case, and the boys from the Office of Natal Intelligence had their feelings hurt.

The Captain said to MacIntyre, "The Executive Officer and I have told you all we know."

MacIntyre nodded. "Thank you."

The Captain turned to me. "Carlson, take that chair and tell our guests what you know. Start from the beginning and stick to facts." Then he added, "And keep it short."

As I sat down in one of the vacant chairs, a cup of coffee materialized in front of my face, put there by one of the hovering messmen. I took it, skipped the sugar and cream they poked in front of my face, and turned confidently toward the others. The Captain ordered the messmen to leave the cabin and close the door. I was beginning to like the way the other half lived in the Navy, and I hoped I would survive long enough to enjoy some of the benefits myself. This was a lot better service than we got in the ward room, but the coffee still didn't measure up to the brew that came out of Howlett's old aluminum pot down in the damage control locker.

I looked around at the spartan but pleasant decor of the Captain's cabin. I pictured myself in the Captain's chair someday, or at least the Exec's.

"Well?" said the captain.

I came back to the present and began to talk. I told them everything, including, in spite of the Captain's instruction, my deductions and suspicions, making sure I gave Doc Hasler full credit for his help. Halfway through my narrative, the Captain sent for Hasler, who appeared a few minutes later and was put through the standard round of introductions. A chair was brought for him, and he sat down next to me. The messmen repeated their the coffee routine and then left the room. I managed to snag a second cup of coffee, this time with all the sugar I could put in it. I figured I'd need the energy.

I continued my story, ending with a description of our visit to the commissary storeroom the night before and what we had found.

I said, "The Executive Officer wanted to go down and verify our findings, but I advised him not to, since you would all be here today."

The Exec nodded in agreement. When I finished, old trap-mouth asked me a few questions, and as I had expected, Agent Ligosi narrowed his eyes a little when I described my search of the crew's records looking for Italian names. His questions were not openly hostile, but I figured I had better watch my step with him.

The Exec said, "Tell them about the attempts on your life." MacIntyre's eyes widened. "Why would anyone want to kill you?" I bristled, thinking my life was as valuable as anyone elses. Then I realized it wasn't a sarcastic remark. I said, "I don't know exactly, but I believe he, or they, must have thought I knew something about Lieutenant Farrington's murder or the drugs, if that's what it is."

I stole a glance at Hasler. Sure enough, his mustache was twitching. Below it I could see his lips moving. It wasn't hard to make out the word he was mouthing. It was "guessing".

I looked at him sternly. He sneered. To hell with him. I'd convince him soon enough.

I went on. "Petty Officer Garrity has confirmed my theory about what happened in the machine shop, and I know Chief Novella was aware that I had the soldering iron in my possession. He saw me take it that night in the machine shop. Whoever it was probably decided to try to kill me because of the evidence I was hiding, or because they thought I knew something. I think I'm safe now because they'll figure that any evidence I had in my possession will have been turned over to you."

Agent MacIntyre turned to the Exec inquiringly.

The Exec said, "I have the soldering iron and the roll of solder in my safe. I'll get them for you when we leave here."

MacIntyre nodded and turned to me, "Now tell us about the attempts on your life."

I started with the two men who had come into my room, went over the knife-throwing scene, and ended with the bucket dropping. MacIntyre laughed when I finished. I must have looked pained at such a light reaction to a serious matter. Evidently MacIntyre sensed my irritation.

"Sorry." he said, "But in my long career I've seen a lot of ways to kill a person. But I've never heard of three such unusual methods tried on one person over such a short period of time. I'd like the details later. They'll make interesting reading for the head of the FBI. Do you have anything else to tell us?"

"Nothing except there may be fingerprints on this knife." I pulled it out of my belt and held it out to MacIntyre.

The Captain and Exec looked at it as MacIntyre unwrapped it.

The Exec whistled softly. "Christ," he said, "No wonder the hole in the paint on the bulkhead was so big."

I was beginning to think that nobody gave a damn about what kind of a hole it might have made in me, or even in Benito. Everything else, even holes in paint, was important and interesting. But the fact that I could have been dead three times over, was incidental and just made for a helluva good laugh.

MacIntyre looked carefully at the knife and then shook his head. "No prints possible here," he said.

The questions put to Doc Hasler were mostly technical, having to do with his examination of Charlie's body in the machine shop, and they were soon terminated by Chief Agent MacIntyre who said the results of the autopsy would answer the remaining questions. Hasler looked relieved.

I had ceased to think of Chief Agent MacIntyre as "old trap-mouth." He was a nononsense professional with a trap-mind rather than a trap-mouth. The mouth was just firm and purposeful. I wasn't sure what he thought of me, but I was glad he was on our side.

The chief FBI agent then turned to the Captain and said they would like to examine the machine shop and the commissary store room. We all trooped out of the Captain's cabin and headed for the machine shop. When we arrived, I pointed to the spot in the passageway that I had thought was blood. It was still there. So were the two scuff marks leading to the door. The chief FBI agent asked the Captain to direct the guard there to continue to keep everyone away from the spot except agents. The party looked around the machine shop with interest, trying not to destroy any evidence. I showed them where I had found the soldering iron and the roll of solder on the work bench, where Garrity's body had been, and where I had discovered Charlie's body.

The agents moved carefully, obviously not wanting to destroy or mask evidence until their experts could come aboard and look the area over for evidence and fingerprints. Then we left for the commissary storeroom. This was going to be my starring role, and I edged up next to the Exec as we walked down the long passageways and ladders to the storeroom.

The Exec apparently heard my firm footsteps, turned, and noticed me.

"Carlson," he said, "I think I might make you the ship's secretary when the new ensign comes aboard in July. The Captain and I need more help."

Each destroyer customarily got one Naval Academy graduate and one NROTC graduate each July after they were graduated by the Naval Academy or their university. During the year, the ship would lose one or two senior officers to shore duty. It would be a big occasion for me when they came aboard. I'd no longer be called 'junior.'

In my mind's eye I could also see that extra desk and comfortable swivel chair in the rear of the ship's office, and Chief Snodgrass and his assistant slaving away to carry out my every order. I liked the thought of it. I said, "Thank you, sir."

"Of course you'll keep your present job, too. The ship's secretary job will be a collateral duty. A ship this size doesn't rate a full time ship's secretary, and I know you'll accept the challenge."

I was taken aback for a minute. That 'collateral duty' stuff was the Navy's way of getting more
blood out of a skinny turnip. But I couldn't
complain.

"Don't worry, sir, I'll do them both to your
satisfaction."

"As ship's secretary, you'll be working directly
under me and also the Captain."

I thought it was the other way around, but this
wasn't the time to quibble.

Lieutenant Ross Barnaby had been summoned and was standing by the door to the commissary store room, keys in hand. The Captain
introduced him, and Barnaby opened the storeroom. The group passed inside, sniffed the atmosphere, and, collectively screwed up their noses.

The Captain called me forward. "Carlson,
show us the can."

I pushed forward, past the chief FBI Agent
and the two guys from ONI. The others, including Ligosi, had retreated to the passageway for
some fresh air. It wasn't that the air smelled bad.
All that good stuff in there couldn't possibly smell
bad. It's just that the combination of odors,
though individually pleasant, overpowered the
nose and made the eyes water. The smells, plus
the gentle rolling of the ship, made some of the
group turn pale.

I looked up at the row of cans. They marched
along the shelves like tin soldiers, each with its

mysterious marking stencilled in black letters.

Something wasn't quite right. I took down the can in the position of the one we had suspected, but it was heavy, and undoubtedly filled with liquid. With a mounting sense of alarm, I lifted down the remaining ten cans and shook them all. Then I shook them a second time and almost frantically clawed at the solder on their tops. There wasn't any doubt about it. Our evidence was gone.

The Captain read the look on my face. He could have had me keelhauled right then and there. Instead, he was astonishingly patient and understanding. All he said was, "Gone?"

I looked for a hole in the deck into which to crawl, but there wasn't anything there but cold, hard, steel.

A MURDER AT SEA

CHAPTER VIII

The walk back to the Captain's cabin seemed endless. No one said a word. Our shoes clattered on the steel ladders and the sound echoed ominously off the bulkheads. To me, the reflections sounded like the muffled drum beat of an escort at a military funeral. Mine. I would have felt better if the Captain had ordered me flogged. I wrote off in my mind a hundred times the Exec's statement about making me the ship's secretary. Even worse, I recalled my earlier fears about being passed over for promotion to lieutenant junior grade. I had blown our chance to collect more evidence or to find out who had placed the can in the storeroom, and worse, we now had no evidence at all.

We filed into the Captain's large inport cabin and sat down. For a moment I thought I ought to remain standing so the Captain could apply the lashes easier, but then I thought, what the hell, I wasn't the only one in on this decision. The Exec had approved it, and he didn't seem to be concerned. Maybe he had just learned to lose a few battles. That sort of thing would be all right if we ultimately won the war, but right now our prospects looked bleak.

The mess attendants hurried in with coffee, but I just couldn't take any, even though my nerves craved it. I felt certain that I would be sent back to the lower levels where I belonged. I even thought about trying to become an FBI agent if the Navy didn't want me. That thought died quickly. The FBI wouldn't want me either.

The Exec looked at me and smiled thinly. Then he broke the ice. "Sorry, Captain, I should have gone down there last night and taken the can into custody."

I was surprised he didn't point out that I had talked him out of it. I felt a new respect for Commander Molesworth and maybe I was beginning to understand a little more about the taking of responsibility in the Navy. The Exec wasn't hiding behind me and telling the Captain the whole thing was my idea. He was right up front and taking the blame.

More help came from an unexpected quarter. Chief Agent MacIntyre took a deep breath spoke up loud and clear, and from then on, he was in charge.

"No, Mister Carlson was right. You had no solid evidence connecting the can with the suspects. While finding the guilty parties in the heroin smuggling business, if in fact that's what it turns out to be, is important, the main thing we're after is Lieutenant Farrington's killer. I assume it is the same person or persons who attempted to murder Carlson. If we lose the evidence as we did, so be it. I think the can is still aboard somewhere and hasn't been thrown over the side. If someone is willing to kill a man for money, he's not going to abandon what drove him to commit the crime in the first place. Breaking up the whole amount into small lots and trying to smuggle them ashore individually would be too dangerous."

"I see," said the Captain, "You think in some ways we're better off having the evidence back in the possession of the culprits." "Exactly," MacIntyre said. "Now hopefully, we can catch them with the evidence either in their possession or under their control and tie the two together."

The Exec was no fool. He knew a life preserver when he saw one, "Exactly," he said.

I liked the idea, too. No, I loved it. What he was saying made a lot of sense, and it certainly took me off the spot. I noticed again that Lieutenant Commander Molesworth sat back in his chair in a posture of relief.

I was even growing to like MacIntyre's steely gray eyes, as long as they weren't focused an me. A few minutes ago I wouldn't have dared to speak, but now I felt a newfound confidence surging through my system. I took a deep breath. "Yes, sir," I said. "That's the way I figured it. Now those who have whatever it is will try desperately to get it ashore in order to collect their money from someone higher up in the system in Norfolk, or even in New York."

MacIntyre scratched his square jaw, "Carlson, who knew about your visit to the commissary storeroom?"

I thought carefully. The list was small, but I didn't want to incriminate anyone unnecessarily or in error. I began, "Of course Doctor Hasler, Lieutenant Barnaby, and I knew. We were in the storeroom. Seaman Benito knew, but he was outside and didn't know what we found there. We didn't talk about the can when we came out or when we were walking down the corridor."

MacIntyre said, "It wouldn't be necessary for the person or person who put the can in the storeroom to know exactly what happened inside. If you were known to have been in there, they'd suspect you found something, or were getting close to finding it, and would move it."

"Then," I said, "We'd have to include Seaman Benito as a suspect. He might have told Novella or Daviglia, and maybe others. We didn't warn him to keep quiet." Now we were bringing Italians back into the discussion again. I didn't want to say anything about the Mafia. I was painfully aware that agent Ligosi was staring at me.

Ligosi surprised me when he spoke. "Whoever is involved aboard ship will be thinking about more than money, and most of our Italian suspects will be familiar with the feeling I'm talking about. Whoever they are, they know their families will be in constant danger if they let this job and all the money involved slip through their hands."

Chief Agent MacIntyre said, "Our best chance now is to catch our suspects in the act of trying to get the heroin off the ship."

Commander Knight broke in. "We have arranged for the ship to moor at an isolated berth at the south end of the Destroyer Piers and for an armed guard of Marines to patrol the pier adjacent to the ship. No one will board or leave the ship without our permission."

"Fine," said MacIntyre. "We'll also arrange to keep the water south of the ship clear of all boat traffic."

Commander Knight looked puzzled for a moment, but then he got the drift. "I see," he said. "We give them a clear way out."

"And in," added MacInytre. "I think the person ashore connected with this operation will try to use swimmers or a rubber boat to take the stuff away. We'll do everything possible to make the route south of the ship attractive to them."

The Exec asked, "How do you know someone off the ship is involved?"

MacIntyre answered, "We can't be one hundred percent sure, but we can be positive that the

men on the ship who brought the drugs aboard
didn't have the hundred thousand dollars it would
have taken to buy it in Naples. Also, they probably don't have direct access to a distribution system in this country. We have to assume that whoever gave it to them is connected with distributors
in the States. Only a large group has that kind of
money and they will have access to the manpower
and equipment necessary to get it ashore."

MacIntyre looked around the room to see if
everyone was listening. He needn't have bothered.
We were hanging on his every word. He turned
back to the Captain and went on. "Also, if it's
heroin, it will bring over a million dollars in this
country once it's distributed. You can be sure that
there is someone waiting for it in Norfolk."

Ligosi broke in. "Well, if it turns out there is
a Mafia or a Mafia-like connection here, there will
be a group ashore putting pressure on those on
the ship to deliver the heroin as soon as possible.
There will be direct pressure on them, as well as
indirect pressure on their families and loved
ones."

"In the meantime, what do we do?" asked the
Captain, obviously relieved that all of us involved
in losing the can weren't to be blamed. He wasn't
alone. I was feeling much more secure, and I
again could see that the Exec's disposition had
improved markedly.

MacIntyre said, "When we get into port, we'll

have to go through the motions of searching the ship and questioning everybody. We might get lucky and turn up something that will lead us to the can, or even to Lieutenant Farrington's killer, but I don't think so. Even if we find it, I think we should just leave it as bait. This ship must have a hundred hiding places not even a dozen dogs could find. If necessary, they'll keep moving the can as we search each part of the ship. We are fairly sure there are two or three men involved. Maybe more."

"We could cordon off part of the ship to prevent that," said the Exec.

"No. We don't want to try too hard, unless someone actually has it in his possession at the time."

The Exec looked puzzled, but before he could say anything, I interrupted.

"I think I'd hang it in one of our fuel tanks by suspending it from a wire," I said.

"Wouldn't work," said one of the ONI agents.

MacIntyre cut him down to size. "Sure would, and it has before. A very clever method. The only way we found out about about it was when the guy who did it died before he could get it off the ship. It was found when the fuel tank was cleaned."

"Where would you secure the wire?" asked the Exec.

"Don't need to," said MacIntyre. "All you have to do is put the can with a wire secured to its handle in the tank with an added weight to insure that it will sink and then attach a float to the top of the wire. Then push the float away out of sight of the access plate. When you want to get it out, open the access plate and fish for the wire with a coat hanger."

"Messy," said the Exec.

"But effective," added the Captain.

"What's an access plate?" asked the second ONI Agent. "And how do you get a five gallon can down a small filling tube?" The other ONI agent inched away from the first one and rolled his eyes to the overhead. His exasperation showed on his face.

"I don't think you'd try to get it down the filling tube." said the Exec patiently. "Access plates are like manhole covers secured to tank tops by bolts. They allow access to tanks for cleaning."

We weren't getting anywhere chasing this red herring, and MacIntyre changed the subject.

"Carlson," he asked, "tell me more about the people you think are legitimate suspects."

I was surprised and not prepared, but I stalled a little and asked for a cup of coffee which I now felt more like drinking. If I could impress them with what I had to say, maybe I could think about the ship's secretary job again, or even being promoted to lieutenant junior grade.

After downing a little of the coffee, I went over the initial visit to my room by the two intrud-

ers and said that at that time I was sure it was
Antonio and Daviglia. I explained that they were
two large men wearing masks and carrying
weapons. Then I recounted my contact with
Novella the night of Charlie's murder, and what
had initially led me to put Novella at the top of
my suspect list.

Next I went over my visit to the ship's office
and what I had found out about the Italians
aboard. I included my later thoughts and suspicions about Lieutenant Abrizzi and told them of
his problem and why I thought he needed the
money. I stole a glance at Agent Ligosi. He didn't
seem to be offended and was listening with interest. By now it was obvious that all he cared about
was solving the case. I decided not to worry about
him any longer.

Hasler stirred vaguely at this point and interrupted to say, "I have a strong feeling that
Lieutenant Abrizzi is involved."

I noticed that Hasler's hands were shaking
again, just like they did those times in Naples
when I had been stuck with the duty and
couldn't go ashore with him. Then I stole a look
at MacIntyre. He was looking at Hasler's hands,
too, but when he saw that I was looking at him,
he quickly looked away and began to examine
something on the overhead.

Hasler's comments didn't get much response,
and he went back to dunking his mustache in

his coffee.

I felt indebted to Doc Hasler and considered him a friend. To cover his embarrassment, I coughed loudly and went on, going back over the knife-throwing incident and how I had found Chief Novella in the chief petty officer's lounge playing solitaire. MacIntryre nodded when I told him about Novella's abnormal breathing and the state of the solitaire game Novella had been playing.

I described again the brief look I had at the top of the head of the bucket-dropper, my visit to Abrizzi's room, and the blue jeans and blue shirt I had found there.

The Captain said, "Well, you've got a good list of suspects."

MacInytre asked, "What about others aboard who aren't Italian?"

I said, "I suppose there are any number of others who might be involved. Anybody in the crew could be guilty. In any event, I know there are at least two people involved. I saw that many in my own room and Garrity saw at least two men go into the machine shop."

MacIntyre asked, "What about motives?"

"As to motives, Lieutenant Abrizzi has a strong motive. He needs money desperately. I'm not sure about the others. Maybe they just like money and what it can buy. But that could apply to just about anyone. Anyway, I don't know if all this helps or not."

"It helps a lot," MacIntyre said. At least we know some of the people to concentrate on. Without your work, we'd have a whole ship load of suspects and no leads. What you did required a lot of initiative and willingness to make a personal sacrifice. As a matter of fact, you almost sacrificed your life."

"Thank you," I said, feeling much better about what I had said, but just a little leery about how the Captain was taking it.

I shouldn't have worried. He spoke up immediately. "Yes, Carlson, I'd like to add my commendation to Mister MacIntyre's. Well done."

"Just doing my duty," I said modestly, lowering my eyes for a few seconds.

I was very relieved. When I had said a few minutes ago that anybody in the crew could be guilty, I was sure the Captain would jump all over me. I had been in the Navy long enough to know that there was a fierce loyalty between a good captain and a good crew. The Lassiter had both, and I had attacked the crew in a very general way. When I had done so, I heard some heavy breathing over toward the Captain's chair, but he hadn't said anything.

Now I turned slightly so that I could see his face. He didn't look mad, and had just paid me a nice compliment. He looked both surprised and satisfied. Surprised that he hadn't known beforehand all that he had just heard, and satisfied, I suppose, because the situation wasn't any worse than it was. I had survived another crisis, and I might still be the ship's secretary.

MacIntyre said, "What we have to do now is go ahead with our plan to flush the guilty parties out into the open where we can deal with them."

Then the telephone call bell from the bridge rang and the Captain picked up the phone. After a minute, he hung up and said, "We're about to enter the channel leading into Chesapeake Bay. I've got to go up to the navigation bridge, and the Executive Officer is needed there also. Carlson, please take our guests topside so they can watch as we steam up the channel and come into our berth at the pier."

"Aye, aye, sir," I said, feeling that I had regained some of the stature I had carefully built up over the last two days, and had almost lost in a few fear-filled seconds in the storeroom.

A MURDER AT SEA

CHAPTER IX

I felt a little overpowered trying to entertain five rather important hot shots all by myself, so I asked Doc Hasler to help out.

He grinned. "I thought you'd never ask. I don't want to miss anything."

"You do the talking. I'll do the escorting. And don't let any of them get lost."

"Sounds good to me."

I led the group to the signal bridge, situated just over the navigation bridge. We stepped up against the forward rail and between the signal bag stations on either wing. That way the signalmen could do their thing with flag hoists, lights, and all the stuff they used without us interfering. I knew the signalmen could get very huffy if you didn't ask permission of the head of the watch to enter their territory, so I asked the big, burly first class signalman who headed the watch if it was all right if we stayed where we were.

He looked at me sort of tentatively for a few seconds and then grinned. "Sure, Mister Carlson. Howlett has told me all about you. Let me know if I can help. Ain't nothing going to happen to you while you're up here as long as you don't get your foot caught in a halliard. Then we might hoist you by mistake."

I didn't think that was very funny, but he said it in a friendly manner and any friend of Howlett's was a friend of mine.

I went back to my party, none of whom had heard the exchange between me and the senior signalman. We stood up tight against the bulkhead to minimize the effects of the cold wind coming over the top.

The wind died down considerably as we began to enter the channel, so it was pleasantly cool, but not so cold that we needed heavy coats. The heavy swells of the open ocean had already been reduced to gentle waves by passing over the shallow coastal shelf, and they shrank further as we entered the shallow waters of the channel. The water had turned from bright blue to light green to dirty green.

Hasler opened his windbreaker, took a deep breath, and said, "Norfolk is funny this way. Sometimes it's almost like summer in December."

I took his word for it. So far, my exposure to Norfolk had been a couple of hours of hectic travel between the airport and the destroyer piers before we had suddenly gotten underway back in the heat of summer. Hasler had been with the ship in Norfolk for almost three years and had

made two Mediterranean tours. The part of the
ship where I had gathered my charges overlooked
the forecastle, and we could see the line handlers
up forward breaking out and readying the large
nylon lines that would be used for mooring. A
detail of men stood by the anchor in case we had
an engineering casualty and lost motive power. If
this happened, they would loosen the large pelican hook, so-called because it was shaped like a
pelican's beak, hold it in, and let the chain run
out until the anchor reached the bottom. Then
they would set the brake on the windlass to hold
the chain, and the anchor dragging along the bottom would set itself in the mud and stop the ship
short of danger.

As we passed Cape Henry, the point of land
marking the entrance to Chesapeake bay to the
south, Joe Barrows, the communications officer,
joined us. It was normal for him to be up with the
signalmen on the signal bridge at times when we
were entering port. At other times he might go to
the radio shack or to the navigation bridge,
depending on where he thought the action in his
department might be. Now I thought he was up
here just to talk to the guests. I welcomed his
presence, because he knew a lot more about the
scenery than I did and and quite a bit more than
Doc Hasler did.

Joe started to talk, and his monologue became
nonstop. I figured he probably had bored those

cattle to death back on the ranch. It wasn't that Joe didn't know his stuff; he just told everyone more than they wanted to know about whatever subject he was holding forth on. MacIntyre's eyes glazed over and he soon excused himself to write some dispatches on the signalmen's desk.

Commander Knight escaped early and wandered around, looking through the signalmen's telescopes and asking a lot of questions of the signalmen on watch. I guess he didn't get to see much as a shorebound legal eagle, and this was a rare treat for him. Ligosi soon got glassy eyed, and the two ONI agents started up their own conversation. Joe went on, in his element and enjoying every moment of his big opportunity to fascinate something other than a herd of cattle.

This looked like just the opportunity I was waiting for. I needed to see Pete Barber, the engineering officer. I knew he would be in the engineering department's central command and control station now. He was always there when we entered or left port, or maneuvered in any way that might call on the engineering plant for rapid changes of speed, or when taking the necessary action in the event of a casualty.

I left Hasler in charge and excused myself from the group. Hasler glowered at me, but didn't say anything. I walked down the ladders to the central command control station. As I had expected, Pete was standing behind the chief of the engineering watch, who was seated in a vinyl-covered swivel chair. In front of them was a mass of dials and gauges, and Pete was sweeping his eyes across them. The scene was as serene and quiet as my mother's living room.

The engineering department of this ship was far different from the steam powered destroyer I had taken a brief cruise on one summer when I had been in the NROTC. Each midshipman was required to stand a certain number of watches in the engineering spaces and to crawl around in the bilges tracing out and making sketches of fuel oil, steam, and water lines. I remembered the smell of my clothes and my hair after a day in the fire room or engine room of that ship. The temperature got up so far above one hundred degrees that I didn't want to know exactly what it reached. I do know that in five minutes we were soaking wet. At the end of the day, or even after a four hour watch, we smelled terrible, and it wasn't just sweat. The exact odor was hard to identify. It was a combination of fuel oil, steam, and wet metal. Somehow, steam on wet steel or copper makes odors that must be smelled to be appreciated. Once identified, they can never be forgotten.

After a watch, there was nothing to do but shuck all of your clothing, get them to the laundry, and head for the shower. I noticed that most of the sailors put theirs into buckets of soapy water and let them soak until they could wash them themselves or get them laundered. The smell on your skin and hair required ten minutes of scrubbing to bring it under control. Even then, you could smell an engineer, or snipes as they were called, half a table away in the ward room or the crew's mess hall.

The *Lassiter* is entirely different. Her gas turbines burned kerosene, or other types of Navy fuel if required when kerosene isn't available. They are just like the big gas turbines on airliners. The products of combustion exited directly out the stack above the turbines into the open air. Even the smell up there on deck is different. More like that of an airport. And instead of the occasional shower of black soot from the steam destroyer's stacks, only a bit of moisture fell.

When I entered the main control room, I realized that even the atmosphere there was different. Instead of the roar of ventilation blowers in the steam destroyer's engine room, or even the loud wail of the machinery and pumps in the boiler rooms of a steam plant, there is a steady singing noise. It is subdued enough so that normal conversations can be carried on in the main control room. Still, all of the persons on watch carry ear pieces around their necks, much like doctors carry stethoscopes in a hospital. If they have to go into the compartments nearby which house the gas turbines, they would need hearing protection. The gas turbines are very self-sufficient, and seldom need close up attention, so the compartments are seldom entered when the turbines are up to speed.

The smell here is also different. More like that of a clean machine shop, with overtones of warm electrical insulation. Since the ventilation is adequate and the insulation between the main control room and the turbine room is so good, the temperature is about like that in the ward room. All the watch personnel wear jump suits of nylon and I've never seen sweat stains on any of them. It is a pleasant way to stand a watch.

I tapped Pete on the back. He looked over his shoulder, recognized me and nodded, but turned back to the panel immediately.

"Pete," I said, "why do you watch those things so closely? They never move."

Pete didn't turn his head. "That's just it. If they move, we're in trouble, and I want to know about it right away."

There hadn't been any trouble in the engineering department in my short stay aboard. This class of ship is propelled by four gas turbines that are simple and reliable. They burn almost any kind of liquid fuel, even bad fuel. If there are impurities in it, they burn those, too, unlike some oil burning steam plants which choke on them and sometimes slow down, spewing white smoke. Also, they don't require engineering geniuses as watch officers like nuclear power plants do.

The turbines are noisy, though. Their whine is as bad as the noise of the turbines on jet aircraft, and so they are isolated, two by two, in specially noise-insulated enclosures. There is also an additional engineering enclosure for each of the two engine rooms containing smaller turbines that generate electrical power. Waste heat from the main turbine exhausts generate steam in a small waste boiler and help make the plant more efficient by evaporating sea water to make fresh water and heating the turbine intakes and equipment topside to prevent the formation of ice in freezing weather.

It is an ideal setup, which can be run by a watch of five men instead of the eighteen or so required in a typical steam plant destroyer. I thought Admiral Rickover had a lot to learn about gas turbine engineering, and I began to think I might even call on him if I ever got to Washington. I don't think he ever admitted that gas turbine propulsion existed.

The main control station was so quiet that I could talk to Pete with out shouting. I tapped him on the shoulder again and started talking to his back. "Pete," I began, "I need some help. As you've probably heard, some unknown person or persons have tried to kill me three times. I think they have some connection with the engineers."

That got Pete's attention, and he swiveled his head away from the dials on the control board. He didn't like any slur on his department.

"What the hell do you mean?" he asked, his pale face clouding up.

Pete spent so much time below that he was paler than most of us. His skin was fair to start with, and his red hair and blue eyes completed the picture of a guy who doesn't tan. There was nothing wrong with his one hundred and eighty pounds of muscle spread nicely on a large frame, and I didn't want to make him too mad. Being a little guy does have its disadvantages.

"I didn't mean to say anything offensive," I said. "It's just that one of the men who dropped a bucket near me was wearing dungarees."

Pete laughed. "I hear it was a near miss. I guess I shouldn't have reacted so quickly to your question. I've heard the details of the attack, and the Exec has asked me a lot of questions. After all, a lot of the heavy spare parts in that bucket could only have come from our storerooms."

"I want to know if you suspect anyone in particular, engineer or otherwise."

Pete scratched his heat rash, which he had almost continuously, even though the control room wasn't hot.

"I can't think of anyone in our engineering gang off hand, and that's what I told the Exec," he said, "but I'll keep my ears open and an eye out."

"What do you know about Novella?"

Pete pursed his lips and thought for a few

seconds. Then he said, "Not much. When he first came aboard it was evident that he didn't know much about gas turbines. He's an old steam plant man. He agreed, and the Exec concurred, that he'd be better off serving as the chief master-at-arms for a while. That way he could do an important job for the ship and still spend some time down here learning about this type of plant. He's been coming down here fairly often, maybe once or twice a week. He talks mainly to the other chiefs and has little to do with the lower ranking petty officers. I think he feels a little embarrassed asking questions of anyone but the other chiefs."

"That makes sense. Do you have any reason to suspect that he might be part of a group involved in smuggling heroin or some other drug?"

"Only that he needs money. He likes to gamble, and I've heard that he owes a lot of money to some big gamblers in Norfolk. Probably some overseas. I heard him grumbling to another chief when he was down here about the 'fixed game' in Naples. I didn't hear him say anything about losing. You could ask the other chiefs about that. They know everything about everybody."

That was all Pete knew, but it was a big help. Novella had a motive, both to smuggle heroin aboard and to do away with me. I couldn't be sure what Novella thought I knew about his involvement. He did know about the soldering iron I had found, and as chief master-at-arms, he had access to all that the division masters-at-arms would be hearing aboard ship, and they hear a lot. Each division had a master-at-arms, and they all reported to Novella. Used correctly, it was a pretty good spy ring.

I thanked Pete and made my way back up to the signal bridge. Just as I got there, I saw MacIntyre hand Joe Barrows several handwritten dispatches, and Barrows left the area reluctantly, still talking, and took them below. I would have given my best white shirt to have read them. The assembled group didn't seem to miss Barrows, and even seemed to be a little relieved to see him go. Now they began to listen to Hasler as he took over again as tour guide. Even MacIntyre joined the group. I stood behind Hasler and listened, too.

This area was new to me, but Hasler knew it well. He livened up his description with a few stories of the history of the landmarks ashore. The mouth of the Chesapeake Bay had seen a lot of explorers and fighting men come and go and they had all left their mark on the local area. I knew that Hasler read a lot, and history was one of his favorite subjects. He made it sound like it all happened yesterday. I kept quiet and enjoyed his stories.

This was the first time I had entered the port of Norfolk, or for that matter, any U.S. port, except on my Naval ROTC cruises. We steamed steadily up the long stretch of the channel fairly close to shore, but between two lines of buoys. The long Cape Charles to Virginia Beach bridge-tunnel was behind us, and the Amphibious Base slid by to port. It was a forest of masts and stacks growing out of a mass of strange looking hull shapes. The alligators of the Amphibious Force, as they called themselves because they operated on both land and sea, were a Navy all to themselves with special ships, landing craft, doctrine, and techniques. Someday, after mastering destroyers, I thought I'd like to check them out.

Suddenly, several puffs of black smoke rose ashore in an expanse of bushes along the beach in front of the Amphibious Base. A few seconds later the sounds of the explosions reached us.

"What the hell is that?" I asked Hasler.

Hasler laughed. "Those are SEALs."

MacIntyre had come over to join us. I think Hasler had reached the limit of his knowledge about seals, whatever they were.

MacIntyre said, "They aren't seals, as in aquatic animals, but as in the acronym SEALs. It means sea, air, and land. The members of the group are trained to land in advance of amphibious operations, destroy beach defenses, conduct guerrilla operations on the beach or inland, and otherwise stir things up. Right now, they are practicing blowing up defenses. They can land by boat, by parachute drop, or by swimming ashore from submarines or boats. You may see something of them soon."

MacIntyre seemed to regret that last prediction as soon as he had said it. I think he was trying to keep something quiet, and didn't trust anyone, including me. I felt bad about not being trusted, and I decided to store the information away. Maybe it had something to do with the dispatches he had been writing earlier or his plan to trap the heroin smugglers.

We all returned to listening to Hasler. I was surprised that the agents and Commander Knight could be so interested in Doc Hasler's narrative. They lived in various parts of Norfolk, Hampton, and Virginia Beach, but I guess they'd never seen their home cities from this angle before, and Hasler was an engaging speaker.

The town of Ocean View was next to port, followed by the north part of the Norfolk Naval Station, with the large row of officer's quarters stretching along the bay side. They looked very impressive, and I made a remark about how well the top brass lived.

Hasler straightened me out. "They are big, all right, but not as comfortable as you might think. They were converted from the buildings left from the Jamestown Exposition, held so many years ago that I can't even remember the date. They are old, drafty, and in need of constant repairs. If you took a vote of the occupants, I think they'd rather tear them down and build smaller, more modern quarters. Then we turned almost ninety degrees to port and steamed down to the end of the Norfolk Naval Air Station.

At the turn, we could see two giant aircraft carriers moored at the long carrier pier. Somehow they seemed bigger than when I had seen them at sea. And certainly less dangerous. I remembered a great many night watches when I had been the assistant officer of the watch, staring out the square bridge windows as the captain or the officer of the deck out on the wing of the bridge yelled in commands to the wheel and engine controls.

Outside, with all ships darkened, and with the light of only the moon and stars, I had been able to catch an occasional glimpse of a huge shape rushing by as we dashed from station to station or took position near it to act as rescue ship in case any of the circling aviators dropped in the water. The radar repeater near me gave a map-like picture of what was happening, but it was nothing compared to seeing the real thing. They were at once comforting, if you remembered the power they could project, but dangerous if you got in their way. They were too big to turn or stop rapidly. It was up to the destroyers to keep out of their way.

As we passed by their sterns, I noticed that there were no aircraft on the flight decks which had been so busy at sea. The others had noticed it, too, and Doc Hasler was busy explaining that the aircraft were all at a shore air station at Oceana so that they could practice flying every day. I kept quiet and listened. I was learning, too.

All of the carriers I had ever seen at sea were also clean-sided and looked like they were either getting ready to accelerate to thirty knots, or were already at that speed. Even in the Mediterranean ports where I had seen them at anchor, they gave that impression. Now they had red paint spots on their sides and were festooned with access brows, mooring lines, and power and fuel lines. Not very glamorous.

A little further south, we passed by the Norfolk Naval Station piers. They likewise held tankers, ammunition ships, large amphibious ships that couldn't fit into the amphibious base, and a miscellany of other ships. They, too, looked shorebound and not at their best. We slowed as we approached the submarine piers and passed two piers full of their sleek black shapes. I had never seen a submarine, even at sea, although we had chased a few. They were larger than I imagined, great powerful beasts. Large as they appeared, I knew that like icebergs, most of their hulls were under water.

Our entire group seemed to be enjoying this very pleasant respite that preceded the grim job that lay ahead. Commander Knight, as a legal spe-

cialist, seldom went to sea, and this was a wel-
come change for him. He stopped moving around
the signal bridge and concentrated on watching
the pier we were approaching. I noticed that the
signalmen seemed to appreciate his steadying
down.

Then we turned to come into our berth. As
Commander Knight had said, it was isolated. We
eased in and moored port side to the pier.
According to the sailors near us, the Captain did
a fine job of making the landing, using a tug
when he needed it. Sailors are uncharitable critics
of ship handlers, and when they approve of a
landing, it must be good. I had never seen us
moor to anything except a buoy, or a backing-in
type of maneuver with our stern near the beach,
the Mediterranean moor we used in Monaco. I
guess this was a simple landing compared to that.

As the men on deck scurried to and fro, secur-
ing and doubling up the mooring lines, I looked
around us again. We were moored directly to the
pier. There were other destroyers across the pier
from us, but none astern or ahead. We had the
whole side of the pier to ourselves, as if we were
quarantined, and I guess we were. On the pier
was a platoon of Marines, in ranks, but standing
at ease, looking sharp in their fatigues, their rifles
slung ominously over their shoulders. A small
party of officers and civilians, obviously more
agents, stood in front of three vans.

MacInytre stirred. "Our lab guys," he said. "Finger prints, search dogs, and all that. They'll be boarding immediately."

I nodded. Just up the pier were two vans with meshed screens separating the rear portions and the driver's compartments. Several dogs were bounding about the rear seats. Others just lay there, sometimes being trampled by the active ones. Occasionally all hell would break loose in the dog compartments, and the drivers would shout at the dogs to quiet them.

Then a white ambulance drove down the pier and stopped near our brow. I knew what this was for. In a few minutes four men came up from below carrying a stretcher containing a green body bag. The handles of the stretcher were so cold they were still covered with frost. So much so that the four stretcher bearers were wearing gloves.

I felt for Charlie Farrington. He had always hated cold weather. Now he was as cold as one can get. Knowing he couldn't feel it didn't make me feel any better.

They paused at the top of the brow and put their burden down. MacIntyre stepped forward and conferred with the ambulance attendants for a few minutes. Then he motioned to the stretcher bearers who picked up the stretcher and carried Charlie's body down the brow to the waiting ambulance.

As the stretcher party left the quarterdeck, all

of us on deck saluted, a final and small tribute to
a fine naval officer and good friend. We would
have a memorial service as soon as the situation
calmed down, but Charlie would already be on
the way home to Tennessee where his family
would bury him. I didn't like to think about it,
but I knew that his first stop would be the Naval
hospital in Portsmouth for an autopsy before the
undertaker went to work on him. I hated the
thought.

I came back to reality and led my group back
to the Captain's cabin. In a few minutes the
Captain and Exec joined us. As we left, the
Marines were being deployed up and down the
pier. The dogs were taken out and began to have
a field day, watering the tree trunk-like mooring
bollards located along the pier.

The Captain's cabin was too small to hold us
all, so we moved to the wardroom. MacIntyre
knew all the arriving agents and introduced them
one by one. All of them wore some combination
of civilian clothes not unlike MacIntyre's. With all
the dark suits, plain ties, and vests, It looked like
a gathering for a small funeral. Then he introduced us to the agents in a sort of a mass intro-
duction, giving the names and billets of all of us
on the ship side and the specialties of all the
agents. He knew more than I thought he would
about ship matters and never used a wrong word
or term.

He briefed all of the new arrivals on what he had learned and then he and the Exec set up a plan for a search of the ship. The dog expert had eight dogs, which confirmed that our communication security system needed some tightening. Helms evidently had a friend somewhere who had revealed to him part, but not all, of what had been contained in a classified dispatch.

The plan called for eight parties of one dog, one agent, and one officer escort to search every inch of the ship, obviously divided into eight sectors. In order to insure quick access to all of the compartments, those in charge of them would unlock them, if necessary, and stand by until the inspection was completed. It was now about noon, and it was expected that the search would be completed by evening. In the meantime, the rest of us would conduct interrogations in the mess hall, as soon as the crew had eaten and the space was cleaned up.

With that, we adjourned topside for a few minutes so the messmen could set up the tables in the wardroom for lunch. I was told by the Exec to join them at lunch, and it would be one of the first times that I had eaten with the first sitting except when I had been due to go on watch. The wardroom could only serve about three quarters of the officers aboard at one time, and the junior officers and the off-coming watchstanders usually ate as a bob-tailed second group.

I sat across from Agent MacIntyre, and I noticed that when he opened his mouth to eat, he had a beautiful set of teeth. The fact that he kept his mouth so tightly closed obviously had nothing to do with his dental work. When he was not talking business, he could be quite pleasant. I began to like him even more, and I thought the success of what we were about to do depended on him and his ability. I didn't know all of the details of his plan, but I trusted him and wanted to do all I could to help. After all, he was trying to catch someone who had tried to kill me.

After lunch, we moved down to the mess hall, where some folding chairs had been set up to augment the fixed seats and tables. I was allowed to sit in a corner and listen. I was surprised when MacIntyre came in, looked around, and came over and sat down next to me.

The two ONI agents sat with Ligosi in the center of the mess hall behind a table. Across the table was a single chair for the person to be questioned.

I asked MacIntyre what kind of interrogation this would be.

"Just an informal inquiry," he answered. "It will be taped, but none of the witnesses will be sworn, and no counsel will be present, since nobody is accused of anything as of yet. We'll just be assisting your commanding officer, who still retains legal jurisdiction over the case and all the persons on his ship."

When all was ready and the first officer had been brought in, Ligosi stood up and started to question him. "Why aren't you doing the interrogating?" I whispered to MacIntyre.

"Ligosi's an expert. Besides, I'd rather watch the guys getting the prod. I can read their body language better."

I squirreled this bit of knowledge away.

Nothing came out of the questioning of the officers. None of them said they had seen or heard anything unusual, except Ross Barnaby, who told about our visit to his storeroom. I commented to MacIntyre on the fact that none of the officers seemed to have noticed anything irregular.

"Not unusual," he said. "You guys get in a cycle at sea. Bunk to wardroom to watch station to bunk. You don't see or do much else, except paper work, at least in wartime or during busy exercise periods."

I scratched my head. He was right.

"How did you know that?" I asked.

"Simple. Just before the Korean War, I joined a destroyer as an ensign from the Naval ROTC, just like you did. I went through the same hardships and all the feelings of excitement, but even more so because we were at war with Korea. A few months after Inchon, I swam away from my sinking ship when a mine blew our bow off. I was picked up by our own whaleboat, which had blown clear. Before I could be assigned to another destroyer, the war was over, and I was still an ensign. I stayed in the Naval Reserve for about a year after I joined the FBI, but I soon became too busy to go to drills. I was never promoted to lieutenant junior grade, and I retired as an ensign. But I think I saw enough to know what you guys go through."

I thought about this a little. One year of wartime experience was probably the equivalent of five years of peacetime service. If so, then my five months of steaming around the Mediterranean, occasionally in a crisis condition, must count for more than just five months of peacetime experience. I felt better and somehow more at ease with myself.

I thought back to all the nights when I was convinced that I would never master the intricate ballet that was going on as our ship moved at high speed around the screen of the carrier, or drew alongside a rolling oiler in the dark of night to fuel, as we plunged up and down even more than the ship we were alongside. But I was making progress. I was allowed to take charge in the daylight when help was available if I made a mistake. And I even looked forward to our next night maneuvers. Maybe I wasn't a candidate to be the next John Paul Jones, but I'd settle for making lieutenant junior grade. After that, we'd see. There was always the FBI.

The last officer to be interrogated was Lieutenant Abrizzi. Ligosi was easy on him. He asked only routine questions and didn't ask about his finances or his whereabouts during certain times. I was a little disturbed. He was one of my suspects, and no one was asking the key questions necessary to either implicate or clear him. I leaned forward to MacIntyre.

"Why isn't Ligosi asking him about his jeans and where he was when the bucket was dropped on me? And what about his debt?"

MacIntyre said, almost in a whisper, "Trust me. We don't want to spook him."

I decided that if I were going to trust MacIntyre, I had to go all the way. I sat back in my chair and listened.

Hasler was sitting behind me. He leaned forward and said, "What the hell was that all about?"

I could see MacIntyre looking at us. He raised his eyebrows. I wasn't sure what he meant, but I decided to play it carefully. I turned to Hasler and said, "Nothing important."

The chief petty officers were interrogated next. They were all cagey and gave the minimum answers. Ligosi was good. I soon figured that he didn't really expect to get anything out of this process, but it had to be done. Most of his questions made it seem that alcohol might be involved, but he said little about drugs. None of the chiefs would admit anything, and some of those who I knew had brought back an occasional pint, made wide-eyed denials of any knowledge of such a thing. Antonio, Novella, and Daviglia got the same treatment as everybody else, similar to that of Abrizzi. Obviously this session wasn't being conducted to find the guilty parties.

Novella and Antonio said they hadn't seen anything to indicate there might be any smuggling of alcohol and left the mess hall with obvious relief. Daviglia smirked and wrinkled his mammoth nose when asked if he had smuggled any alcohol aboard.

"Nah," he said. "I ain't seen none aboard, and I don't drink."

The lie of the century. I had seen him carried back to the ship in Naples, and it hadn't been from sunstroke.

After all the officers and enlisted men who were in any way involved, or who might be able to contribute information about either Charlie's death or the smuggling of drugs or alcohol had been questioned, MacIntyre stood up.

"Ligosi," he said, "I'll take over now and question Ensign Carlson."

Ligosi sat down, obviously tired in the feet and glad to have a rest. I started to go over to the witness chair, but MacIntyre put a hand on my shoulder and stopped me.

He whispered in my ear, "I'll be careful in my questioning. I don't want you to say anything about your search of the personnel records or say anything at this stage that will indicate that we suspect Abrizzi, Antonio, Daviglia, Novella, or anyone else in particular."

I went over to the witness chair, still trying to figure this one out, but still trusting MacIntyre. He started me off with the usual question, "Tell us what you know about this case." I gave them the whole ball of wax except the parts MacIntyre had put off limits. It came out pretty well, and I noticed that the Captain and Exec hung on my every word. They were a little puzzled by why parts were left out, but then so was I. Still, I thought I was making progress with them.

When I had finished, it was obvious that a lot of information had been recorded, but that almost no progress had been made toward finding out who had killed Charlie or who had smuggled the contraband aboard. In addition, it seemed there was no evidence to indicate who had tried to kill me. I seemed to be the only person who cared about that.

It was about 1800 when the questioning concluded, and we went back to the wardroom for dinner. After dinner, the wardroom was cleared, and we began to receive reports from the various search groups. None had found anything. We settled down to a discussion of the results, and Doc Hasler got a lot of information from the agent in charge of the dogs. I looked forward to hearing about it later.

The dogs got in the news right away. About 2000 the First Lieutenant came in the wardroom and whispered loudly in the Exec's ear. "Sir," he said, "Those damned dogs are crapping all over my decks. Can't we get rid of them?"

MacInytre, like all the rest of us, overheard the complaint. "Sure," he said. "We don't need them any more tonight. He turned to the chief dog specialist and gave orders for the dogs to be returned to their kennels."

It was obvious that we weren't getting anywhere, and that MacIntyre wasn't really expecting to see any results. After a decent interval, he leaned over to the Captain and whispered to him. I couldn't hear what he said.

Then he straightened up and said. "That's all for today. All of my agents can leave."

He looked at the head ONI agent, who nodded and said, "My agents can go."

The captain cleared his throat. "Commander Molesworth, please join me, Commander Knight, and the two chief agents in my cabin."

As we all rose and those named to join the Captain began to leave, MacIntyre glanced at me. I thought there was a gleam of sympathy in his eye. Still, I felt ignored, and I was sure there was something in the wind that I didn't know about. I didn't like not knowing what was going on, and I was being left out for the first time since all this began.

I went down to my room to pout a little about being left out of the conference. I figured I was back on the second team.

A MURDER AT SEA

CHAPTER X

On my way to the wardroom for evening meal, I went topside to check on the situation. I was wearing the normal uniform of the day for evening meal in port, blue service. I felt a little conspicuous in case someone still had killing me in mind, but I figured that they would think I had already told the authorities all I knew, and that there was no point in harming me now. Also, there were many other officers and enlisted men either standing about watching the activities on the quarterdeck or going about their duties topside.

Seamen of the deck force always caught it when we came into port. No matter what time it was, the boatswain's mates of the various deck divisions were never satisfied until the topside was clean, swept clear of all debris, and all gear was neatly stowed. I didn't think this was unusual. My mother thought the same way, and I never left my room until it was neat and clean. I found that the Navy calls this condition 'shipshape.' There must have been a sailor somewhere in my mother's past.

As I walked around the upper level, I could see that someone had considerably reduced the number of Marines on guard on the pier. One man was opposite the brow, one man at the stern, and another man across from the bow. I thought I could see another man well up the pier, but in the gathering dusk, I couldn't be sure. At this time of year and without daylight savings time, darkness came very early in Norfolk.

In addition to those working on the cleanup detail, a few small groups of men were gathered here and there on the weather deck talking, as was normal. The crew ate before the officers and tended to drift topside after their evening meal for a smoke and some bull-shooting sessions. I could hear small gusts of laughter drifting up from the various groups. Conversation among sailors tends to be predictable, particularly after a long time at sea, but the American sailor still maintains a keen sense of humor. Separate the inevitable sexual chaff, and the rest is usually very humorous.

As I watched, a group of agents in civilian clothes walked down the brow and climbed in the last van. There was no mistaking what they were, in their dark suits and vests, plain ties, close shaves, and neat haircuts. Cookie cutter stuff.

As the van drove away, I could hear the voice of the Executive Officer passing the word on the loudspeaker, "Now hear this, the investigation and search have been completed for today. Both will be resumed tomorrow starting at 0800. All hands be prepared to open and to stand by all locked spaces at that time. There will be no liberty until further notice."

Usually the petty officer of the watch or the officer with the day's duty passed the various messages over the loud speaker in port, but apparently the Executive Officer thought this was important enough for him to do the honors himself. As usual, his voice was firm and commanding. Someone at the wardroom table once said he had been a high ranking midshipman officer at the Naval Academy, and gave a lot of commands at their parades. He certainly hadn't forgotten how, and the loud speakers on the bulkheads seemed to jump to attention when he spoke. I could see his even white teeth in my mind's eye. There must be something wrong with Lieutenant Commander Molesworth, but I hadn't found it yet.

There were groans from the knots of sailors as the Exec reached the part about no liberty. After five months of abstinence, they had a lot of business to take care of ashore, both bachelors and married men. On the other hand, they had no legitimate gripes. Their dependents and girl friends didn't know they were in port; our early arrival had not been published in the papers, and they had not been allowed to send messages ashore. The other ships of the division wouldn't be in port until late tomorrow, a time well known

and published in all the papers well in advance.
The next day there would be hundreds of anxious
dependents, women and children, of the men on
the other destroyers of the division filling the pier-
side, waiting for their men to come ashore. By
that time, I hoped the case would be sufficiently
solved to allow our men to go ashore, too. This
would depend on MacIntyre. I couldn't do much
to help solve the case if they wouldn't tell me what
they were up to.

As I was about to leave the area topside for the
wardroom, a van came down the pier and stopped
at the brow. Three men got out and opened the
back doors of the van. I could see the name
'Norfolk Laundry and Dry Cleaning' on the sides
of the van. The men were wearing blue jump suits
with the company name on the back. They
unloaded several paper-covered packages of what
looked like finished laundry and carried them up
the brow and then forward out of my sight. It was
obvious that they were straining under their loads.
Heavy starch, I thought. Then I wondered why
they would be delivering laundry and dry cleaning
to the ship at this time. No one aboard could have
sent anything to them ashore unless it had been
sent by airmail from the Mediterranean.
Ridiculous. There had to be some other explanation.

Besides, all of the officer's and crew's laundry
was done by the ship's laundry, and it was a very

good one considering its limited equipment and facilities. All dry cleaning of blues for both officers and enlisted men was sent ashore. It made sense for the laundry and dry cleaning men to be picking up dirty clothing, but what were they bringing aboard? It was damned heavy, whatever it was.

I remembered Commander Knight's statement earlier in the day that no one would be allowed aboard without his permission. This arrival must have something to do with MacIntyre's mysterious master plan.

There was something else peculiar about the men from the laundry. I could have sworn that one of them looked a lot like one of the agents who had been aboard this afternoon, except that now he was wearing glasses and had a bushy mustache. On an impulse, I stayed around until they left the ship and the van departed. I watched carefully, and of the four who had arrived, only two left, although they had all made a show of going up and down the brow several times with other small loads of packages.

Then an old sedan came down the pier and two men got out carrying packages of papers and magazines. They were dressed in old clothes and there was something a little off-key about them. I didn't stay around to see any more. My stomach was sending me urgent signals, and I knew that I would need a lot of energy for the long night ahead. I made my way down to the wardroom and arrived in time for the second sitting.

I ate my evening meal in silence, lost in thought. Doc Hasler was eating with the late sitting because he had been treating a patient. He asked me once or twice if I felt all right. Then he said, "What are you worried about? We know pretty well who the smugglers are and we turned a lot of evidence and information over to the FBI. There's nothing left for us to do."

I put down my fork. "That's great, but what about Charlie and me? I want to find out who killed Charlie and who tried to kill me, and I want the smugglers and the guys who tried to kill me behind bars, not just some names on a suspect list."

"That's the FBI's business."

"It's mine, too. It's my life, and I've been part of the case for too long to be left out now."

"Oh, so that's what's bothering you. Well, I guess you're right, but I don't know what you can do about it." He gave up trying to talk to me and turned to the guys on his other side.

I was sure that MacIntyre wasn't going to sit on his butt until the next morning, but he hadn't said anything to me. On the trip up the channel he had given Barrows a lot of dispatches to be sent ashore. They must have set some sort of plan in motion, and I could only guess at what it was. The only clue I had was MacInytre's remark about about seeing more of the SEALs, a remark which he quickly regretted. There had been indications in his manner, his glances at me, and the way he had conducted the questioning that afternoon, that something was afoot. But he hadn't told me about it. Then there had been the bringing aboard and stashing away of extra agents. I found out when the off-going duty officer came into the ward room for dinner that the quarterdeck watch had been told by the Exec to let the laundry men and the newspaper men aboard. Nobody had shown any interest in making sure that they all left.

At the end of the evening meal, I drank three cups of coffee to make sure I would stay awake late that night. One cup was normal for me at dinner. Two would always keep me awake until midnight, and three usually kept me wide awake and made me jittery till dawn. I didn't like that coffee jag feeling, but this was an important night.

After the meal was over, I went to my room and stretched out on my bunk for a few minutes of rest. But I was so hyped up by the caffeine in the three cups of coffee I had to get up and walk up and down in the narrow confines of my room. The movement seemed to help me think more clearly and it used up some of the caffeine.

As I walked, I went over in my mind the events of the past few days and particularly the last day. I kept coming back to the routine manner in which MacIntyre had conducted the search and questioning today. His heart hadn't seemed to be in it. The old trap-like mouth hadn't opened and shut as it had in the early hours when he had first come aboard. He seemed to be going through the motions. During some of the interrogations he had almost dozed off. I got the feeling that this was all stage setting, and that only now was he starting to get down to business.

It had to be that he was setting a trap to catch someone trying to smuggle the can of drugs ashore. I was insulted that he hadn't seen fit to include me in his confidence, but maybe the fewer who knew of his plan the less chance there was of tipping off the culprits.

Nevertheless, I wasn't going to be left out. I'd get involved somehow. I stopped pacing the deck and laid down again. I tried to settle back for a few hours of rest even if I couldn't sleep because of the coffee. I didn't think anything was going to happen before midnight. It never did in the detective novels I read. I set my alarm clock for midnight just in case the coffee in my system didn't work. It was already rumbling in my gut. I tossed and turned, but never lost consciousness. At midnight my alarm jangled, and I heaved my weary frame out of my bunk.

This was probably going to be a hell of a night, and I wanted to be ready for it. I took a benzedrine pill which I had cadged from Hasler on an earlier occasion when it had been essential that I stay awake on one of our shore excursions.

I felt a little guilty about it, but it would do the trick.

I put on an old suit of blues, or what passed for old for a six-months ensign. Under it I wore a heavy blue sweater. I put sneakers on my feet, and a blue baseball cap on my head trying to be careful with my stitches. Junior officers aren't issued .45 caliber automatic pistols in peacetime, so my armament had to be improvised. I took a ten inch letter opener I had bought in France and secured it to my left ankle with two rubber bands. I practiced pulling it out from under the bottom of my trousers several times and finally settled for putting it in with the handle pointing down. With the handle pointing up I had to pull up my pants leg to get at it, and that was too awkward.

As I straightened up, I remembered the butcher knife the man I had thought was Antonio had carried the night my room had been invaded. I needed something better to cope with guys like that. Just a letter opener wouldn't do. I would be outreached. What I needed was a weapon that was longer than a butcher knife. The only other weapon I had and knew how to use was my dress sword. I reached up and took it out of its scabbard. The point was pretty sharp, even if the edge of the broad side was dull. A saber user is trained to attack using either the point or the side, and I could get along with just a sharp point if necessary. I said a silent prayer of thanks for all the hours I had spent in college learning the art of fencing. I was no Errol Flynn, at least in the fencing department, or in the romantic department either for that matter, but then who was. Besides, I had seen a lot of his pictures and I didn't think he was that good a swordsman. Most of his opponents seemed to be taking a dive.

Movies on the *Lassiter* ran largely to John Wayne cowboy pictures, Errol Flynn costume operas, and Doris Day "comedies". The exchange rate when two ships came together to trade movies usually ran to three John Waynes or two Errol Flynns to one Doris Day. Flynn was a little more popular than Wayne because Flynn's movies usually featured at least one bodice-ripping scene, or at least one costumed lady who threatened to lose something out of the top of her torn dress. The crew always cheered, although they knew nothing would happen.

But even if Flynn himself was a laugher as a swordsman, I was grateful that he had at least given me the idea of using a sword.

I loosened my belt a little and shoved the sword upwards under it. The point came up to my armpit, and the sharpness was unpleasant. If I carried the sword around much it might even dig a hole in my tender skin. I put a wad of cotton over the end and secured it with masking tape. That made it bearable if I was careful. I knew I couldn't put it down through my belt because it would be visible hanging alongside my trouser leg.

I took off my blue uniform jacket and substi-
tuted a blue windbreaker. I couldn't zip the bottom up over the hilt of the sword, which was just
below my belt, so I let the sides flap loosely. I
checked myself in the mirror. I sighed. Errol
Flynn I wasn't. If I carried my forearms close to
my sides and my hands in front of me, the bulges
of the sword hilt weren't too noticeable. I looked
like I had a sore gut, which I did. The coffee still
bothered me. I couldn't see how the older officers
drank as much as they did. Practice, I guess.

I was ready to go. Where, I wasn't quite sure.
I decided to start with a position as high in the
ship as I could get to. There I'd be able to see
what was going on below. I made my way up to
the signal bridge just above the navigation bridge,
using darkened passageways and little-used ladders
to conceal myself. There weren't any patrols or
sentries along my route, and I looked carefully up
and down each leg of my trip before stepping out
in the open. This wasn't exactly the way Hawkeye,
the Indian, would have done it. The silence of the
forest was replaced by the gentle whirr of ventilation blowers, and no moonlight shone through
the leaves of the trees. Just red lights placed at
intervals along the corridors for travellers like me.

I got to the topside area without seeing anyone
and carefully made my way to a point outboard of
the starboard signal bag. Signal bag was an old-

fashioned expression from the days when the signal flags were actually kept in bags. Now it was a
large metal structure in which the flags were hung
by their metal fittings, quick release hooks and
eyes, which rested in notches for fast removal and
attachment to the signal halyards. The halyards
themselves were long lines used to raise the
groups of signal flags to the yard arms above.

There were no signalmen on watch at night in
port. Any necessary communication between
ships was done by telephone or messenger, and
the signalmen only came up to the signal bridge
during the daytime to hoist certain special flags
indicating what the ship was doing, such as the
crew was at chow or the ship was transferring fuel
oil. They were always some signalmen up there for
morning and evening colors and some even came
up to get out of work elsewhere. At any rate, none
of them ever came up late at night.

I had the space all to myself. It was eerie to be
standing in the middle of all that unusual silence.
At sea, the signal bridge was a bustling center of
activity. Signalmen shouted at each other, repeat-
ing signals and message texts being sent and
received. The communication 'squawk boxes'
spewed forth a constant torrent of information to
and from the navigation bridge. Now there was
only the occasional rattle of a signal halyard
against its block up on the roost indicating that it
had not been secured tightly enough.

The sword in my belt had made the trip up to the signal bridge awkward, but not impossible. I was glad I had it, and I took it out from under my windbreaker, tightened my belt, and laid the sword on the deck close by. I sat down facing aft with my back to the signal bag and looked around. The night was very dark and overcast covering the moon and stars. There were light's on the ships up the pier, but I noticed that our usually more than adequate topside lights were at a bare minimum. I couldn't even see around our decks down below very well, even after my eyes had adapted to the dark. This seemed planned rather than accidental. There was a light over the brow on the pier side, but the side of the ship away from the pier and toward the open water was very dark. I couldn't see bow or stern sentries on the ship, although the Marines were still on the pier.

In the ship under me I could hear the usual night noises. We were taking power from the pier, so no auxiliary turbines were running, and this was the first time since I had come aboard that I had not heard the soft whoosh of stack gasses from either the main turbines or the auxiliary turbines. Now they were all secured. Occasionally there would be a snatch of quiet conversation floating up from the quarterdeck where the watch was stationed. Still, I didn't think I could hear a single man walking about down on the main deck. I would have to see him to know he was there, and that was going to be difficult.

The adjacent commercial pier across the water was very dark. Only a dim light or two lit the vast area. Now I was sure this was planned. If it was a trap, who was going to spring it? Though no trapper was in sight, I could guess who it was. Old trap-mouth I'll bet, and this time I thought about the name I had given MacIntyre with affection. I knew he had to have a good reason for not including me in his plans. For a moment I thought that I should let well enough alone and go back to my bunk, but the feeling passed quickly. I would not miss what was going to happen even if they caught me watching and busted me to seaman.

I felt for the sword at my side. It was better than nothing, but I would rather have had a gun. I zipped up my jacket to keep out the air which was growing steadily colder. This might be a long vigil, and I might as well be as warm and comfortable as possible. I stood up and took a half dozen signal flags out of the flag bag. I wrapped two around each leg and one around my neck. I folded the last one and sat on it. When I sat down, the cold deck was insulated from my frozen backside, my legs felt warmer, and my neck came to life again. The signalmen wouldn't have liked my use of their sacred flags, but they would never know, unless I forgot to put them back in their proper order. There was a specific notch for each

flag in the bag, and I realized that I couldn't see
them in the dark. Oh well, nothing I could do
about it now.

The silence around the ship seemed to close
in on me, and to pass the time I began to recall
our various port visits around the Mediterranean.
For some reason our second visit to Naples
nagged at me. It had been a hectic time, but very
pleasant. We had arrived in port early on a
Saturday. Just after Captain's inspection, Hasler
and I had gone ashore together to the Orient
Hotel, a fixed-rate place according to the tour
guide. It was in downtown Naples. We'd had a
couple of quick beers and lunch. Then we went to
the car rental desk to rent a car for a trip to
Pompeii, Salerno, and back to Naples via the
Amalfi Coast. We had been to Capri by boat the
first visit.

The car rental desk was manned by two young
ladies. Another stupid Navy expression. These
ladies were not "manning" anything. They were
obviously a hell of a lot of woman, even from a
distance. One I liked right away. The other was on
the phone with her back to us. I shouldered
Hasler aside and began to try to arrange our trip
in rudimentary Italian. The girl laughed and said,
"Try English. We'll make less mistakes."

As I talked to her I realized that she might be
the girl for me. The part of her above the desk was
superb. Long black hair, thick black eyebrows over

dark eyes, an intelligent expression, red lips even with no lipstick, and teeth that flashed with abandon as she smiled at me.

"That's fine, but I need to know your name. Mine's Carl." "Arabella," she said. "You must be Swedish."

"Of Swedish ancestry, but I'm an American."

"Of course. With that haircut you must be from the American destroyer that just came in."

Then the other girl put the phone down and turned around toward us. For a minute I thought I had made a mistake, for she was a stunner. Still, there was something lacking in her face that Arabella had and she had just a hint of hardness that I didn't like. "I see you've all met. My name is Maria," she said in perfect English.

Hasler's jaw dropped, and he stepped in front of me. "Harold Hasler," he said, with a silly grin on his face. I knew the expression. It was meant to put new female acquaintances at their ease before he began his usual operation. I didn't think it would work with Maria. He had met his match, and I'd have to keep an eye on him.

Hasler said, "I hope we can get together later." Maria smiled. "What kind of car do you want?"

Hasler was obviously smitten. "Anything that can carry four people," he said.

We made arrangements to keep a Renault sedan for the weekend. Even with the keys in Hasler's pocket, we stayed around the desk talking. There were no other customers, so we had the girls to ourselves. Both had long black hair and pretty faces. Both wore long-sleeved white blouses and pleated black skirts. Sort of a uniform for the car rental company, I thought. I leaned over the counter far enough to see that two pairs of rather spiffy legs supported the swirling skirts.

By the time we left, we had made arrangements to pick the girls up at the end of their shift, 1900, and take them out for dinner and dancing.

The trip to Pompeii, Salerno, and along the Amalfi coast was superb, but we both wanted to get back to Naples. We made it back a few minutes early and cleaned up at the Orient Hotel's men's room, a cavernous, tile-lined Roman bath.

The girls were ready on time, and we piled into the Renault. Hasler insisted on driving, and that was fine with me. Arabella and I fitted into the small rear seat like two peas in a pod. We were thigh by thigh, and I had to breathe deeply to control my libido as Hasler started the engine. After all, we had been at sea for a long time, and Candace Terry was but a memory.

"Where to?" Hasler asked from the front seat. I was glad I hadn't argued about who was to drive. I had wanted to concentrate on Arabella in the back seat. But now that I had what I wanted, I found that to avoid embarrassment, I needed to concentrate more on the scenery and less on Arabella. The problem would take care of itself in due time.

Maria didn't hesitate. "Let's go to Mariguano. It's about twenty kilometers east. I know the manager of a café there, and it's the best place in town. The food is better than any place in Naples."

Hasler put the car in gear and we were off, scattering shoeshine boys, pimps, and tourists with equal abandon. Hasler was merciless when he was on the prowl.

Still, with the terrible Neapolitan traffic, it took us an hour before we rolled up in front of the Paradiso Cafe in Mariguano.

We unloaded, with me stooping over to help control my passion. By the time we got to the door I had come back to normal, although the sight of Arabella's gently rolling hips made it difficult to stay that way.

We got a fine table in the back of the room and settled down to a little heavy drinking. A young man brought over a giant bottle of Chianti and offered the first round of drinks. He sat down as if he owned the place. Maria introduced him as Emilio. It turned out that he did own the place.

I was glad she told me. Otherwise I would have thought he was a local pimp or dope pusher. He was a little too sharp looking, with wide coat lapels, a bow tie, and pointed shoes. Even his nose and chin were pointed. Over all he looked like an Italian fox. In downtown Naples that getup would have been about average, but out here in the country it was a little out of place. Even the waiters wore long, flowing shirt sleeves and longer hair. But I wasn't worried about Emilio. My attention was focused on Arabella.

After another round of drinks, Emilio got up, excused himself, and walked off.

Hasler and Maria seemed to be hitting it off well, and we had a good time, stopped drinking only long enough to enjoy a wonderful dinner. Emilio came back and joined us for dinner. I didn't mind his presence, because I figured we would get the best service in the house. We did. We started with minestrone soup. It was as good as my mother's. She had learned to make it from an Italian friend in San Francisco.

Emilio recommended the house salad. We went along. When it arrived it was fresh, well mixed, and lightly covered with a superb oil and vinegar dressing. I looked at Emilio, who was wolfing down his salad. "This is so fresh it must have been picked this morning," I said.

Emilio raised his eyebrows, still chewing as he spoke. "This morning? If it's that old I fire the chef. He is supposed to pick it from our own garden just after you order it."

I believed him. The ravioli with Paradiso sauce was just as good, and then Emilio recommended linguine with clam sauce. It, too, was great. I said, "Emilio, this is so fresh the clams are still wiggling."

Emilio looked at me like I had dropped the butter plate on the floor. "Very funny," he said. I figured I'd better cut the humor. Emilio didn't look very happy with me, and I thought I could see the outline of a knife handle in his belt under the back of his tight jacket.

We finished up with some delicate cannolis for dessert and cafe cappuccino. It was the greatest Italian meal I had ever eaten. Arabella's company only made it better.

About the time we were on our second cup of cappuccino, a party of tourists walked in. I don't know how they found the place, and they didn't seem to be impressed. One, who was the largest and the loudest, asked the waiter what they had on the menu. The waiter was obviously over his head trying to converse in English, and Emilio went over to help. The big American looked him over and sneeringly asked, "Whatta you got, chico?"

I could see Emilio's neck turning red. "Hamburgers," he said.

"Damn," the big guy said, "We can get those at home."

"That would be a good idea," Emilio said. I could see Emilio's right hand curled up behind his back. As the American got up, I was afraid Emilio was going to reach for his knife, but instead he kept his hand behind his back and stuck out his middle finger in the royal Italian salute.

Hasler almost broke-up. It was just as well the American couldn't see it. He sneered again at Emilio and said, "Thanks for nothing, chico." I was proud of Emilio. He was a real diplomat. He kept his cool and bowed politely.

Hasler stopped laughing and wiped his eyes. "Greatest put down I've ever seen," he said.

During the next round of cappuccinos a three piece combo came in and started to play, an accordion, a drum, and a violin. We danced the evening away. Arabella was good, and I tried to show her some of the latest American steps. In return, I learned a lot of the older Italian dances. It was a great evening.

About 0300 Hasler and Maria disappeared. I excused myself to go to the restroom and went out to the parking lot to check up on the Renault. It was gone.

When I got back to the table I asked Arabella, "What happened to Hasler and Maria?" Arabella giggled. "They've taken a room upstairs, I guess."

I knew that was unlikely with the car gone, but the idea of a room was great. "Is there another room?"

There was, and it didn't take me long to sign "Mr. and Mrs. Smith" on the dotted line.

When I came out of the head, Arabella was hanging her dress and slip in an armoire. What she had on was skimpy but dazzling, a lace brassiere and a pair of beautiful white panties.

She beat me to the bed, but not by much, and then only because I stopped to take off my trousers.

It was a night I'll never forget. All thoughts of Candace Terry rapidly faded away. Arabella's dark hair wrapped itself around me, and her liquid eyes swallowed me up. She had a slim, but shapely body, and she knew how to use it. Where Candace had been muscular, Arabella was soft and yielding. I didn't have to persuade her to do anything. She knew what to do, and it all came naturally. We made love until dawn. Then in the growing light we talked until the sun was well up. Her English was good, and I learned a lot about her and her family. Maybe more than I wanted to know at that stage of our relationship. I wasn't planning to become a permanent part of it just yet. After all, I was just an ensign, and I needed a few more years to expand my horizons.

Later that morning at breakfast downstairs, I looked for Hasler. The car was still gone, and so was Maria. Emilio was nowhere in sight. The desk said Hasler had checked out, but I doubted that since I didn't think he had ever checked in. There was no message. There was something fishy about the situation, but I didn't care. Breakfast with the beautiful Arabella awaited me.

When I went back to her, I thought she was more beautiful than she had been the night before. As I seated her, I told her so. She blushed slightly. "I'm glad you think so, but you seemed to have ruined my hairdo."

"Sorry," I said.

She giggled. "I was only kidding. I don't care about it."

I sighed with relief. This romance stuff was new to me. It wasn't exactly my first time, but it was the first time I had ever spent a whole night with a woman. It certainly beat the old college try I had been giving the girls on the University of California campus in the back seats of various cars.

Fortunately, there was a bus to Naples, and I delivered her to the Orient Hotel in time for her next shift.

Hasler and I had planned to go shopping that day, but with no Hasler I had no stomach for shopping. That would have to wait. I decided that since Hasler had taken the car and left me, he could pay for all of it.

Late Sunday evening Hasler came back to the ship, carrying an armload of packages. I was walking up and down on the forecastle thinking about Arabella when he came into view walking up the pier towards the ship. Chief Novella, also carrying several packages, was walking with him, and they were laughing and talking. I didn't trust myself to face Hasler when he came aboard, so I went below and waited for him in his room. He showed up a few minutes later, came in, and tossed his packages on his bunk.

"Well!" I said.

He looked at me like nothing unusual had happened. "Hello. How the hell are you?" he said.

"Okay, but that was a long bus ride back to Naples. And I did want to go shopping today."

Hasler laughed. I had never seen him so happy. His eyes sparkled, and his mustache flapped as he smiled. "Sorry. I had a very big deal on, and I forgot about you. I paid for the car rental, and you don't owe me anything."

"I wasn't planning to pay you."

I had the duty the next day, but Hasler was gone again and brought back more packages when he returned. This time I avoided him. I couldn't stand his 'up' periods.

Naples had been a hell of an experience, and I'd never forget Arabella.

Then my thoughts turned back to the stillness and darkness of the night. Certainly nothing unusual was happening about the topside, but I felt abnormal. Then I realized that my feeling was physical. My bladder was sending me a message about the three cups of coffee it was carrying around. It was telling me it was past time to get rid of them.

I unwrapped myself from the signal flags and stood up. I didn't want to go below, so my only alternative was to use one of the signal bridge scuppers. They were small drains at the edges of the deck to carry rainwater down to the water's edge. I unlimbered and started to fill one up. Before I was half empty I could hear the patter of drops down below in the water. In the unusual silence they sounded like a waterfall. Now that I had broken the silence, all I could do was finish the process, and it seemed to take forever.

When I had finished I stood quietly for a few minutes, but couldn't hear anything unusual. I went back to my signal flags and burrowed down in their warmth. I felt better.

I looked around the adjacent piers at the sleek destroyers nested in pairs and snugged up to the pier sides. I shuddered to think how many billions of dollars of taxpayer's money had been put into them. But from what I had seen of the Navy so far, it was all worthwhile. My naval experience was limited to two short summer cruises, one on a destroyer and one on an amphibious ship, and four years of Naval ROTC courses. Now I had completed a six month deployment to the Mediterranean, and I felt good about it. This was my Navy, the surface Navy, and if I could just survive the next few days, I might just get good at it.

Now there was nothing left to do but wait and try to stay awake. I felt something would happen, but I didn't know when. I would probably not be a part of it except as an observer, but if I needed to I knew I could defend myself. I put a hand on my trusty sword. We were ready.

A MURDER AT SEA

CHAPTER XI

The deck got awfully hard and cold after an hour, even with the signal flags between my butt and the icy cold deck. Also, I couldn't see too much of the side from where I was sitting, so I moved to the outer edge of the signal bridge platform. Even then, the platform was about ten feet inboard of the ship's side. About 0200 my eyes were getting tired from staring into the dark, and the caffeine from the earlier coffee had worn off, but I forced myself to stay alert.

Suddenly I was rewarded. I thought I could see a faint movement on the upper deck level amidships. I blinked my eyes, but I couldn't make the image any clearer. I didn't want to be left out if something was about to happen, so I got up carefully, picked up my sword, and slipped it into my belt, this time point down. I tested its position once or twice. I couldn't make the same smooth draw as Errol Flynn, but I could get it out easily.

I tried to put the signal flags back in their proper notches, but I couldn't see the symbols on the notches. I decided to hell with the signalmen,

and I threw them into the bottom of the bag, trying to be quiet. The cotton material flopped in
easily, but some of the metal connectors clinked
together softly.

At the forward corner of the signal bridge, I
climbed over the life lines, lowered myself to the
deck edge, hung by my hands, and dropped the
remaining two feet to the deck of the navigation
bridge. I was as quiet as I could be. The only real
noise was that of my breath being expelled as I hit
the deck, and a noisy pounding which I soon
identified as my heart. But I felt I was safe because
I didn't expect anyone else to be up there either
on the signal bridge or on the navigation bridge.

There was a door leading into the closed part
of the navigation bridge about three feet aft of
where I had landed, but I ignored it and headed
for the edge of the wing of the bridge. There I
would be able to see down to the waterline of the
ship all the way aft.

I didn't quite make it. I heard a sound behind
me. By the time I had figured out that it was the
door to the bridge opening behind me, it was too
late. Before I could turn around, an arm reached
out and snaked around my throat. I fought it as
best I could, but it was strong, and it pulled me
backward into the bridge enclosure.

Just as my heels were dragging over the coam-
ing of the door, I managed to get my sword out of
my belt. I was in an awkward position and could

only manage to grasp it about midway up the blade. I jabbed the handle of it into the gut of whoever was on the other end of that powerful arm. He gasped in pain and released me, falling backwards to the deck as he let go. I was able to keep my feet, and I crouched and turned toward the middle of the navigation bridge.

I looked around in the faint light coming in the navigation bridge windows from the ships across the pier and saw a second figure standing in front of me. He was crouched low in a karate stance and looked as if he meant business. I decided now was not the time to test my white belt qualifications. After all, he might have a black belt and I'd end up spreadeagled on the wheel or flat on my back. Instead, I went with my strength, transferred my grip on my sword to its handle, and whipped the point of the blade by his head a couple of times in fencing fashion. This was no time to try the Errol Flynn stuff. He seemed impressed, or at least confused, and I pressed my advantage with a feint to his gut and then brought the point up under his chin and said in my best authoritative command voice, "Don't move a muscle or I'll shove this up your throat, through your head, and clear into your brain."

There was a groan from the figure still lying on the deck. Not exactly a groan of pain, but more like one of disgust.

"Carlson, is that you?" the figure said.

I froze. The voice was one I had recently become accustomed to. None other than that of Lieutenant Commander Molesworth.

"Yes, sir," I said.

The Exec groaned again, but I knew I couldn't have hurt him too badly. It didn't take much to figure out that I was holding my sword under the trembling chin of Chief Agent MacIntyre. I lowered my sword, and laid it on the deck.

"Sorry, sir," I said.

I bent over to help the Exec to his feet.

"Don't come near me!" he said.

"I'm just trying to help you up, sir," I said.

"Thanks, I'll make it myself."

MacIntyre took out a slim pencil light and played it up and down my sword lying on the deck. Then he laughed.

"I feel relieved," he said. "At least you've got the point covered with something."

I looked down. The padding I'd put on it earlier to protect myself was still in place. I would have looked stupid trying to shove it in MacIntyre's throat, or anybody else's for that matter.

I said, "If I'd known it was you, I wouldn't have tried that."

MacIntyre laughed quietly. "I think after all the trouble you've had, you were justified in trying whatever you wanted, but I'm surprised at your choice of weapons. I can't figure out why you had to use a Navy dress sword instead of a pistol."

I said, "Ensigns don't rate being issued a pistol. Besides, I had a standby weapon. I have a letter opener up my trouser leg."

That really broke MacIntyre up. His shoulders heaved as he tried to keep his laughter quiet.

The Exec took pity on him. "I guess we'll issue him a pistol in the morning."

"Thank you, sir," I said.

By now Lieutenant Commander Molesworth was up and adjusting his clothing and tentatively feeling his bruised middle. "Carlson, what in the name of hell are you doing up here?"

"Sir, no one told me I couldn't come up to the bridge area, and I wanted to find out what you all were up to."

MacIntyre laughed quietly, more a subdued sniffle than a laugh.

"I told you he'd figure it out. We should have included him after all he's done to help."

I said, "I only guessed that you were doing something. I don't know exactly what's going on."

"All right," said the Exec. "I guess Mister MacIntyre is right. We wanted to keep the number of people who knew about this to a minimum so it wouldn't leak out. Tell him."

MacIntyre explained to me briefly what was going on. The two of them were up on the bridge watching the scene below, just as I had been, but they had stayed inside the bridge structure so that they could communicate with the rest of their men by hand-held radio without making too much noise. As MacIntyre was speaking to me, he stopped now and then to listen to an ear piece he was wearing and then to murmur quietly into a walkie-talkie radio he was carrying in his pocket.

"We've got a dozen of these aboard," he said. "Also twelve agents and half a dozen Marines. Each is carrying a radio and a strong flashlight and is armed with a machine pistol. Two men have Polaroid cameras with specially sensitive night film. They are scattered around the top side in positions where they can see over the side of the ship.

"There are two Zodiac rubber boats manned with SEAL, or Navy underwater demolition experts, shoved back into the pilings at bow and stern far enough so they can't be seen. There are also five free-swimming SEAL divers in the waters around the ship. Across the open space in the commercial yard are several observers spotted to see any approaching boats from that direction."

"Yes," I said, "I remember what you said about the SEALs this morning. It indicated to me that you were carrying out some sort of plan."

MacIntyre said, "I thought it would. At first I was concerned because I had violated our own security. Then I thought maybe it was a Freudian slip. Maybe I owed you a chance to figure out what we were doing, and it looks like you did. I just hope you haven't told anyone else, even your best friend."

I assumed he was talking about Hasler, but I couldn't figure out why that would be bad. I stopped trying to solve this problem and said, "I didn't know exactly, but I knew approximately what you were doing. It seems I knew enough to come up here and get in trouble."

MacIntyre shook his head. "It'll be all right, and I think we need your young eyes to help us see down below in the dark." MacIntyre looked at his radium-dialed watch, "It's time to move back out onto the bridge. When we get there, speak very quietly."

The Exec said, "We haven't heard a thing except for some small disturbance in the water a while ago."

I figured he didn't need to know what it was, and I had had no other choice. I hadn't wanted to go below to empty my bladder, and it had been about to burst. I cleared my throat, "Maybe some small fish jumping."

The Exec said quietly, "Harumph!" which I interpreted as his not agreeing with me.

MacIntyre carefully opened the door out to the bridge wing, and I followed them out the door and over to the side of the bridge. I stood next to MacIntyre as he looked over the side. It was still so dark over the starboard side that I couldn't see anything but dark water.

"What did you mean when you said it was time?" I whispered. "This evening we allowed the ship to take aboard two portable phone booths and to place them on the quarterdeck.

The Exec, who had come over and was standing on the other side of MacIntyre, said, "That wasn't anything unusual. We always have two telephone booths on the quarterdeck when we're in port."

MacIntyre went on. "Two of our men came aboard with the telephone workmen and quietly lost themselves after milling around the booths for a reasonable interval."

I grinned in the dark. "Along with a newspaper man and a couple of laundrymen."

"How did you know?" he asked.

"I was topside looking at what was going on around the quarterdeck about that time, and I figured that's what you were doing. You were trying to convince the suspects that all of you had left the ship and that they would have a quiet night before the resumption of the search of the ship tomorrow."

"I hope the suspects aren't as observant as Carlson," The Exec said.

For a man with the sore gut I had given him, I thought he sounded fairly friendly.

MacIntyre said, "About 2100, Novella made a phone call. Of course we had tapped both the telephones and we made a recording of his conversation which will give us both evidence of what he said, and also an opportunity to make a voice-print of his voice."

"Will this be good enough to identify him?"

"Good enough to stand up in court. Also, one agent was in a position to identify him by sight when he went into the booth and to record the time of his conversation. Novella talked briefly in what had to be a prearranged code. The number he called turned out to be another telephone booth in downtown Norfolk."

"Fortunately he didn't try very hard to disguise the time of whatever it is they're going to try. We could figure it out as 0300, about fifteen minutes from now. We don't know exactly what he and his group have planned, but we can guess."

MacIntyre looked at his watch. "Five minutes to three," he said. "Now you as know as much as I do. Help us look over the target area, and pipe up if you see anything. You'll probably see something before I will. My eyes aren't what they used to be."

I asked, "Do we know if anyone else aboard the ship is involved?"

"Not for sure," MacIntyre said after a slight pause. "But we have to assume two or three others are in on this in some way."

There had been something evasive about MacIntyre's reply, and it had come just after I had thought the two were beginning to level with me.

They were using binoculars, so I went back inside the bridge and outfitted myself with a pair. Back outside, I wedged in beside them and scanned the topside and the water alongside. For awhile I saw nothing at all. It was still almost coal black over the side and on deck on the starboard side. The clouds still obscured the moon and stars. Gradually my eyes became better adapted, and I recognized some of the shadows on deck because I knew what equipment was there. Then, a light flared up momentarily somewhere up the pier but not on our ship, and in the slightly higher light level, I could make out a man in a blue jump suit. He was flattened against some equipment on the deck above the main deck, but I could still read 'Norfolk Laundry and Dry Cleaning' on his back.

I nudged MacIntyre and pointed downward. "One of your boys from the 'Norfolk Laundry and Dry Cleaning' company," I said.

"Great company," MacIntyre said. "We give them all our business. Laundry, cleaning, and otherwise."

"I take it this is otherwise."

"Yep. This and other covert stuff."

The atmosphere on the bridge tensed as 0300 came and went without incident. The last of the coffee in my bladder wanted out, but there was nothing I could do about it. I tensed my gut muscles and willed it to stay put.

Then MacIntyre pressed his earpiece to his ear and listened intently. In a few seconds he took the earpiece from his ear and turned to us. In a barely audible voice he said, "A boat just landed at the other side of the commercial pier across the way. Two swimmers in complete scuba gear got into the water. We ought to be seeing some action soon. Our men over there will take the boat and its crew into custody as soon as it's safe to do so without alerting the swimmers."

We watched the dark harbor water between the commercial pier and the ship for almost fifteen minutes. The surface of the water was ruffled by a slight breeze fighting a cross tide. The calm and quiet in the air were almost oppressive even in the cold air of winter. I knew that something was happening out there, but I couldn't see or hear anything. There wasn't enough light to see below the surface of the water.

The Exec was shuffling his feet nervously, but MacIntyre seemed to be made out of stone. I guess a lifetime of such nights makes you blasé. Damned if I was. My heart was beating way above normal, and my hands gripping the binoculars were wet and clammy. I'd even forgotten about my bladder.

Suddenly there was a shout down on the main deck, and at least three flashlights stabbed the darkness on deck and over the side. A camera flash went off. Then the voice that had shouted first said loudly and clearly, "Don't make a move, or we'll shoot your masks off! This is the FBI, and you're all under arrest!"

I leaned over to get a better look and so that my view would not be blocked by the bulky shoulders of the men beside me. Through my binoculars, I could see two black-clad figures swimming in the water alongside the ship. Both were wearing diving masks, which reflected the light of the flashlights like mirrors. I could see enough through the illuminated harbor waters to make out their black-finned feet moving slowly to keep them afloat, but they weren't going anywhere. I could see at least six machine pistol muzzles pointed at them.

Suddenly several swimmers surfaced about thirty feet away. They closed in slowly on the other two swimmers in the water.

"Some of our backup," said MacIntyre. "They're some of the SEALs I was talking about."

Around the stern and the bow appeared the two Zodiac rubber boats filled with more swimmers. The boats were outfitted with outboard motors, but they weren't needed. Four paddlers generated all the speed they needed to close in on the swimmers.

"I guess this is what you were arranging this morning with all those messages you were writing up on the signal bridge."

"Yes, and I'm sorry I couldn't tell you about

it. We couldn't risk a leak. I know you wouldn't deliberately let it out, but you might have been forced to. Anyone desperate enough to try to kill you wouldn't stop at torturing you for any information they thought you might have. Also, you might have inadvertently told someone something that would have given away our plan."

I didn't know anyone I might have talked to that fit that category, but I had to trust MacIntyre. He still knew something I didn't. "I see," I said, but I still wasn't happy about the whole affair.

I turned and looked over the side again. If the occasion hadn't been so serious, it would have been beautiful with the various light reflections, the dark water, and an occasional camera-flash explosion as the cameramen recorded what was going on.

On the main deck, just above where the group over the side was swimming, there were two figures dressed in dark clothing. They were immobile, too, and surrounded by three figures with three machine pistols. One of the two central figures held a thin piece of line which dangled over the side and was attached to a five-gallon tin held in the hands of one of the swimmers. There was a life jacket tied around the tin, so the swimmers couldn't get rid of it, even if they were foolish enough to try to drop it and let it sink.

One of the figures on deck turned his head toward us and looked up. "Daviglia," I hissed.

"You can speak as loud as you want to now. It's all over," said MacIntyre.

"Thank God!" said the Exec.

"Well, it's not quite time for that," MacIntyre said. "We still have to find out which one of them killed Lieutenant Farrington and tried to kill Carlson, here. We may not have them all. Let's go down to the main deck and get a closer look at our catch."

We walked carefully in the dark, MacIntyre leading us with his small pen flashlight. We went down to the starboard side and joined the group there.

By the time we arrived, several agents had Daviglia and Antonio spread-eagled against the nearest bulkhead and were searching them carefully for weapons. Antonio had a finely sharpened, large kitchen knife in his belt. An agent removed it gingerly.

Daviglia was easier to search. His weapon was a two foot length of pipe of the kind stored near each water tight door and meant to move the dogs which secured the door. Some of the damage control equipment that I was always having to replace. Those pieces of pipe were the most popular items on the ship. It was sticking out of his back pocket like an off-center iron tail.

An agent had taken the line from Daviglia and carefully hoisted the can to the deck. He bent over it, removed the line, took out a pocketknife, and scratched his initials on the top surface. He would be able to identify this particular can in court by his mark. He picked it up and headed for the mess hall.

After the weapons search was complete, Daviglia and Antonio were handcuffed and taken away to the mess hall.

I leaned over the side. A Zodiac rubber boat was alongside the ship and the two swimmers were being hoisted into it. Their fins and masks had been removed, and they, too, were searched for weapons. A ladder was lowered over the side and they climbed up to be greeted by a handcuffing party before heading for the mess hall.

As soon as the prisoners were clear and the lights had been turned out, we filed into the mess hall for the next act in the play. One problem had been resolved, who had the drugs; but the other problem, who killed Charlie and who had tried to kill me, was still a mystery.

I felt safer as soon as I saw Daviglia and Antonio in custody, but I still didn't feel secure. Novella and Abrizzi weren't around. There appeared to be too much evidence against them to clear them of Charlie's death and the attacks on me. On the other hand, much of it was circumstantial. I decided I still had to be careful until we found out what Daviglia and Antonio knew. Until we found out, I was going to stay close to the FBI agents and their machine pistols. I felt foolish

carrying my dress sword, and I hid it as best I
could under my windbreaker until I could find an
opportunity to get rid of it.

A MURDER AT SEA

CHAPTER XII

The crew's mess hall on a destroyer at 0400 is not a very inspiring place to spend time. I had heard that the *Lassiter* had as fine a mess hall as there is in destroyers. It is clean, efficient, and nicely decorated, but this morning it was crowded and more than a little cluttered. Some movable chairs had been brought in and were scattered around the room instead of being neatly arranged as were the fixed chairs and tables, all of which were bolted to the deck.

I followed MacIntyre and the Exec into the mess hall, and they headed directly for the agent who had the five-gallon tin can in his custody. MacIntyre bent over it and placed the long blade of his pocket knife along an upper seam. He hit the end of the knife with his closed fist, and the big blade penetrated the tin top. Then he pulled out another blade in the knife shaped like a can opener and began cutting the tin top.

"Boy Scout knife?" I asked.

MacIntyre grinned. "Yes. You ought to get yourself one. Every sailor should have a knife, not just a dress sword."

"I've got a long, sharp letter opener taped to my leg if you need it."

MacIntyre laughed. "Yes, I can see it sticking out from under your trouser leg. You look a little silly. Maybe you should get rid of it. I won't need it. This can-opener blade will do the trick. I see you've gotten rid of the sword."

"Yes, temporarily," I said. I guess I blushed a little, because the Exec asked me if I was all right.

I said, "Yes, sir. I feel a lot better, but I'll feel better still when we find out who killed Charlie." He said, "Be patient. We're getting there."

I walked to the back of the mess hall, bent over, and removed the letter opener. I felt a little better, but I thought I'd keep it in my belt until this whole affair was settled. I felt a little safer too, when I noticed Howlett standing quietly in the back. I went back to the center of the mess hall and bent over the can next to MacIntyre.

He had managed to saw around the top of the can until he had a gap of about eight inches. He bent the triangle of tin back to make an opening. I bent over his back trying to see what was in the can. I raised myself on my toes, and I could see the edges of a neat row of cellophane packets.

MacIntyre took one out, slit the top with his knife, and put a little of the white powder on the point of his knife. He raised the blade to his mouth and tasted the powder. "Heroin?" I asked.

"Yes," MacIntyre said. "The lab will confirm it. I think this is very pure stuff. Probably worth about a million dollars when it's cut and distributed. Maybe more."

He turned to the agent who was guarding it. "Take it to the lab and call me with the results."

I looked around the mess hall. The four men who had been taken into custody were seated on folding chairs along one bulkhead. The two swimmers were on one side, blankets wrapped around their wet suits, and their legs secured to their chairs with leg irons. Antonio and Daviglia were seated in the center of the room along the same bulkhead, their legs also fastened to their chairs with leg irons. All four had their hands in handcuffs. Across from them, MacIntyre had placed chairs for himself, Commander Knight, the Captain, who had mysteriously appeared out of nowhere, and the Executive Officer. I guess captains don't want to be bogged down with details. They only want to be there for the kill. I pulled up a chair and sat down behind MacIntyre, and no one objected.

For the first half hour, messmen served coffee to all hands in the mess hall including the prisoners, who had a tough time getting their mugs up to their mouths with their hands in handcuffs. The ones from the water were shivering badly, but the coffee helped warm them up.

I could see Howlett talking to one of the messmen, Larosa, who was carrying two coffee pots. I knew they were watching me carefully. For a minute the master-at-arms brassard on Howlett's arm gave me some comfort, but I remembered that Novella had worn one, too. But I felt better. If the FBI didn't give a damn about my safety, at least someone did, and I trusted Howlett and Larosa.

Howlett was in the mess hall because he was now acting chief master-at-arms in place of Novella. Getting him appointed had been easy. "Commander Molesworth," I had said last night. "He's just the man for the job. Novella is under too much suspicion to keep the job."

Molesworth's eyebrows had shot up. "Maybe Howlett will do. He knows everything that goes on aboard this ship."

"With him in the job your troubles will be over."

Molesworth's eyebrow's lowered a little. "But, he'll have that damned damage control locker extended clear back to the master-at-arms shack."

"And then he'll rent out all the space."

The Exec's eyebrows went back up.

"No," I said quickly. "I was just kidding. I promise to keep him under control."

"Sure, you'll take ten percent." Now I knew he was kidding too, and that he had given in. At any rate, Howlett was back there at the rear of the mess hall wearing a master-at-arms brassard.

Doc Hasler examined each one of the four men as carefully as he could with them seated and restrained. MacIntyre explained that he would have to later certify that the men being questioned were physically able to answer questions and had not been physically coerced, whatever the hell that meant. Otherwise a smart counsel would claim that his clients were too cold and wet to know what they were saying, or come up with some other excuse.

A complete physical examination was not mandatory, but as long as Doctor Hasler was available, a partial examination was added insurance.

While this was going on, I looked around the room. There were about eight FBI agents moving around, talking in low tones, and unlimbering equipment from their waists and pockets. All were dressed in dark blue jump suits and baseball-type caps, and two had 'Norfolk Laundry and Dry Cleaning' on their backs. I watched them all as they moved about, but my eyes kept coming back to a short, slim agent. There was something different about this one. As this agent bent over to talk to another one, a light flashed in my tired brain. This one was a woman. That rear end couldn't have belonged to a male agent. It was broader than a man's, but not by much. Even in the baggy jump suit, I could tell it was shapely and beautifully proportioned. I knew then I might like to become better acquainted with its owner. Her front might be even better than her rear.

Now, as she stood up and turned around, I looked at her more carefully. There were a few strands of jet black hair peeping out from under her baseball cap. I couldn't see the color of her eyes, but I guessed they were black, or maybe dark brown. Her complexion was free of any makeup, and when she smiled, I could see a dazzling array of white teeth. She walked across the mess hall. Her stride was firm and not particularly feminine, maybe because of the boondocker shoes she was wearing. Her jump suit was very loosefitting, but, there was no mistaking that she would look just fine in something a little tighter.

I leaned forward and whispered in MacIntyre's ear. "One of your agents is a woman."

I couldn't see his face, but the back of his scalp twitched, and I knew he was laughing. "Ensigns are slower than they were in my day. It took you a long time to figure that out."

"I didn't know you put women agents in the field," I said. "This operation was a little dangerous."

"Why not? The Navy is almost ten per cent women. She graduated from the FBI Academy about six months ago and was assigned to my office. Now she pulls her weight there and in the field. And since she's taken charge of the office, I finally have time to sit back and think. When she heard about this case, she assigned herself to it because she said she wanted to learn something about the Navy."

"I'd like to teach her."

MacIntyre reached inside his jacket and hauled out his wallet. He extracted a card and handed it back over his shoulder to me. "My phone number is on this card. She'll answer my telephone if I'm not in. We have a secretary, but Matt thinks letting a secretary answer the telephone while we are there is sexist. Now we all answer our own phones. Also get our own coffee. I'm getting used to this new way of conducting business, but I don't know if I like it."

"Sounds to me like she'll be taking your job soon."

MacIntyre sighed. "Maybe sooner than you think. I'm getting too old for this all night stuff. By the way, her full name is Matilda Moffett, only don't call her Matilda unless you want to get thrown over her shoulder. She's called Matt, and she's a knockout in a dress."

"Oh, no, not another karate expert!"

"Black belt, and also women's intercollegiate fencing champion. Foil, I think."

"Well, I'll avoid the karate, but I think I can hold my own in fencing. It's said that in free fencing a saber can beat a foil."

MacIntyre snickered, "Don't forget to take the cotton off the end of yours first."

"Sorry about that," I said, "But I noticed that you stood pretty far back when I was waving my blade around up on the bridge."

MacIntyre shook his head. "If you'll forget about that, I'll leave it out of my report."

"It's a deal."

"On second thought, I can't leave it out. The Chief will laugh himself sick over it, and he needs a few good laughs." "Okay by me. I always like to make people happy."

I settled back to watch the proceedings. Hasler had completed his physical examinations and had come over to tell MacIntyre that the four men to be questioned were in reasonably good physical condition. Ligosi seemed to be ready to give them his beetlebrowed best. He started by reading them their Miranda rights.

I bent forward, "Is this Miranda rights reading necessary? Aren't you just making a preliminary investigation?" "It's not really required as long as we don't ask any questions that might tend to incriminate them, and we haven't formally accused anyone. We're really only informally investigating a murder at this time."

This didn't make me feel very good. Charlie had been murdered and I'd almost been killed three times and, as of now, no one was officially looking for the perpetrators.

Also, one suspect was missing, Novella, and as far as I was concerned, Abrizzi was still a suspect, too. Maybe there were others as yet unknown.

MacIntyre went on, "We have a right to ask questions which might help us find Novella and any other possible suspects. Remember, your commanding officer still has legal custody of all the suspects and so far hasn't formally accused anyone of anything, not even Antonio and Daviglia, even though they were caught with the heroin. Legally, your commanding officer is only conducting an informal investigation into the facts surrounding the smuggling of heroin, and we are only acting as his agents and assisting him in this affair." Commander Knight was listening. "That's right," he added. "Then you aren't investigating the murder of Lieutenant Farrington?" I asked.

"No, not formally," MacIntyre said. "We don't have any evidence to connect any of these men to it yet. That's what we're looking for."

I looked at the Captain, who had been listening. His face was as black with rage as I had ever seen it. His large hands were on his equally large knees, and his fingers were almost tearing at the flesh of his knees.

"Damn!" he said explosively.

Maybe damn wasn't even strong enough to be used on the lower decks any more, but for him it was heavy oratory, and indicated that he was about to chew someone out. Then a bell rang in my head. Something about investigations. I slipped quietly out of the mess hall and went back to my room. I opened the top to my desk and took down a copy of the *Naval Officer's Guide*. I didn't have a copy of the *Manual of Naval Justice* which would have explained in long, boring detail all about investigations. It was locked in the ship's office, and I couldn't take Chief Snodgrass away from the mess hall now. *The Naval Officer's Guide* would give me all I needed to know in a hurry. I turned to the section in the back which covered military law and specifically to the part on investigations. Sure enough, it said that an informal investigation, or board, could be formed of two officers appointed by the commanding officer and could interrogate witnesses who did not need to be placed under oath. The proceedings could be informal, which meant not in a court room, and counsel didn't need to be present. There wasn't anything which prohibited interrogation under oath, only that it was not necessary. For what I had in mind, the trick would be to get witnesses to agree to take an oath even if they didn't need to.

I sat back and thought a moment. I didn't like the way the investigation was going. If it adjourned with out finding out who the killer was, I'd be left aboard with the killer still free. Even Howlett and his troops couldn't protect me all the time.

My Viking blood began to boil, and I could see why the Captain was so mad. I had read a lot of the history of my Scandinavian ancestors, and I remembered that the Vikings killed a lot of enemies. They always attacked first and asked questions later. Damned if I was going to let them down. If I were cornered, I was going to attack.

I slammed the book into its vacant slot on my bookshelf and headed back to the mess hall. Ligosi was conferring with MacIntyre, and people were still milling around, so I hadn't missed anything.

Howlett eased up beside me and whispered out of the side of his mouth, "Next time you leave here that fast give me a little warning. My messman spilled a whole pitcher of coffee trying to keep up with you."

"Thank you," I said. "I didn't even see him." "You're not supposed to see him, but we need a little warning." "O.K. I'll try to remember."

"If you'll just keep your mind off that FBI broad it'll easier."

Howlett left my side, moving to the back of the mess hall, where I could see him hovering like a mother hen, giving unobtrusive signals to his helpers.

At present, I wasn't sure just exactly what I would do with my information about investigations, but the situation was very fluid, and anything could happen. Whatever it was, I didn't want it to happen to me, and I felt very dependent on Howlett. MacIntyre didn't seem to be much interested in what I did.

I asked MacIntyre if Novella had been found.

The Exec overheard my question and said, "We're still searching the ship. I have yet to hear from two of the search parties that were assigned to the forward part of the ship." I noticed that Snodgrass was seated at a table near the prisoners, monitoring a tape recorder. Then, on a signal from MacIntyre, Ligosi got up, carrying a portable microphone connected to the tape recorder, and stood in front of the two swimmers. Both of them regarded him with stony stares.

"What are your names," he asked.

One of them, obviously the leader, smirked and said, "I'm Sam Smith and that's Joe Jones."

Ligosi didn't flinch. He went on after looking at Snodgrass, who nodded to indicate the tape recorder was functioning.

"Do you have anything to say about why you were in the water at the ship's side holding a can of heroin when you were apprehended?"

The two men looked at each other. Finally the leader smiled and said, "Just out for a midnight swim. We bumped up against this big boat here, and someone threw a big can at us."

The other one laughed and said, "They ain't supposed to throw no trash over the side. Besides, we ain't goin' to say nothin' more without our mouthpieces."

Ligosi got red above the back of his collar, but

didn't say anything further. Instead he turned and looked at MacIntyre, who shook his head. Ligosi left the two divers and walked over to Antonio and Daviglia.

MacIntyre turned to the Captain on his left and said, "We don't need anything more out of those two swimmers at this time. We have enough evidence to send them away for years. When we get them downtown, we may be able to sweat out of them who they were working for, but I wouldn't count on it. There's a lot of loyalty and fear among gangs like the ones they probably belong to."

Ligosi began to interrogate Antonio and Daviglia. They admitted to their names, but after that Daviglia said, "We ain't sayin' nuthin'. We want a lawyer."

"Me, too," echoed Antonio.

MacIntyre turned to the Captain again. "I can't legally go much farther now," he said.

The Captain squirmed in his chair so hard it creaked. He was even madder than he had been just a few minutes before. "I'd give anything to find out which of those two bastards killed Lieutenant Farrington."

Again, not a word about the fact that I had been in danger of losing my life three times. Ensigns just don't rate. Just then an officer walked in and bent over the Exec's shoulder. All of us nearby could hear him. "Commander, we found

Novella a few minutes ago. He was lying unconscious on the floor in the paint locker. We
dragged him out in the fresh air and revived him.
Claims he was conducting a search and passed
out from the paint fumes. Frankly, I think he was
hiding up there and got overcome. With the door
closed and the ventilation off, the fumes would
overcome anyone not using a rescue breather." A
rescue breather was the sort of thing you could
find in my repair lockers. It was like a gas mask,
sort of, except it had a canister of oxygen attached
to the mask through a hose so that the wearer
could breath even though he was walking in
smoke or fumes. I felt a little better. Novella was
now one more who couldn't hurt me. Although
MacIntyre hadn't said it yet, the fact that Novella
had been caught making the telephone call would
be enough to put him out of circulation. Only
Abrizzi was still out there.

The Exec turned to Hasler. "Go look him
over."

Hasler got up reluctantly and left.

The Captain said to MacIntyre, "Will finding
Novella help? Maybe we should postpone these
proceedings until we can question him."

"Maybe a few minutes," said MacIntyre.

The Exec announced a fifteen minute recess,
and we all got up and got fresh cups of coffee. I
wandered over and started to talk to agent Moffett.
Up close she was everything I had guessed she

was from across the room. The eyes were black, and the smile was warm and genuine. When she took off her baseball cap, I could see that her hair was cut in a very neat bob. I was beginning to forget all about Candace Terry and Arabella. It took a lot to make me forget Arabella, but Matt had it all. As I looked at her, I began to regret my thoughts about her splendid rear end. Not that it wasn't attractive, but I liked the rest of her more, and I felt guilty.

She was more than a sexually attractive female. She was a beautiful woman. Not pretty in the sense Candace Terry was. Not as passionate and sensuous as Arabella had been. Matt's features were almost plain. Well proportioned, but still plain, and to my mind classically beautiful. The remarkable thing about them was that they seemed to change as she talked and expressed her thoughts. I had the impression that I was talking to her inner soul, not just her face. This was the first time I had felt like this with any woman. I had read about such relationships, and all of them had been labeled love. All this was happening and I hadn't even introduced myself yet.

I took a deep breath, looked into her eyes, and said, "Sorry to be so forward. I should have introduced myself. I'm Ensign Carl Carlson."

She said, "Yes, I know about you. Mister MacIntyre has a very high opinion of you."

"High enough so that I might ask you out to

dinner soon?" She grinned impishly, "You sure
don't waste any time. I'll think about it."

We talked for almost twenty minutes, the
most enjoyable time I'd ever experienced with a
woman. Well, almost the most. On second
thought, it was the most, even better than sex. I
found out that she had a degree in criminology
from Northwestern and had lived all her life not
too far from there. I made a mental note that she
needed to travel, and, as a naval officer, I could
sure fix that. She was interested to find out that I
had been raised in a small town near San
Francisco in Northern California and had attend-
ed the University of California. I had a hard time
reassuring her that the jerks who used to populate
the Berkeley campus were almost all gone, and
that the University was regaining its lost prestige.

Her parents were still living, and I hoped I'd
be meeting them soon with a big question for her
father. I knew I was getting way ahead of myself,
but that's just the way it was.

Somewhere far away I could hear someone
loudly clearing his throat. MacIntyre. I looked
around, and he was looking at me with a half
smile, half smirk. He cleared his throat again, this
time not so loudly, and said, "If it's all right with
you two, we'll reconvene."

I said to Matt as we parted, "Please think hard
about that dinner date."

"I already have. I'll meet you at the Officers'

Club at eight." I liked that. It showed she was self-sufficient and could make up her mind. She'd provide her own transportation. It was going to be a great night, provided I survived the rest of the long day ahead and didn't fall asleep in my soup.

Then Doc Hasler returned and reported to the group, "Novella is in fair shape, but very groggy. I don't think you can question him yet without running into legal complications."

"Damn!" The Captain said for a second time that morning. Now he was really mad. "Everybody's a smart-assed lawyer," he snapped.

I thought somebody had to do something. I tapped him on the shoulder and leaned forward. He turned around and looked at me, the remains of his bad temper still showing in his face.

"Sir, if you will appoint Doctor Hasler and me to conduct an informal investigation in the case of the death of Lieutenant Farrington, I can question Antonio and Daviglia without their lawyers being present. They will have to answer me as long as we haven't accused them of anything and haven't officially turned them over to the Commandant of the Fifth Naval District for further action. If I question them, they will have to answer me under penalty of not carrying out your orders."

Doctor Hasler scowled and looked at me like I had lost my mind, but he didn't say anything when I mentioned his name.

The Captain looked at Commander Knight

and then at Chief Agent MacIntyre who raised his eyebrows. "Can't hurt," MacIntyre said.

"It's legal," Knight said, "but I don't know what you expect to prove. Remember, the proceedings are informal and not necessarily under oath."

Those words "not necessarily under oath" were all I wanted to hear. I was sure he would go along with me when I reached the critical point I knew was coming.

I looked at Commander Knight carefully. Something about going to sea had rubbed off on him. Gone was the meek lawyer who had boarded us the day before. There was a little salt water coursing through his veins now, and he was willing to take chances. Maybe not a John Paul Jones type chance, but a large jump for a lawyer. If I goofed, it would be his legal tail that got caught in the wringer. I would suffer, too, but I would be thought of, and dealt with, just as 'that stupid young ensign' who wasn't expected to know any better.

I tried again. "Captain, please trust me. It won't hurt, and it might help us to find out who killed Lieutenant Farrington."

That did it. The Captain literally would have done anything to find out who killed Farrington. He turned completely around and looked at me directly and searchingly. His bad temper was gone, but there was a new look of doubt. I began to regret what I had started.

He cleared his throat and adopted his best official manner. "Doctor Hasler and Ensign Carlson are hereby appointed an informal board of investigation in the case of the death of Lieutenant Charles Farrington. I will confirm this in writing as soon as possible."

Hasler looked at me in panic.

"Doctor Hasler," I said, "with your permission I will begin the questioning."

Hasler's face lit up with relief, and he sat back in his chair.

I got up from my chair. My knees were shaking and my mouth was dry. I took a sip from my coffee mug and put it down on the floor under my chair. I walked over to the table in front of Chief Snodgrass and picked up the portable microphone and several coils of its long cord. Chief Snodgrass looked up at me like he never wanted to see me again. His fingers were nervously playing with the button on his tape recorder. I grinned weakly at him. Then I walked over in front of Antonio and Daviglia, playing out the mike cord behind me. They looked up at me, but paid little attention, apparently deeply lost in their own black thoughts.

I walked back and forth in front of them in my best courtroom manner, moving the microphone cord around skillfully to avoid tripping over it. Actually, I was just trying to think of what the hell to say. If I screwed up too badly, I would no longer be ship's secretary. Maybe not even Ensign Carlson. Matt Moffett would laugh me out of her office, and Head Agent MacIntyre would lose his respect for me. The latter was the hardest of all to take. I stole a glance at both of them. MacIntyre was sprawled in his chair, looking at something on the overhead, but Matt was sitting forward in hers, her eyes glowing. I hitched up my trousers, cleared my nervous throat, and began my questioning.

"Daviglia and Antonio, the Captain has appointed Lieutenant Hasler and me to conduct an informal investigation into the death of Lieutenant Charles Farrington. You are still in the custody of the commanding officer and not accused of the murder of Lieutenant Farrington. Therefore, under the Universal Code of Military Justice, you are required to answer all questions I ask you regarding the subject of the investigation, which is to determine the circumstances under which Lieutenant Farrington died."

"As of this moment, since you are not charged with any offense regarding Lieutenant Farrington's death under the Uniform Code of Military Justice, you are not entitled to have counsel present. Do you understand all of this? If you don't, Commander Knight, who is a lawyer, and the legal representative of the Commandant of the Fifth Naval District, will answer your questions."

Daviglia looked at Commander Knight. There was a mask of surprise beginning to spread across Daviglia's face, broken only by the vast, inexpressive expanse of his large nose.

"Is that right, Sir?"

"Yes," Commander Knight said.

Antonio didn't trust lawyers any more than the Captain did. He bypassed Commander Knight and looked directly at the Captain.

"Is that true, Captain?"

The Captain nodded. "Yes, it is, and at this point let me remind you both that you are not entitled to counsel and that you must answer all questions asked of you as long as they do not incriminate you and are only about the death of Lieutenant Farrington."

I knew that I didn't have to swear in either witness, but I thought that I'd try. If they objected, I would have to pull back. If I succeeded, and they confessed, or revealed important information, I would have produced a dramatic result for a later trial. If they implicated someone else, it would be invaluable evidence for a later prosecutor.

I looked at Snodgrass. Sure enough, he had a small Bible in front of him. He was a jackass, but he knew his business. I thought I'd keep him on when I became ship's secretary. I walked over to his table, picked it up, and handed it to Daviglia. "You don't have to be sworn in to give evidence before this investigation, but if I were you, I'd think about taking the oath. There will be other persons questioned here too, and they may say something which will incriminate you."

This didn't make much sense to me, and as I glanced back at Commander Knight and MacIntyre, I saw that it didn't make sense to them either. There was a growing concern in their eyes, and MacIntyre had stopped looking at the overhead and was looking at me. But it did what I hoped it would. It persuaded Antonio and Daviglia to be sworn in.

"Okay," said Antonio. Daviglia looked sideways at Antonio and nodded his head.

I moved quickly before wiser heads sitting behind me could interfere or Daviglia or Antonio could change their minds.

"Repeat after me," I said, and I rattled off the oath, which I remembered from my course in Naval justice at the Naval NROTC. Daviglia looked a little confused, but he raised his right hand and repeated the oath.

Antonio had a little more time to think, and started to say something, but I hurriedly transferred the Bible to him and repeated the performance.

I straightened up, and looked back at the group around the Captain. He beckoned to me. I walked over to him.

"Why the oaths?"

"I think I may get them to say something incriminating about Novella, and I want it to be under oath." The Captain looked at Commander Knight. Knight shrugged his shoulders. "He did it and got away with it. If they say anything useful, having it under oath will help us prosecute whoever is charged."

Now I knew Commander Knight was completely full of salt air. He was really swinging. The Captain didn't say anything else and nodded to me, so I walked over to Antonio and Daviglia, first looking at Matt to see how she was taking all this. I gave the microphone cord another twitch. I was a little heavy on the twitch, but fortunately Snodgrass grabbed the tape recorder before it slid completely off of the table.

"Daviglia," I said, "This is being recorded. Please state your name and naval rate."

Daviglia looked at me like I was off my rocker, but decided to humor me, and answered the question. I asked the same question of Antonio and he answered. They both looked at each other and grinned, obviously wondering why I would ask such a stupid question. I decided to explain.

"Asking your names is just a legal procedure. I have to establish for the record who you are."

I pointed at the tape recorder. Daviglia shrugged. Antonio just sat there.

I gave my microphone cord another flip, this time being more careful. Snodgrass was ready for me and had a hand over the tape recorder. He looked relieved when it didn't move. I walked up and down once, and stopped in front of Daviglia.

"Daviglia, what do you know about the death of Lieutenant Charles Farrington?"

"Nuthin," Daviglia said.

"You were in the machine shop the other night when he was stabbed with a screw driver."

Daviglia looked at me like I had thrown cold water on him. "Can't prove it," he sputtered.

"Don't need to," I shot back. "Novella will say so. Do you still deny it?"

"Yeah! I didn't do nuthin."

I knew I was skating on thin legal ice. I hadn't accused him of a crime, only of being present when one was committed.

I went on. "Soon we're going to turn you over to the FBI. They have enough evidence against you regarding smuggling drugs to lock you up for twenty years. A lot of things can happen to you when you are in prison.

I was guessing at the possible sentence, and when I stole a look at MacIntyre, his eyes were almost rolled up in his head, but he said nothing.

I went on. "The sentence for murder will be for life. The murderer may get the death penalty and hang. Is it worth it to you to protect someone else? I know all about the Mafia if they are behind this. Maybe you are just afraid they will come after you if you tell the truth about the murder."

Daviglia sneered. "Them bastards. They're all Sicilians. I'm a Neapolitan. They give all Italians a bad name. I ain't afraid of them."

I felt I had set the stage now, or rather the saber duel. My next move had to be like the closing moments of a tight saber match, with both swordsmen having exhausted all of their ploys and with the match still undecided. The one who would then make the winning thrust would have to do so by first diverting his opponent's attention. A turn of the knee, a flick of the wrist, a slight jerk of the head. Then when the opponent is diverted, the front foot snakes forward, the body lunges towards the opponent, and the sharp point or edge finds its mark.

My next move in this legal fencing duel had to be carefully crafted. I figured Daviglia was my best chance and the one most likely to crack. I'd have to break him. Antonio was too smart. First, a diversion, then a thrusting question. The trouble was, I'd get only one such question out. It would trigger Commander Knight's sense of legal propriety, and he'd have to stop me, no matter how he felt.

I glanced across the room. Commander Knight's glasses reflected the overhead lights so strongly that I couldn't see his eyes, but the rest of his face looked eager and expectant. This legal business was his home turf, and he was enjoying the unfolding drama. Frankly, it was tearing at my gut. Or maybe it was the three cups of coffee I had taken aboard last night. I made a mental note to learn how to drink coffee. I'd have to if I were to stay in the Navy. In any event, my career would depend on my performance over the next few minutes. I took a deep breath, stole a quick glance at Matt for inspiration, and then looked at Commander Molesworth.

Commander Molesworth looked interested, but not overly concerned with the legal implications. I knew his busy, executive officer type mind was probably mulling over more mundane details, such as how he was going to get us all out of the mess hall in time for the crew's next meal to be served.

MacIntyre was still sprawled in his seat, looking more relaxed and confident than he had a right to be. He had lost interest in the spot in the overhead.

The Captain was sitting forward in his chair, both meaty hands planted firmly on his knees. I got the impression that if either suspect admitted to killing Charlie, the Captain would spring up and execute him on the spot with his bare hands.

My question had to be legally correct, or at least enough so that Commander Knight wouldn't have to intervene too quickly. Under the rules of evidence, I couldn't ask any question that would directly accuse either witness of Charlie's murder. I only had a few more seconds to come up with my question. Those in the room were beginning to stir impatiently, and I could hear a few coughs and deep breaths. I couldn't wait any longer, so I started my maneuver.

I walked back in front of Daviglia. As I did so, I switched the microphone cord out of my way so that it snaked across Daviglia's feet. He recoiled as if it had actually been a snake, looked down at it, and then raised his face to me as if expecting at least an apology. He didn't get one. I had made my feint. Now I would thrust.

"Daviglia," I said, "You said a few minutes ago that you weren't afraid of the Mafia. We've found Novella and he is talking to us. What are you going to do when he is brought in here as a witness and accuses Antonio of killing Lieutenant Farrington?"

The question was way out in left field. It didn't directly accuse either witness, and certainly not Daviglia, but if Daviglia stopped to think, he'd realize I didn't have any basis for predicting what Novella would do. I was counting on my deduction that he wouldn't think about it, and his emotions would take charge.

I knew I'd get a reaction from the group behind me. They would also know that the question was flawed, and their minds, rather than their emotions would motivate them. Out of the corner of my eye, I could see that the Captain and the Exec were both scowling and MacInytre suddenly sat forward. I knew I had only a few seconds left when I noticed that Commander Knight was slowly rising, his mouth beginning to open, and his finger raised.

I turned back to Daviglia. His mouth was hanging open, and there was surprise in his eyes. Antonio had paled. My thrust had deliberately been aimed, not at Daviglia, but at his friend Antonio. But still it was Daviglia I was working on. I judged somewhere inside of him lurked some good qualities. He wanted all of us to know that he wasn't going to be intimidated by the Mafia, and, better yet, he was loyal to his friends. I was counting on this. He didn't disappoint me.

Daviglia suddenly closed his mouth and shook his head. Somewhere inside the wheels were turning. I held my breath. Commander Knight was on his feet now.

Then Daviglia said abruptly, "No! No! Antonio didn't do it!"

"You mean Novella did it?"

"Yeah, that bastard did it."

I realized I had been holding my breath, and I let it all out in one big sigh. It was over, and for the first time in two days I could live without fear. There were sounds of relief behind me. In the corner of the room I could make out Matt's smiling face.

I turned slightly and looked at the Captain. His face was a weltering sea of emotions. Relief, that the murderer was now known, the desire for revenge, but still the knowledge that he, of all those present, had to maintain some sense of order and dignity. I knew then what a high price commanding officers sometimes had to pay for the honor of commanding. Commander Knight was still standing, but there was a slight smile below his glasses, and I knew I was home free, at least legally.

Now I had to get back on more solid ground and produce a few facts while Daviglia was still in the mood.

"Tell me what happened," I said.

The words began to spill out. "Mister Farrington came into the machine shop when Novella was solderin' up the can. When Mister Farrington bent over to see what was in the can, the bastard struck Mister Farrington in the back. Then he went outside, bashed Garrity over the head, and dragged him back inside the machine shop. Then he expected us to take all the chances gettin' the stuff off the ship while he laid back and stayed clear."

I looked at Antonio. "Is that right, Antonio?"

The cat was out of the bag, and Antonio couldn't do anything but confirm Daviglia's statement. "Yeah, Novella did it all right. Me and Daviglia tried to stop him, but I was too far away to get to him, and Daviglia couldn't get between him and the screw driver. It's true what Daviglia said about Novella puttin' us on the spot, too."

Now the dam had burst, and I hoped I could get some more information before someone behind me turned me off.

"Daviglia, what were you and Antonio doing in my room the other night?"

"Novella sent us there lookin' for evidence that he said you took from the machine shop. A soldering iron and some solder. He knew you had it, and he thought you had it hidden in your room. He thought he might have left some fingerprints on it. If we couldn't find it, he wanted us to kill you. We wasn't goin' to hurt you, but you leaped up outta your sack and yelled, so we took off before someone could come in your room and catch us. We was glad to have an excuse to give to Novella about why we hadn't knocked you off. He said we was a bunch of goats, and he would take care of you himself."

"Who dropped the bucket of heavy fittings near me yesterday?"

Antonio broke in. "Novella. He found out by questioning Benito that you had been down to the commissary storeroom. By the way you were acting, he thought you knew all about the can of heroin but that you weren't tellin' anyone else. We thought maybe you wanted the heroin all to yourself."

I laughed inadvertently. This was a thought I hadn't had before. Suddenly visions of a million dollars passed before my eyes but just as rapidly disappeared. Before they left I had one fleeting thought of Matt and me on the Riviera, counting the income from our heist.

I shook my head. "It never entered my mind," I said.

"Well, whatever," said Antonio. "We didn't know too much about you, and you looked like you could use some money."

"Let's get back to Novella," I said.

Antonio took a deep breath. "He tried to get me to do it by threatening me. He said he would turn me over to the Mafia, but I said hell no. He didn't have as much hold on me as he did on Daviglia. I'm only part Italian, and I don't have any relatives in Italy."

Daviglia scowled. "The bastard threatened my grandfather in Naples if I didn't help him. Said the Mafia was behind this and he would sic'em on my family. I didn't think I would have to do much, so I went along. Then he killed Mister Farrington, and we were all floatin' in the mine-strone. After that, both of us had to do whatever he said."

"Did Lieutenant Abrizzi have anything to do with the murder or the attempts an my life?"

Daviglia snorted. "Nah. He don't know noth-in'. He's just a stupid northern Italian. Nice guy in a lot of trouble."

"What kind of trouble?"

"Owes a lot of money, just like Novella."

"To whom does Novella owe money?"

"A dozen gamblers in Norfolk and some in Naples. A couple with the Mafia."

I heaved a sigh of relief. We had all the suspects in hand, and my life was now safe. I turned to MacIntyre. There was a combination of a smile and disbelief on his face. I walked shakily over to him. He put his hand on my shoulder and said, "Son, I wouldn't have believed it could be that simple. Out of the mouths of babes . . ."

I knew the quotation, but I didn't think I was that bad. Neither did the Exec or Captain. They were both smiling when I walked over to them and stopped in front of the Captain. "Sir," I said, "the investigation is complete. You'll have a written copy as soon as Chief Snodgrass can type it up and Doctor Hasler and I can sign it."

A MURDER AT SEA

CHAPTER XIII

Those in the mess hall rose and stretched, and the tension seemed to flow out of the people and down the deck drain like so much water. For the first time I could hear laughter and casual conversation. I, too, hoped the case was over, but there was a nagging feeling of unease and incompleteness in the back of my mind, and I looked at MacIntyre to try to get some feeling of what was happening.

He wasn't as relaxed as I thought he should be. He whispered to some of his agents, and they went off on some unknown errands. I remembered he hadn't taken me completely into his confidence before, and I resolved to keep an eye on him.

The big shots standing around shook my hand, and the Captain asked if there was anything he could do for me.

I decided to take him up on his offer before he came down off of the cloud he was on and changed his mind.

"Yes, sir, I'd like fifteen days leave to recuper-

ate from the recent blow on the head which I suf-
fered in the line of duty."

The Captain turned inquiringly to the Exec,
who was standing at his side.

Commander Molesworth said, "Well, I think
we can spare him. He was scheduled for the second leave party anyway, so I'll just move him up."

"Thank you, sir," I said. "When I get back,
I'll get the ship's secretary job squared away."

Hasler nudged me and grinned, "When do I
get a chance to ask some questions?"

"Next case," I said. "You have to brush up on
Naval Justice first."

I looked over at Matt, who was talking to
some other agents. I pointed to her discreetly.

"Doc, that's the woman I'm going to marry."

"I noticed you couldn't take your eyes off of
her for long, but that's a pretty quick decision on
a very important matter. The last I heard you
could hardly wait to get back to Naples and
Arabella."

"Yes, but the situation has changed, and I
know Matt's face is the one I want to see on the
pillow next to mine for the rest of my life. She's a
wonderful woman."

"I hate to remind you that you have several
years left on your obligation to the Navy, and you
will be making more five-month tours to the
Mediterranean. There won't be any pillow next to
yours for many a month."

He might as well have stabbed me with a knife. I think he sensed that some of the air was coming out of my balloon.

He said, "Well, of course she'll be able to make a trip to the Mediterranean at special tour rates once or twice during your absence. I think you'll both like the beach at Menton, or maybe the countryside outside Naples."

I knew Hasler was just digging at me, and in spite of his digs, life was suddenly brighter. Anyway, you'd never catch me taking Matt to Menton. At least not until she had an overall tan.

"Well," I said, "the old goats like the Captain and the Exec have survived a lot of separations. I guess your libido wears out and you don't miss your wife so much."

Hasler sighed. "You've got a lot to learn. Just watch the Exec when his wife walks down the pier tomorrow. I saw them together in Monaco, and he didn't look worn out, except maybe temporarily. All my medical books say it gets better as you get older."

It amazed me how little sex meant to me at that moment. In the back of my mind I knew life in the sack with Matt would be wonderful. But that wasn't as important to me as it would have been yesterday. My feelings for Matt transcended sex, but still included it. And here was Doc Hasler telling me it lasted practically forever. Or at least until you were a commander. Life looked good.

Time was moving on, and the Exec began to push people out of the mess hall because a late breakfast for the crew was due to be served any minute. The Captain invited MacIntyre up to his cabin for breakfast, but MacIntyre declined.

"I've got to get my agents off the ship and back to their day jobs," he said. The Exec said, "Carlson, show Mister MacIntyre and his agents up to the quarterdeck and give them any help they ask for."

On the quarterdeck, I watched some of the agents taking the suspects off of the ship. Each one was securely handcuffed with an FBI agent or Marine on each elbow. The two swimmers had been put in dungarees and old shoes. They looked preoccupied and downcast. Antonio and Daviglia were next. I felt sorry for them. They had been caught up in a situation where they were at the mercy of Novella. Maybe a good lawyer could help them.

Then came Novella, separated from the others. Perhaps for his own safety. He was pale and unshaven. There was a third agent just behind him. This last group stepped off the bottom of the brow and headed for the last van. Novella looked back at the quarterdeck and seemed to recognize me. Hasler was standing beside me. Novella's face darkened and there seemed to be a sneer on his lips. His mouth moved slowly, but I was too far away to guess what he was saying. I thought it was meant for me, maybe a Sicilian curse, but I looked back at him boldly. Curiously, I didn't hate him. He, too, had his problems, and he would spend the rest of his life with them in a cell. That would be more than enough punishment.

Just as the last van had closed its doors and driven away, there was a tap on my shoulder. I turned, and there was Lieutenant Abrizzi, neatly dressed in shore-going blue service, two large bags at his feet.

He smiled hesitantly. "I think I owe you an apology for being so short with you the other day in the wardroom."

I wasn't yet comfortable with Abrizzi so close to me. A couple of hours ago I had thought he might be a smuggler as well as a killer.

I cleared my throat a little nervously. "Thanks, but don't worry about it. I'm glad you'll get to see your family soon."

Now Abrizzi really smiled. "Yes, I'm detached from the ship, and I'll be home in an hour. I also want to thank you for doing so much to solve the case so fast. Without you there wouldn't have been any liberty for the crew and no detachment for me."

"I was glad to help. Would you mind answering a few questions to clear up a couple of points?"

"Sure. Shoot."

"Where did you go in Naples? We saw you leave every time liberty started and you never came back until liberty was up."

Abrizzi grinned again. Three times in one day he had smiled. I was beginning to like and understand him.

"I went out to my uncle's farm, got into my Levi's, and helped him farm."

"Dungarees," I said softly.

"What was that?"

"Nothing important. Why your uncle's farm? I thought your family was from northern Italy."

"It is. My uncle left Venice years ago to come to the United States. He established a restaurant in Washington, D.C. A good one. It made money. A year ago his arthritis got very bad. He leased the restaurant to another relative and went back to Venice. It was too cold and damp there for his arthritis, so he moved south to Naples and bought a little farm. Just a few vegetables. We had a good time working in the open air and swapping stories."

"That explains a lot. Thank you."

"There's more," he said. "Next year I'm getting out of the Navy and taking over his restaurant. In a few years I'll be out of debt."

"Great. I guess you'll be glad to see the last of the Navy.

He looked pensively over his shoulder at the bulk of the ship, rising gracefully behind him.

"No. I liked the Navy, and I liked this ship. But my wife hated having me away, and she couldn't cope with the children's health by herself."

I thought about Matt. Would she hate having me away? I didn't think so. If she didn't like something about the Navy, she'd straighten it out. Probably straighten me out, too.

Abrizzi said, "Well, I've got to go. Good luck."

We shook hands warmly, and he carried his bags down the brow, much as I had carried mine up five months earlier. I thought, maybe I'd visit Washington someday, drop in on Admiral Rickover, and have dinner at Abrizzi's restaurant.

Howlett had been watching Abrizzi and me, and after Abrizzi left, Howlett eased up beside me and said, "Well done, Mister Carlson. Now I can call off my watch dogs."

"Howlett, I can never thank you enough. I always felt safer when I could see you and your guards."

Howlett cleared his throat. "Glad to have been of service, Mister Carlson. We don't expect thanks, but if it isn't too much trouble, there is something you can do to show your appreciation."

I could feel it coming, but I didn't care. "Yes?" I asked.

"Mister Carlson, since you're going to be the ship's secretary, could you get the Captain to sign an order authorizing the damage control locker to have a coffee mess?"

I thought about that a moment. I owed Howlett and his troops a lot. Maybe they had kept me alive. I said, "I sure will try, Howlett, as soon as I get back from leave."

Howlett grinned. "I know you'll be able to do it, sir."

This was the first time he had bothered to call me sir in a respectful manner, and I liked it.

I said, "I'll try to arrange for permission for you to have your own electric coffee pot and your own coffee mugs. That way you won't have to 'borrow' those mugs from the mess hall each week."

Howlett shook his head. "You mean I wasn't fooling anybody?"

"Yeah, that's what I mean. I'll bring my own mug down. Please thank all of your men who helped guard me."

Howlett shrugged. "Don't mention it. We wouldn't want to lose you. Good ship's secretaries are hard to come by."

Yes, I said to myself, particularly one who is in your debt. Aloud I said, "Chief Snodgrass will be at your service."

Howlett scratched his head. I knew something else was coming. "Mister Carlson, after you get back off leave, I would like to ask you about enlarging the damage control locker."

"Okay, just as long as you don't try to install

a dance floor."

Howlett laughed, "Nothing like that. Just a few more of the comforts of home."

Then MacIntyre came up beside me and watched the departure of his agents. "Before you ask," he said, "She can have all the time off she wants. By the way, I'm in favor of long engagements. I'll need her around the office for at least six more months."

I grinned. "Maybe she'll be there longer than that. Ensigns don't make much money, and the housing allowance isn't much. Could she have leave from the FBI to join me in the Mediterranean for a couple of weeks?"

"You're getting a little ahead of the game. You haven't even had a date with her yet. But if you can persuade her to come, she can have the leave."

When the last agent had filed off, MacIntyre walked to the head of the brow, pulled in his slight gut, and saluted the petty officer of the watch with as smart a salute as I'd ever seen. Even the Annapolis types couldn't do better.

"Sir," he said to the petty officer of the watch, "I request permission to leave the ship."

The petty officer of the watch almost dropped the telescope he was carrying under his arm, but he managed to get off a good return salute.

"Permission granted, sir," he said.

I stepped forward to watch MacIntyre salute the colors and walk down the brow.

"Just who the hell was that?" asked the petty officer of the watch.

I sighed. "An Ensign of the United States Naval Reserve, Retired."

Then the remaining agents debarked. One of them looked back at me, raised her hand slightly, grinned, and twiddled two fingers in a personal salute. I knew I loved her. In the few minutes we had stolen at the hearing, we had exchanged more information about each other than I had done with Candace in four years. All I had to do now was persuade her that she felt the same way about me. It didn't seem impossible. Men had been doing that with women since before recorded time.

All the vans loaded up and cleared the area. As they left, I looked up the pier after them. There was a group of women and children in gaily colored clothing gathered at the head of the pier behind a restraining line, held by military police. Suddenly I remembered. This was the morning the other ships of our division were due to arrive in port and they were there to meet their men.

At almost the same time, I heard the boatswain's mate of the watch announcing over the ship's address system, "Liberty will start for all hands in the liberty section at ten hundred. Stand by to receive the other ships of the division alongside."

There was a shout of joy from the groups of

men standing around the topside. I looked aft toward the end of the pier. Sure enough, the bow of the first one was peeking around the end of the pier, and men hurried to their stations to receive their mooring lines.

The atmosphere aboard ship had changed from somberness and disappointment to one of happiness and expectation. I thought about Charlie Farrington's body lying in the morgue of the Portsmouth Naval Hospital. I felt bad about the sudden change in the mood of the crew, but I knew in my heart that Charlie would have wanted it that way. One of his favorite expressions was "on with the dance." Today he would have said the same thing.

I sighed deeply, took one last look at the ships approaching our berth, and walked as fast as I could, without running, down to the ship's office. Snodgrass was there, fiddling with the tape recorder. When he saw me, he leaped to his feet and said, "Yes, sir, Mister Carlson, what can I do for you?"

"We'll discuss that when I get back and take charge of this place. Right now type up some leave papers for me with the Bachelor Officers Quarters at the Naval Station as my local address and take them to the Exec to get signed. He'll be expecting them."

Snodgrass was impressed, or at least bamboozled. He started to work on the papers even before I left to go down to my room.

I shaved, showered, dressed in my best civilian clothes, and packed a bag. The last things I
put in were a packet of twenty dollar bills, the last
of my cash, and a bottle of perfume, the infamous
"Eau de Sin," both from my safe. The money I
had saved from five months of my pay, or at least
from the pay I had not spent foolishly ashore.

I had bought a couple of bottles of the perfume in France for Candace, and it was valuable
enough to keep in the safe. She would have to
understand. I needed it for a more important
cause. A one hundred and twelve pound package
of black-haired, black-eyed dynamite.

While I waited for my man Snodgrass to
deliver my leave papers, I sat down and put my
feet up on the lower bunk. The Navy was getting
to be a downright pleasant place to be. I virtually
had the Captain and the Exec working for me, not
to mention good old Snodgrass. I was serving in
a magnificent ship that I liked driving around at
high speed. And right now I was about to embark
on the most important campaign of my career.
Life was good if you were lucky. Even better if you
worked hard.

Then a queer sound intruded on my reveries.
A dog barked. I couldn't believe it. Certainly all
the dope-sniffing dogs had left the ship. I put my
feet down on the deck and, still holding the bottle of perfume, walked over to my door and out

into the corridor.

Then I knew there was a dog aboard, or at least a part of one judging from the muzzle and neck that was sticking out of Doc Hasler's door. The sight so unnerved me that I dropped the bottle of perfume. It broke when it hit the steel deck and splattered all over my shoes and trouser legs. In an instant I was overwhelmed by the smell rising from it. So was the dog. It curled its lip and sneezed slightly. Apparently the smell was too much for it, because it withdrew inside Hasler's room. I made a mental note to check the perfume. Maybe it was too cheap for Matt.

I shook as much of the perfume off of my shoes as I could and walked up to Hasler's door. As I neared it, I could hear a voice reading the last portion of the Miranda rights. The voice was familiar. MacIntyre. No doubt about it. But he had left the ship an hour ago.

I looked in the door. Hasler was sprawled in his chair, looking at the floor. His face was white and his face slack, with his mustache limper than I had ever seen it. The door to the safe over his desk was hanging open, and an agent was poking around inside it. The dog had lost all interest in me and was lying at the agent's feet.

Commander Molesworth was standing behind Hasler, and for the first time I could remember, he looked unsure of himself and of what was going on. MacIntyre, who had been standing in front of Hasler reading the Miranda rights from a card, heard me walk in and turned. He looked a little guilty.

He stuffed the card in his pocket and said, "Oh, there you are. We tried to find you before we did this, but I guess you were in the shower."
I was so surprised I was shaking. I took a deep breath to steady my voice and said, "What the hell is going on?"

MacIntyre gave it to me straight. "We've just arrested Doctor Hasler for possessing and attempting to smuggle heroin into the United States and for complicity in the murder of Lieutenant Charles Farrington."

I knew my mouth was hanging open, so I closed it as best I could. My world had suddenly come apart. My best friend was sitting there, accused of terrible crimes. Worse yet, he must have been involved in the attempts on my life. I couldn't take it all in. All I could say was, "I don't understand."

MacIntyre said, "I don't blame you, but now you know why I couldn't tell you all of what we were doing aboard. You might have inadvertently tipped off Doctor Hasler. And we wanted him very badly. We've had him under surveillance since the ship's last Mediterranean tour."

"We were fairly certain that on his last cruise to the Mediterranean he brought in a good-sized load of heroin in his safe mixed with the routine narcotics he kept there. Unfortunately, he got it off the ship before we could move on him. Then he started thinking it was so easy that he could move into the big time. But in order to make a big enough buy, you have to involve the Mafia, and that can be fatal. Our informants tipped us off, and we were going to move in on him when the ship arrived in Norfolk, but the murder changed everything.

I had stopped shaking now, and my mind was working again. "But how did you find out he had something to do with the murder?"

"We broke Novella. It wasn't hard. He didn't want to take the rap all by himself. Hasler had picked up some of his gambling notes with the money he made on his first smuggling job, and he had a strong hold over him. By the way, my agents report that Novella looked toward you and Hasler when Novella was being led up the pier. He threw a Sicilian curse your way."

"I remember that. He looked pretty serious, and I hoped I'd survive it."

"The curse wasn't meant for you. It was meant for Hasler."

"I don't see how Hasler could have gone so far overboard. I tried to take care of him when we went ashore together."

MacIntyre shook his head. "You weren't with him every night. When you had the duty he did all his business. We had a couple of agents following him in Naples. You, too, but we thought you were innocent."

I shook my head sadly. "Yeah, just too damn innocent," I said.

Hasler stirred and looked up at me. "Yes, a good kid, but a screwy one."

I didn't know whether being screwy was better than being innocent, but I didn't like either description. Hasler sighed deeply and went on, "I'm sorry about how it all came out. I tried to keep Novella under control, but after he killed Charlie, I had trouble with him. He seemed to feel that after he'd murdered one man, another wouldn't matter. You wouldn't keep out of it, so he wanted to kill you, too. I'm just glad you survived."

I said, "I'm sorry, too, Doc, but at least I'm glad to know you didn't turn on me completely."

"Forget me. Go ashore and get on with your life. And hey, maybe you can write to me now and then in prison."

MacIntyre said, "By the way, your friend Emilio from the Paradiso Cafe near Naples was a drug dealer. Not the biggest, but big enough."

I bristled, "He wasn't any friend of mine."

MacIntyre grinned. "Our Neapolitan contact thought he was, but I doubted it. Maria was working with Emilio. She led Hasler to Emilio and they both ditched you while they went to make the drug deal in Naples."

"Was Arabella a part of the plot?"

"No, she had only worked at the car rental agency for a few weeks."

I started to say that I was glad Arabella had liked me for myself and hadn't been entertaining me as part of the plot, but I decided to keep this to myself, and I changed the subject. "I suppose Hasler brought the stuff back in his shopping packages the next day right under my nose."

"No. Part of the deal was that Novella had to carry it aboard and keep it in his custody. The Mafia didn't trust Hasler."

"I guess Hasler made a separate small buy to put in his safe for his personal use."

"Right. He must have dipped into it from time to time. Some of it is gone. Couldn't you tell?"

"Now that I think back, yes. There were several times when he seemed was pretty high. I just thought that his condition was a carry-over from the booze we had taken aboard when we were ashore. I remember now that his hands shook when they shouldn't have, and he had some manic periods I couldn't account for."

"Couldn't you see the pupils of his eyes?"

"No. Now that you bring it up, he kept his glasses on or his head turned away."

"I can see why you might not have seen it. Sometimes your best friend is the last one you'd look for. We caught him because we could see him a little more objectively than you could."

Then my heart sank. My God! If they knew all about Hasler, Maria, and Emilio, they knew all about Arabella and me, and I mean all!

MacIntyre must have noticed my face. "What's wrong?" he asked.

"You know all about Arabella and me?"

"And you? Oh, yes." He paused and looked at me like the father of a daughter who had been wronged. Then he grinned, and I knew he was just putting me on. Maybe he was paying me back for the bit of sword play on the bridge.

"Please!" I said.

"All right, relax. My lips are sealed. Matt will never know. Even if she finds out, I'll claim it was in line of duty."

I heaved a sigh of relief that started in my heels. "Thanks, I'll never forget it."

"What's the big deal? You may not believe it, but I was young once, too. Besides, you didn't know Matt then."

I couldn't take much more of this, so I said to the Exec, "Sir, if you don't need me, I'd like to go on my leave."

The Exec looked at MacIntyre.

MacIntyre cleared his throat. "I think you have some important business ashore to get on with."

"All right, permission granted," the Exec said, clearly glad to get me out of his hair. "But for the love of Pete, get rid of that awful smell."

I walked back to my room. Obviously my first move would have to be to the shower. I stripped off all of my clothes and spent a solid five minutes under the hot water. At sea, shower time was strictly limited, but in port water came from ashore, and I could make sure all of the perfume was off of me. After the shower, I went back to my room and dragged out my second best civilian suit. I only had two, so it would have to do. I finished dressing and sat down in my chair with my feet up on my bunk. It was amazing how my life had changed in just one hour. I thought of poor Doc Hasler.

What had made him turn from my best friend into someone willing to have me killed? I didn't have an answer. Then I remembered a favorite saying of my father, "Thank God the young are resilient." I would have to be just that and get on with my life. Matt was waiting, and I didn't want to be late. I pulled my feet off of my bunk, sat up, opened my safe, and pulled out the other bottle of "Eau de Sin." It would have to do until I could save up some money and buy something more expensive. I straightened my already straight tie, picked up my bag, and headed for the quarterdeck. Life had to go on, and after I had recovered from all of this, I knew it would be pretty damn good.